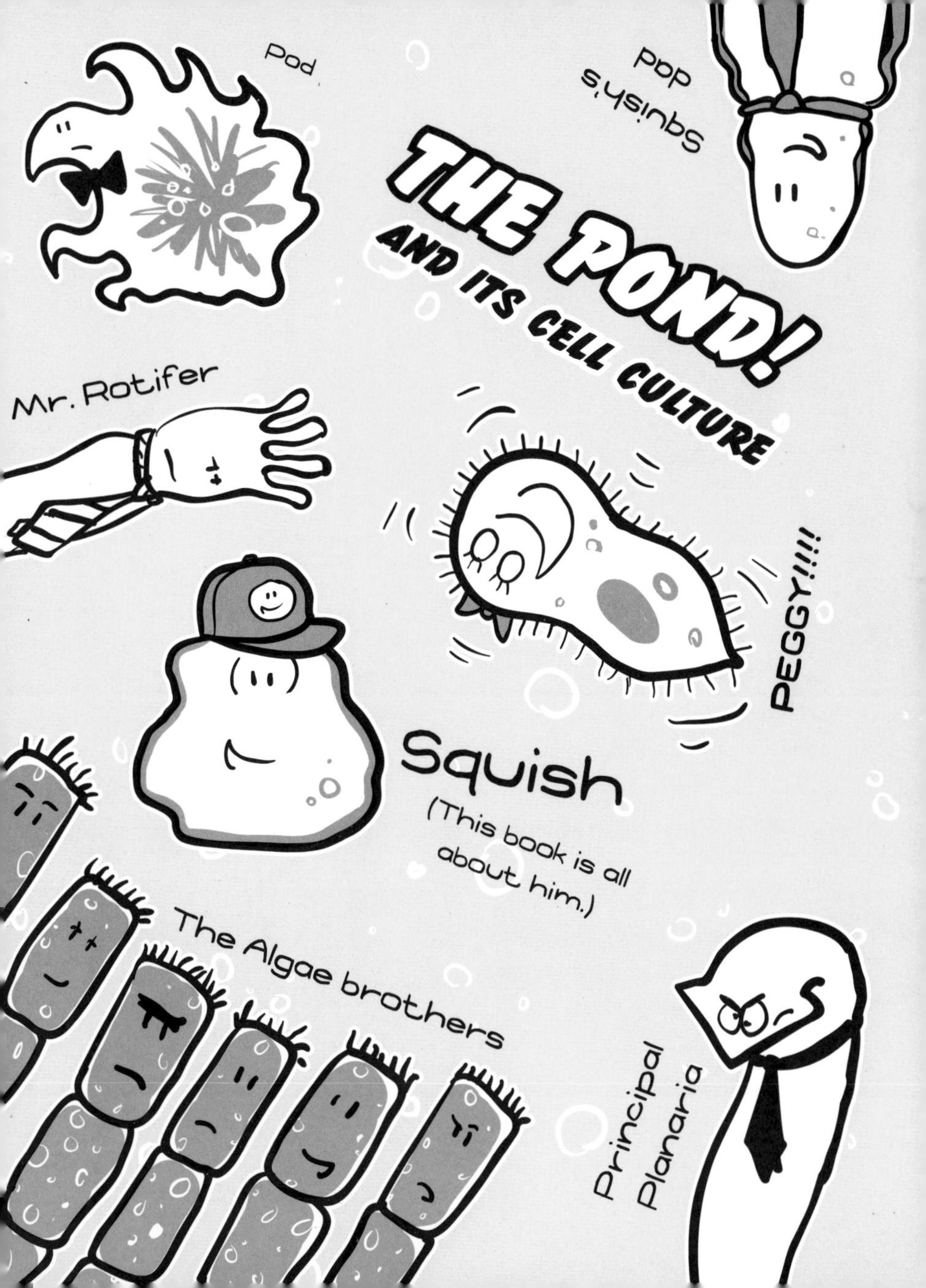
THE POND!
AND ITS CELL CULTURE
Pod
Squish's dad
Mr. Rotifer
PEGGY!!!!
Squish
(This book is all about him.)
The Algae brothers
Principal Planaria

Read ALL the SQUISH books!

#1 SQUISH: Super Amoeba

#2 SQUISH: Brave New Pond

squish
BRAVE NEW POND

BY JENNIFER L. HOLM & MATTHEW HOLM

RANDOM HOUSE NEW YORK

This is a work of fiction. Names, characters, places, and incidents either are the product of the authors' imagination or are used fictitiously. Any resemblance to actual persons, living or dead, events, or locales is entirely coincidental.

 Published in the United States by
Random House Children's Books,
a division of Random House, Inc., New York.
Random House and the colophon are
registered trademarks of Random House, Inc.

Visit us on the Web! www.randomhouse.com/kids
Educators and librarians, for a variety of teaching tools,
visit us at www.randomhouse.com/teachers

Library of Congress Cataloging-in-Publication Data
Holm, Jennifer L.
Brave new pond / by Jennifer L. Holm and
Matthew Holm. – 1st ed. p. cm.
Summary: Starting a new school year, Squish, a meek amoeba
who loves the comic book exploits of his favorite hero,
"Super Amoeba," is determined to get picked for kickball
and hang out with the cool kids.
ISBN 978-0-375-84390-7 (trade) –
ISBN 978-0-375-93784-2 (lib. bdg.)
1. Graphic novels. [1. Graphic novels. 2. Amoeba—Fiction.
3. Popularity—Fiction. 4. Superheroes—Fiction.
5. Schools—Fiction.] I. Holm, Matthew. II. Title.
PZ7.7.H65Br 2011 741.5'973—dc22 2010028084

MANUFACTURED IN MALAYSIA 10 9 8 7 6 5 4 3 2 1
First Edition

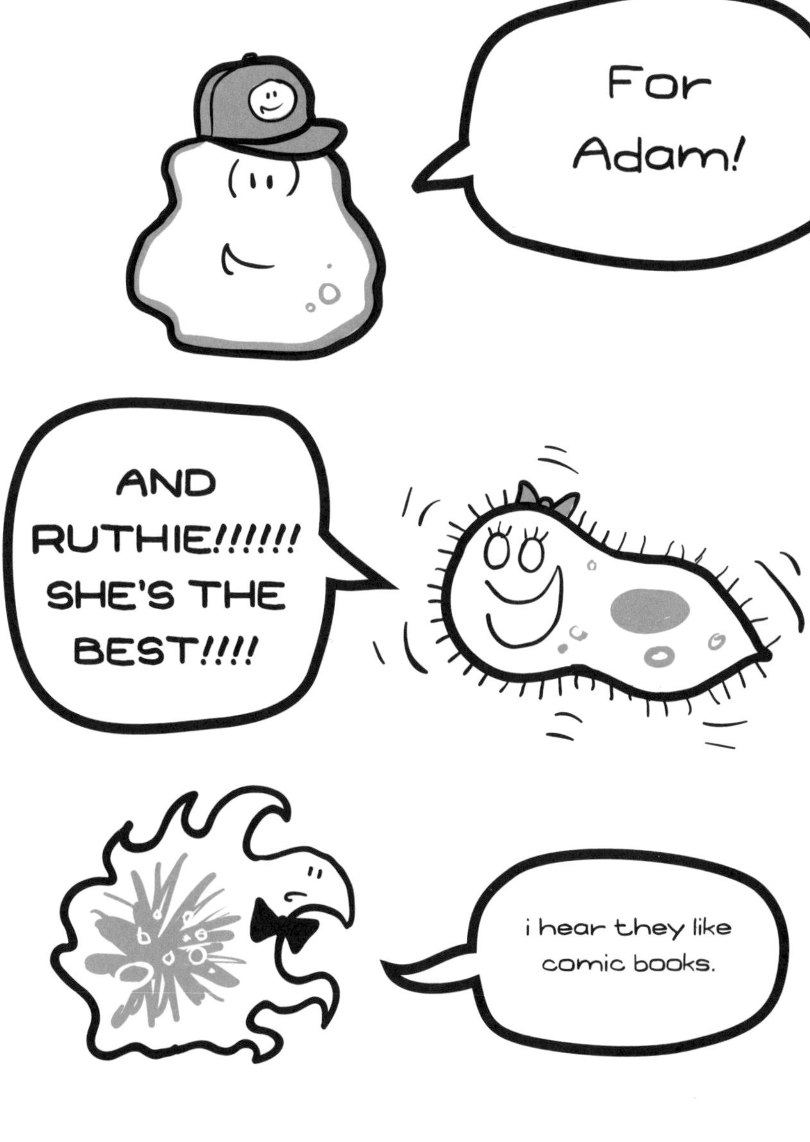
For Adam!
AND RUTHIE!!!!!! SHE'S THE BEST!!!!
i hear they like comic books.

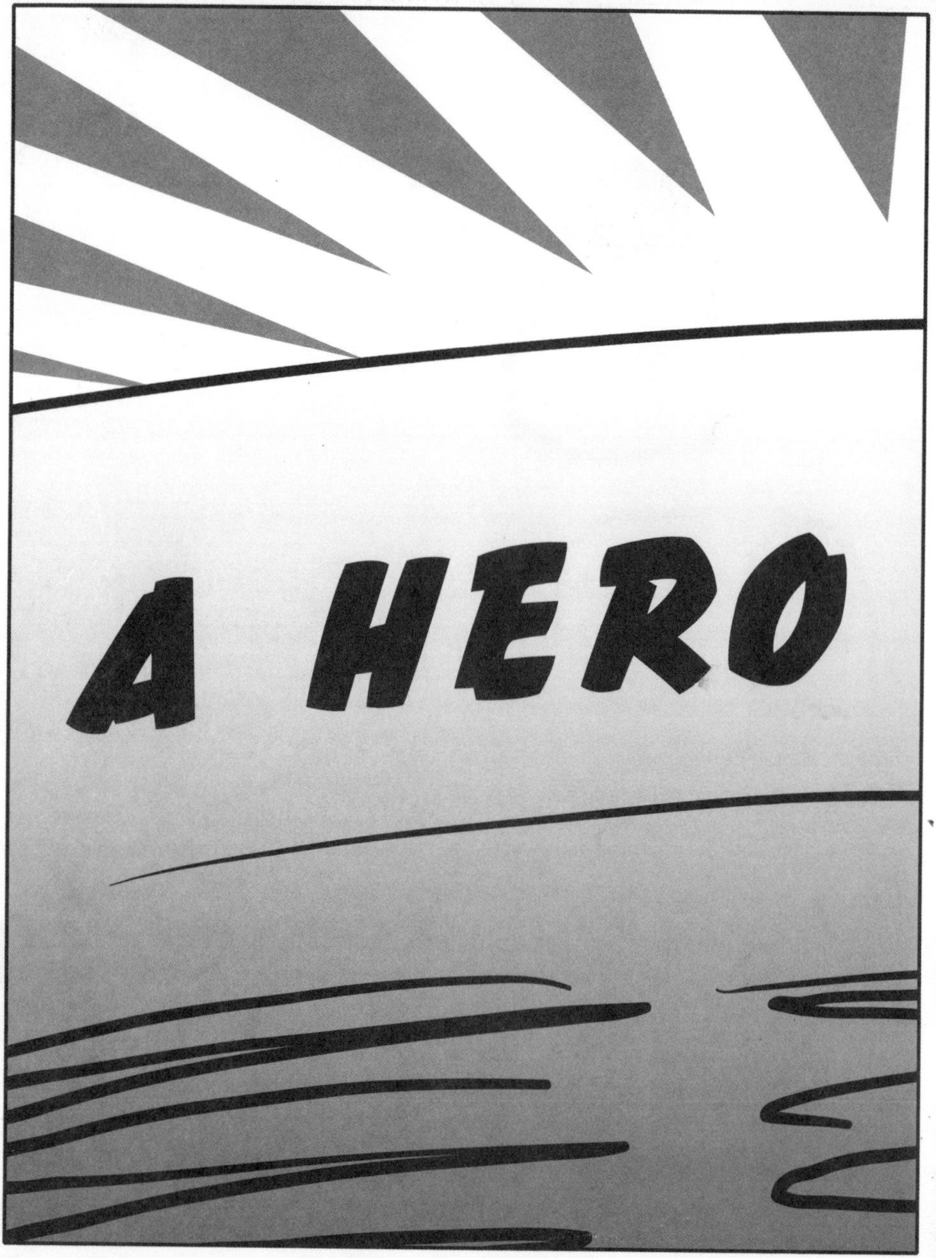
A HERO

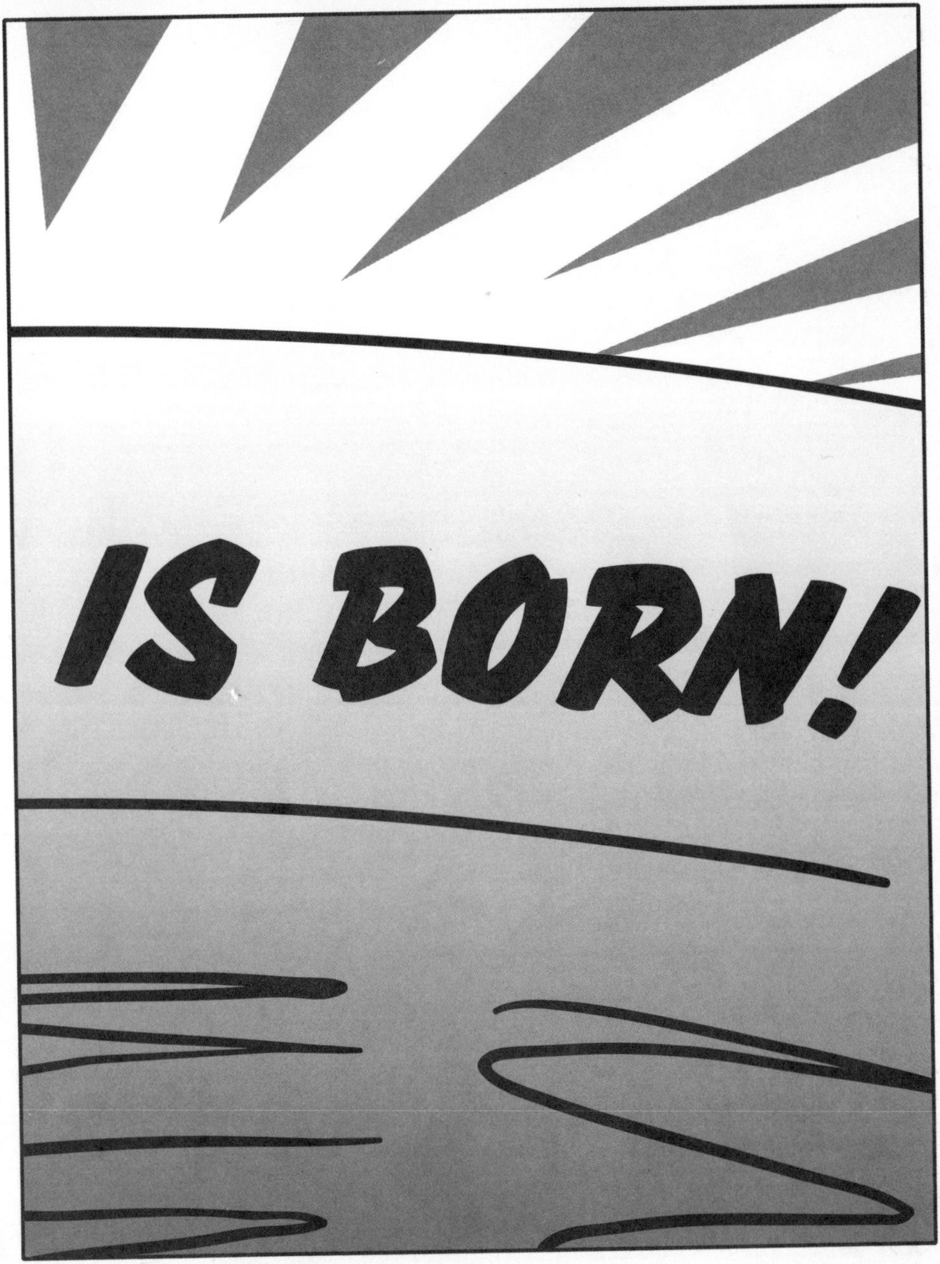
IS BORN!

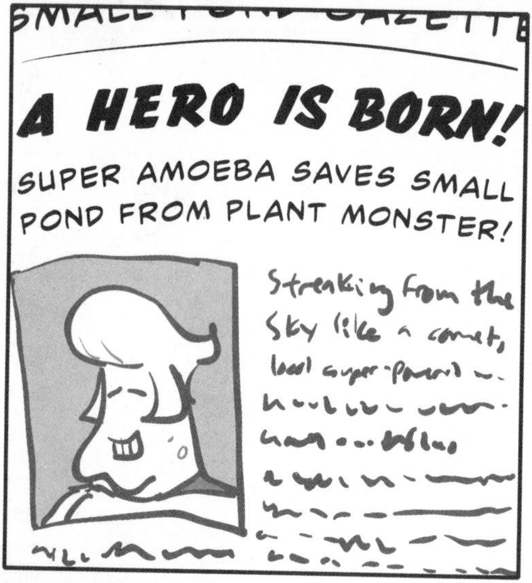
A HERO IS BORN!
SUPER AMOEBA SAVES SMALL POND FROM PLANT MONSTER!
Streaking from the Sky like a comet,

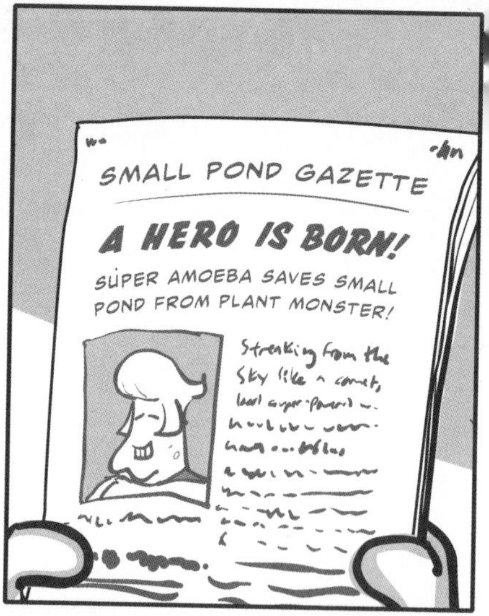
SMALL POND GAZETTE
A HERO IS BORN!
SUPER AMOEBA SAVES SMALL POND FROM PLANT MONSTER!
Streaking from the Sky like a comet,

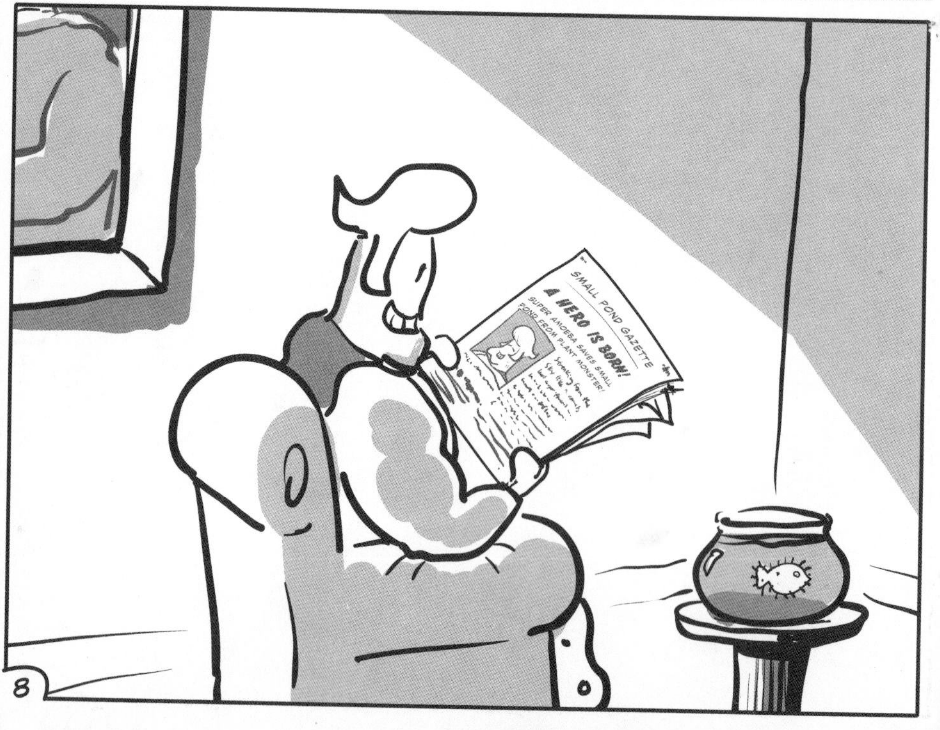
SMALL POND GAZETTE
A HERO IS BORN!
SUPER AMOEBA SAVES SMALL POND FROM PLANT MONSTER!

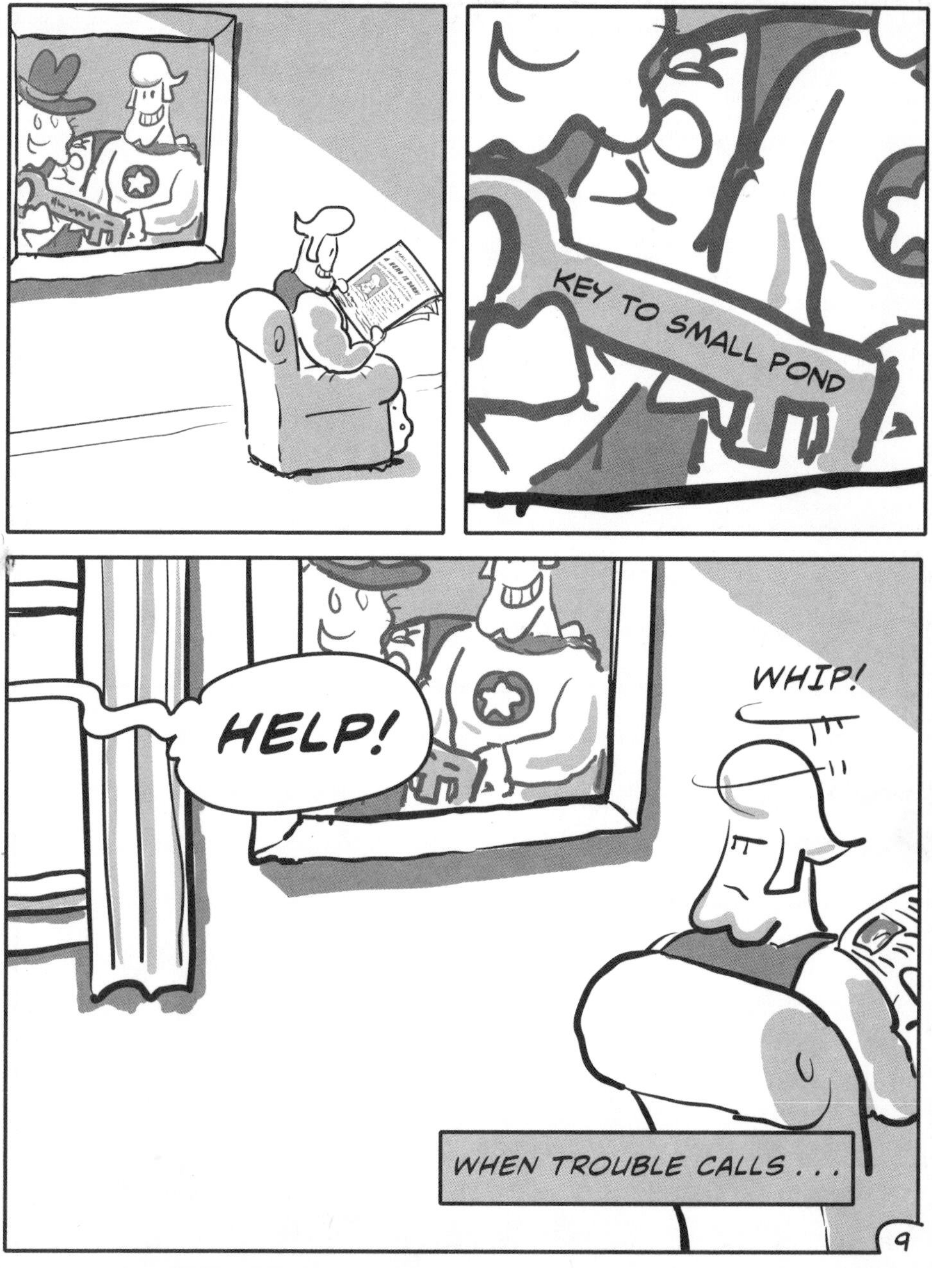
KEY TO SMALL POND
HELP!
WHIP!
WHEN TROUBLE CALLS . . .

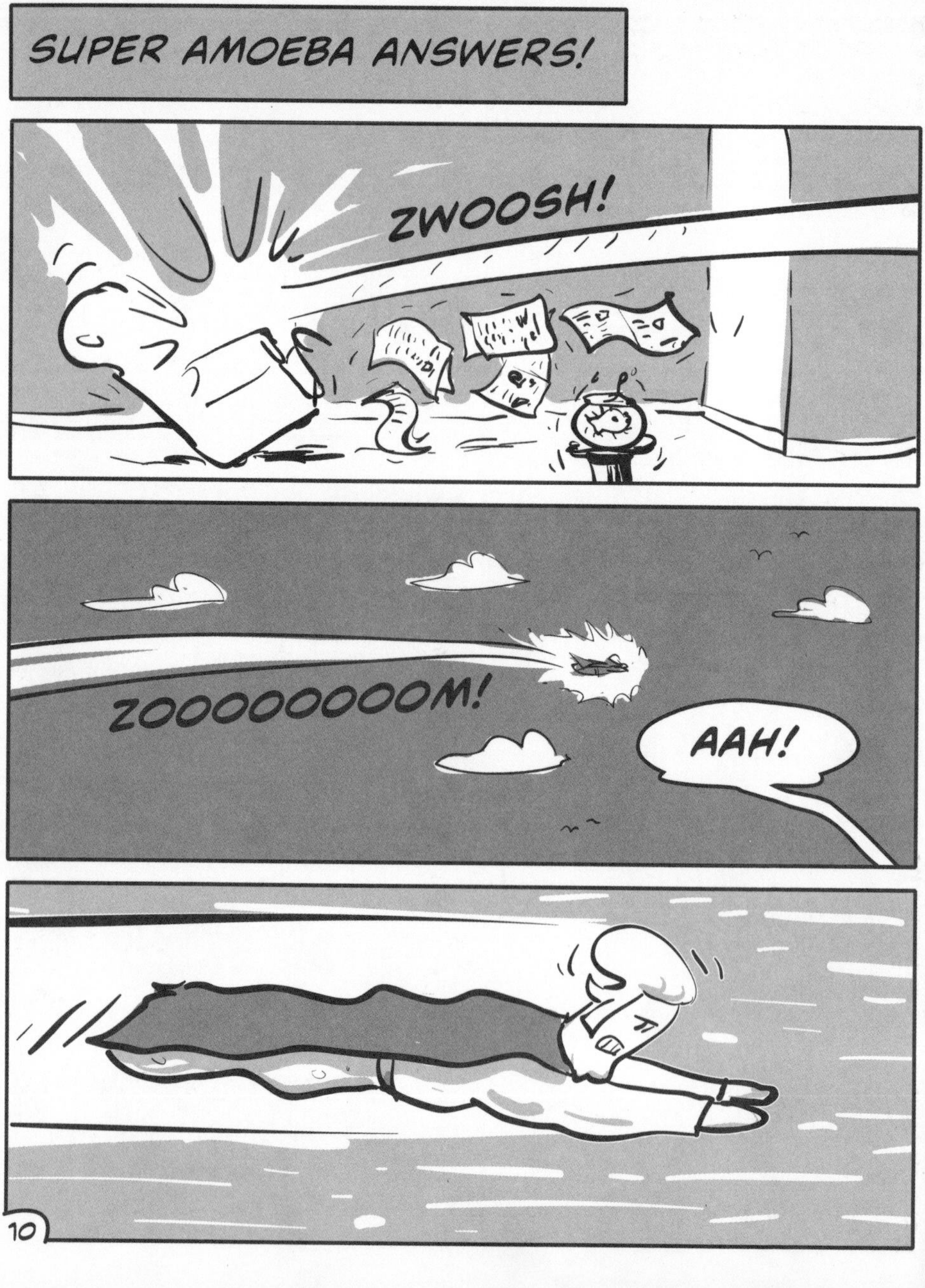
SUPER AMOEBA ANSWERS!
ZWOOSH!
ZOOOOOOOOM!
AAH!

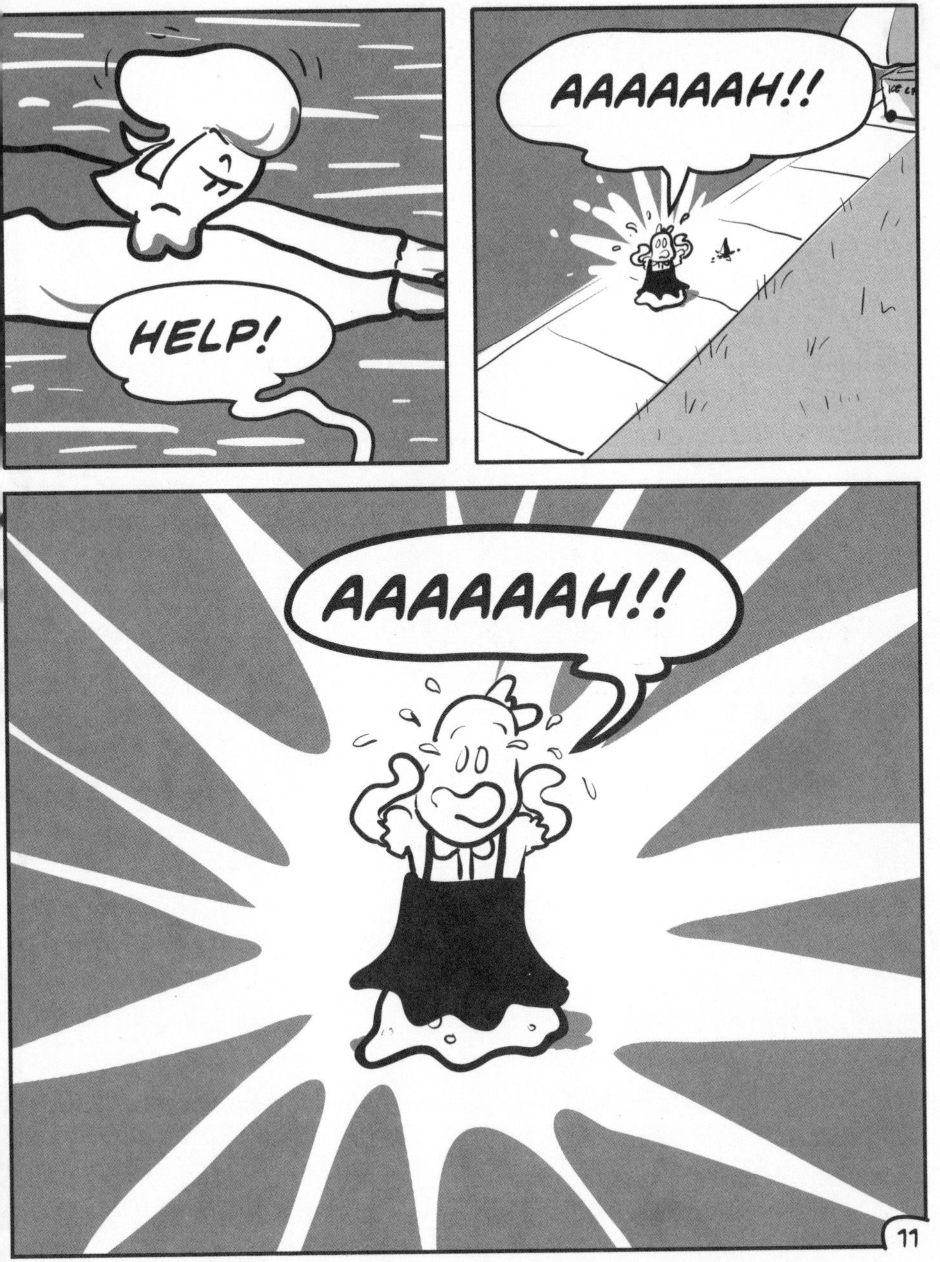
HELP!
AAAAAAH!!
AAAAAAH!!

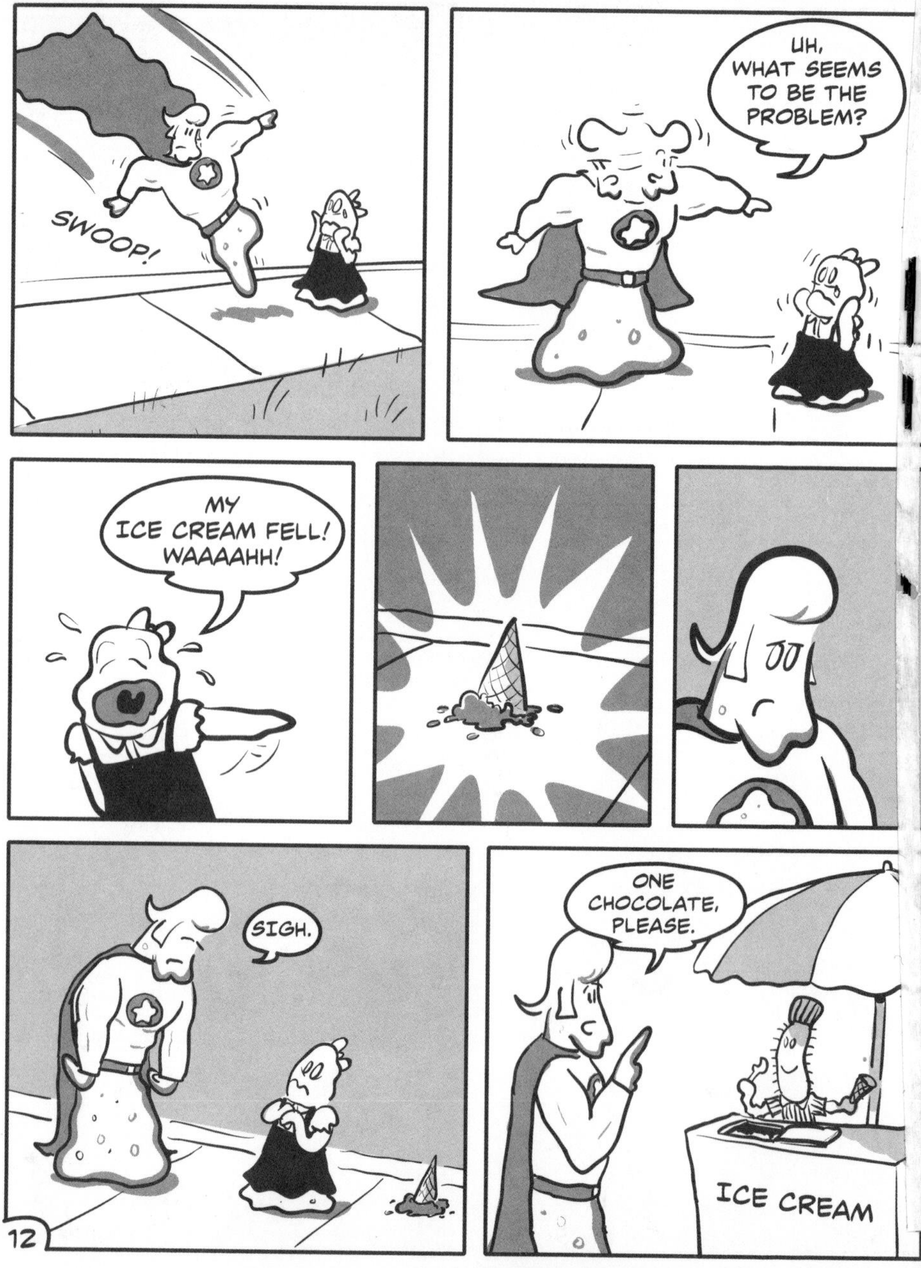
SWOOP!
UH, WHAT SEEMS TO BE THE PROBLEM?
MY ICE CREAM FELL! WAAAAHH!
SIGH.
ONE CHOCOLATE, PLEASE.
ICE CREAM

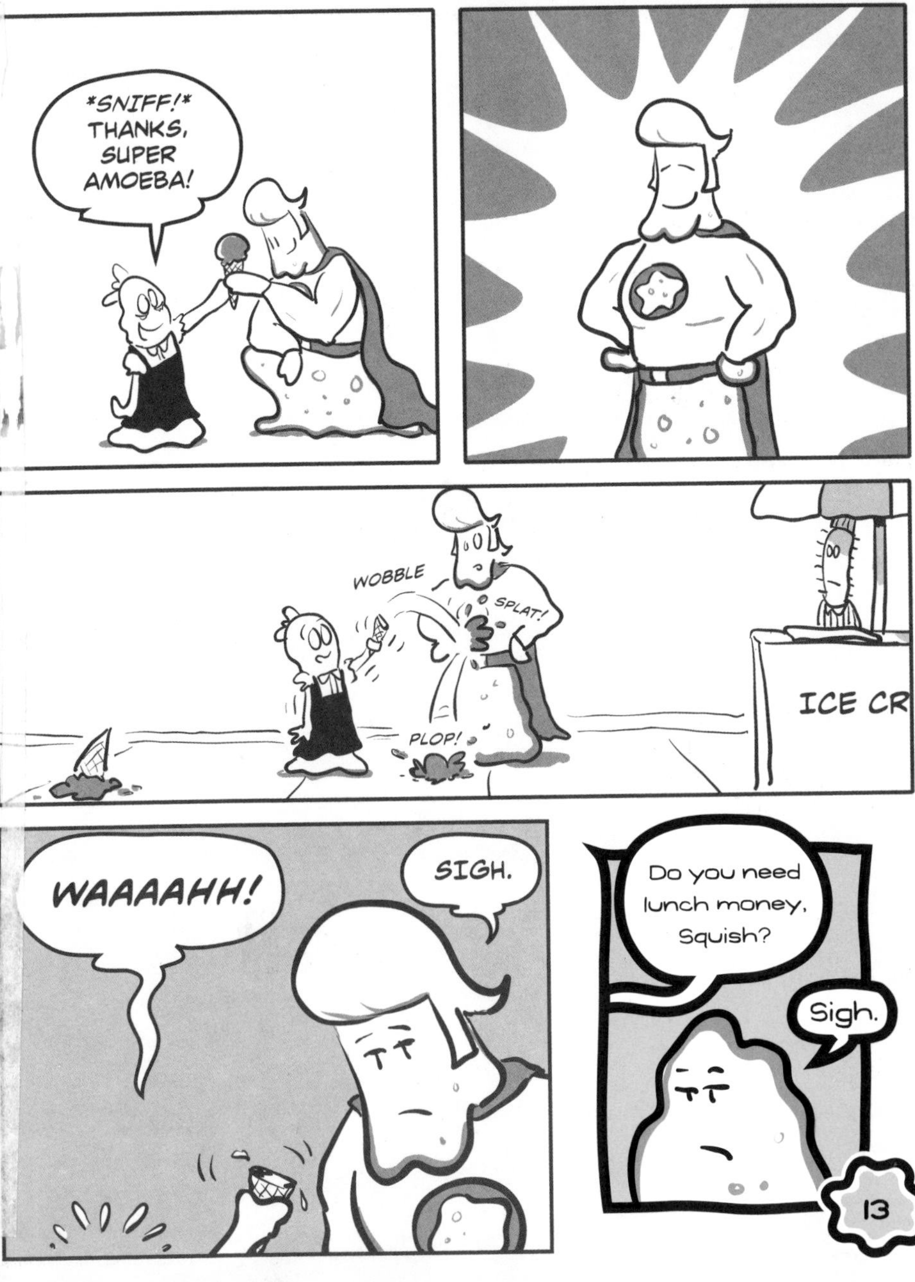
SNIFF! THANKS, SUPER AMOEBA!
WOBBLE
SPLAT!
PLOP!
ICE CR
WAAAAHH!
SIGH.
Do you need lunch money, Squish?
Sigh.

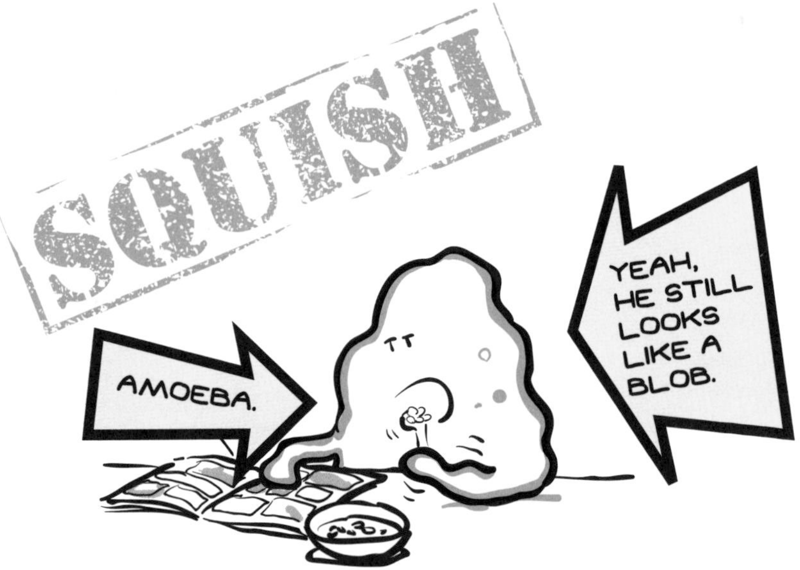
SQUISH
AMOEBA.
YEAH, HE STILL LOOKS LIKE A BLOB.

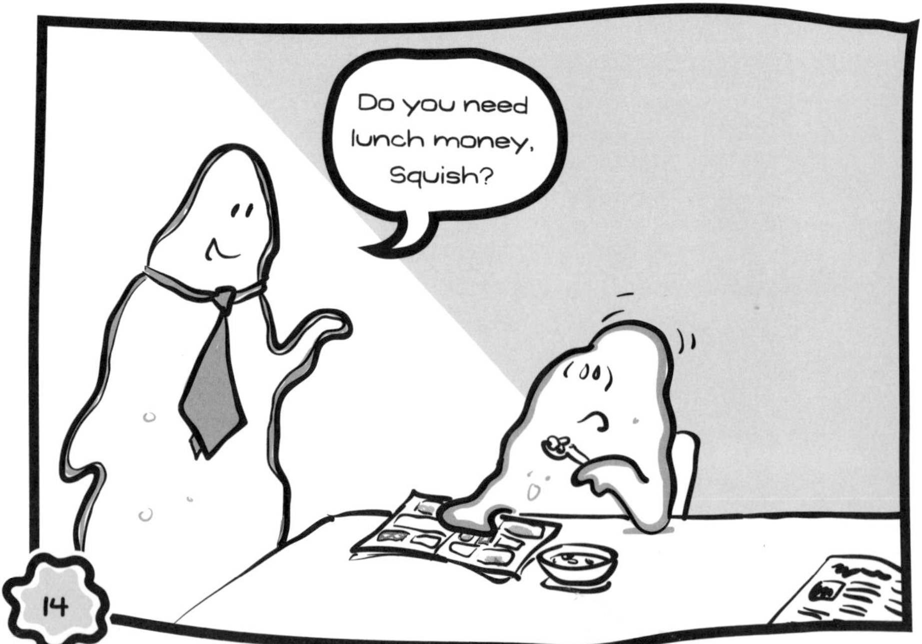
Do you need lunch money, Squish?

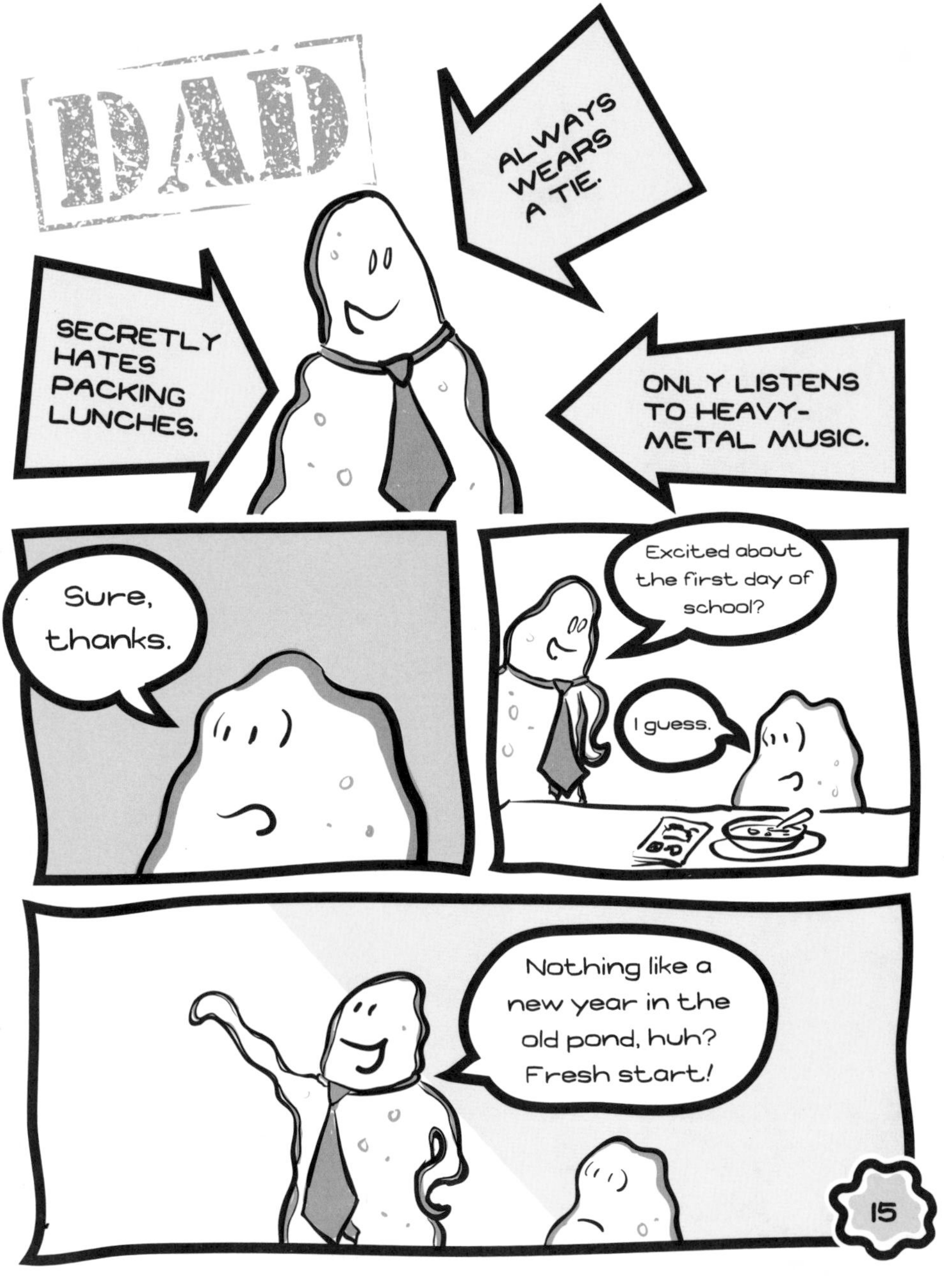
DAD
ALWAYS WEARS A TIE.
SECRETLY HATES PACKING LUNCHES.
ONLY LISTENS TO HEAVY-METAL MUSIC.
Sure, thanks.
Excited about the first day of school?
I guess.
Nothing like a new year in the old pond, huh? Fresh start!
15

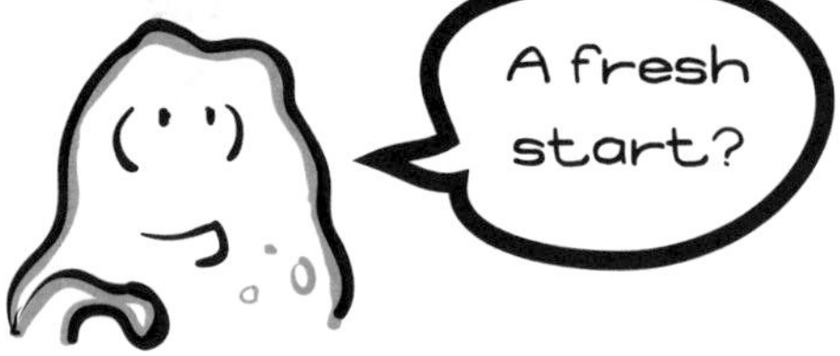
A fresh start?

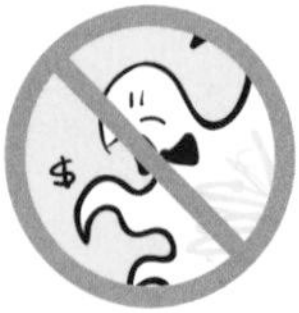
NO TRADING FOOD WITH POD!

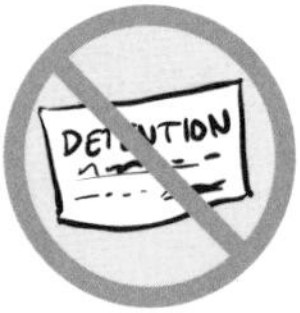
NO DETENTION!

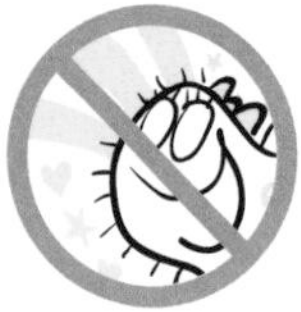
DO NOT LET PEGGY EMBARRASS ME!

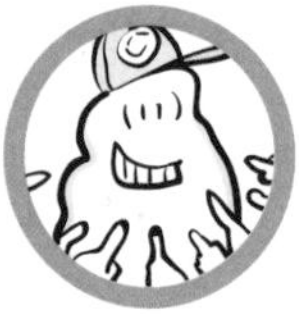
GET PICKED FOR KICKBALL AT RECESS!

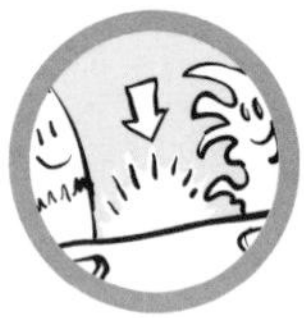
SIT WITH COOL KIDS AT LUNCH!

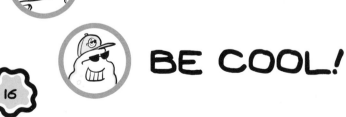

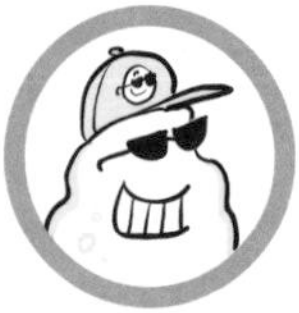
BE COOL!

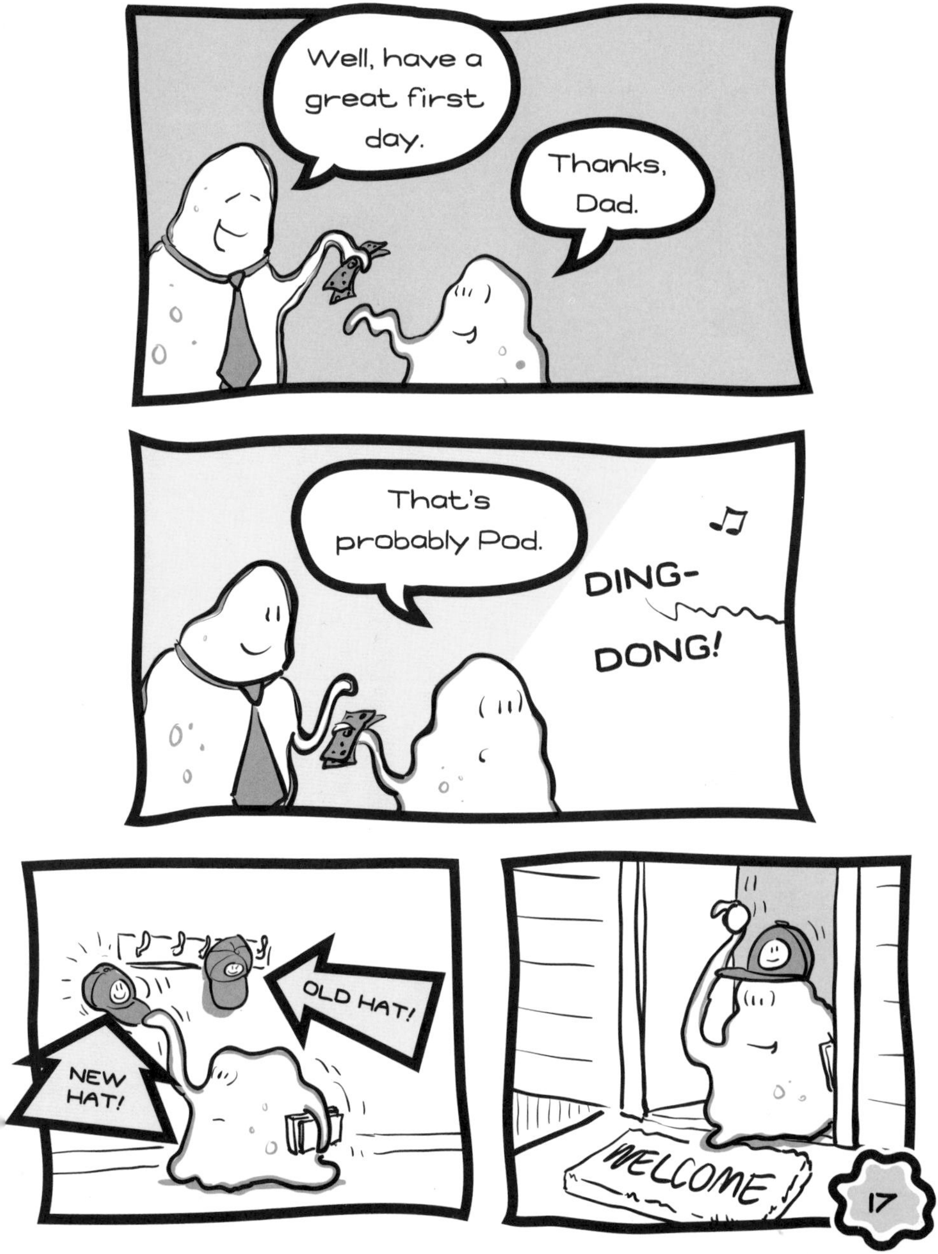
Well, have a great first day.
Thanks, Dad.
That's probably Pod.
DING-DONG!
NEW HAT!
OLD HAT!
WELCOME

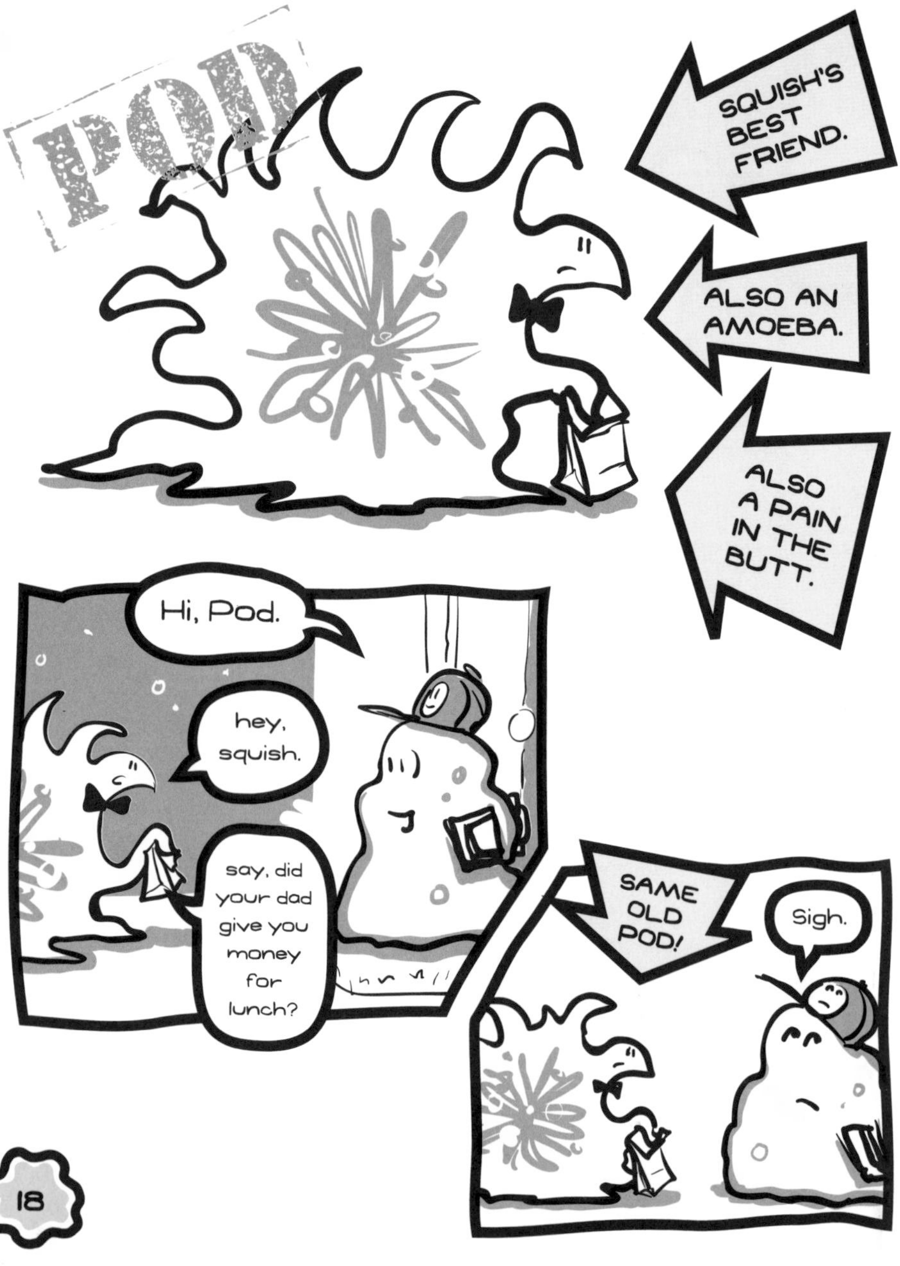
POD
SQUISH'S BEST FRIEND.
ALSO AN AMOEBA.
ALSO A PAIN IN THE BUTT.
Hi, Pod.
hey, squish.
say, did your dad give you money for lunch?
SAME OLD POD!
Sigh.

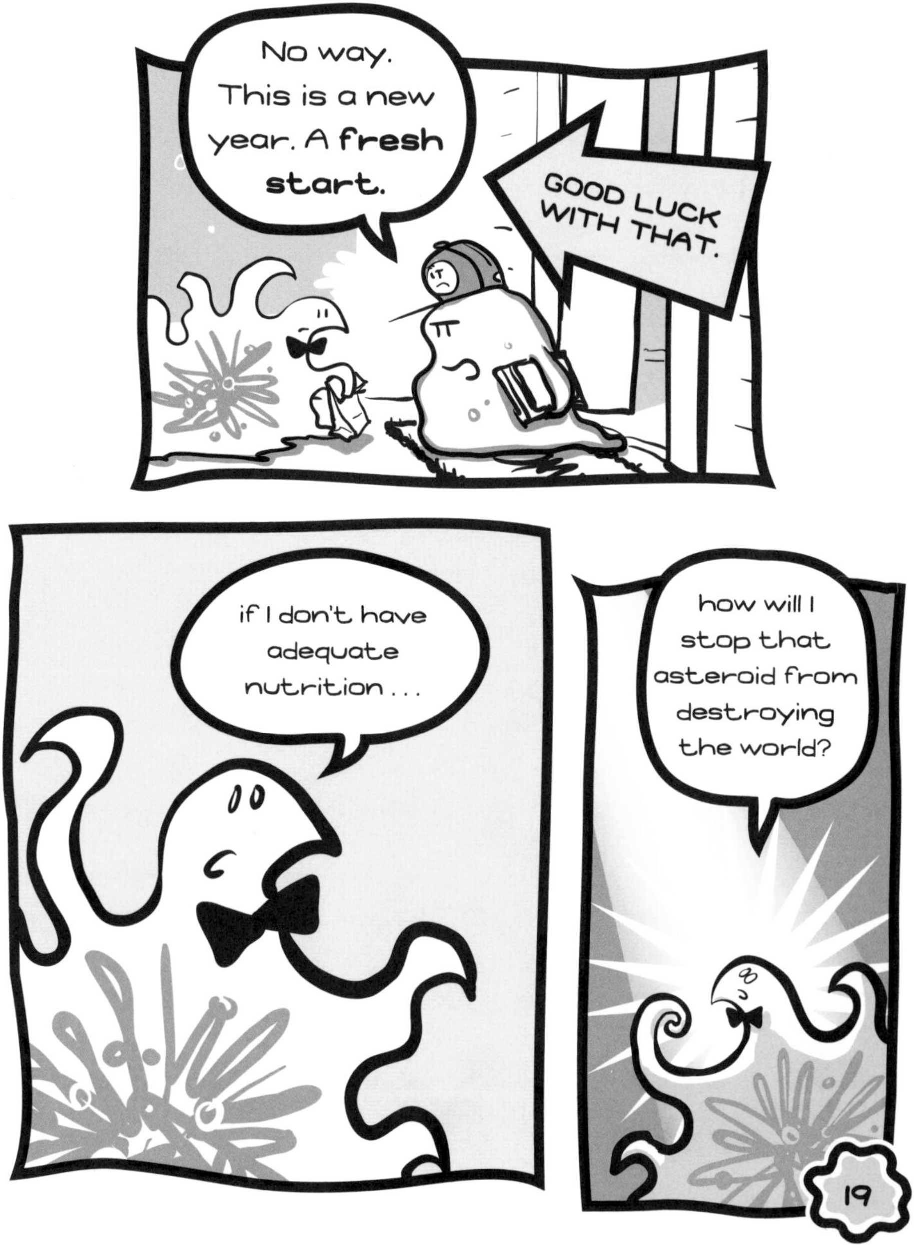

No way. This is a new year. A **fresh start.**
GOOD LUCK WITH THAT.
if I don't have adequate nutrition . . .
how will I stop that asteroid from destroying the world?

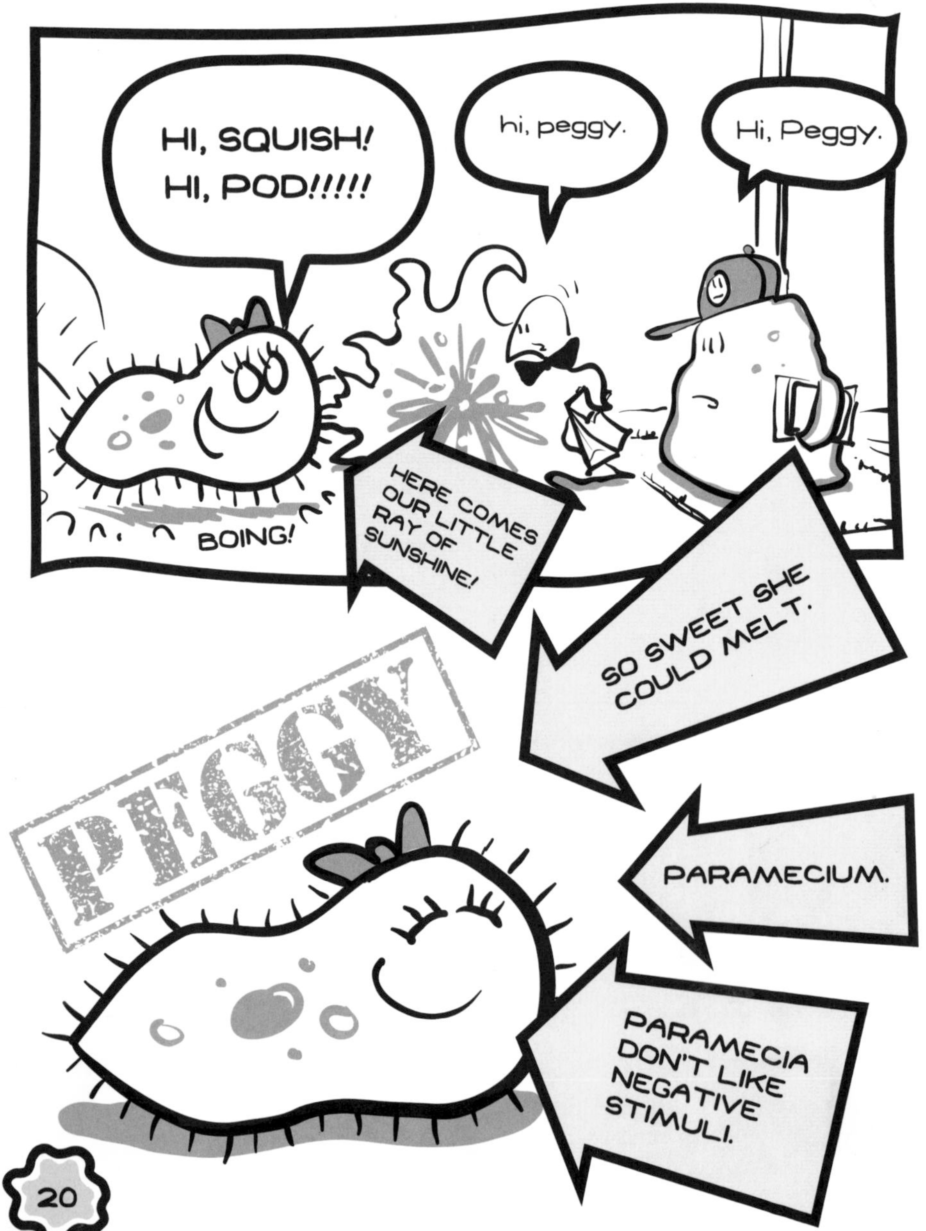
HI, SQUISH!
HI, POD!!!!!
hi, peggy.
Hi, Peggy.
BOING!
HERE COMES OUR LITTLE RAY OF SUNSHINE!
SO SWEET SHE COULD MELT.
PEGGY
PARAMECIUM.
PARAMECIA DON'T LIKE NEGATIVE STIMULI.

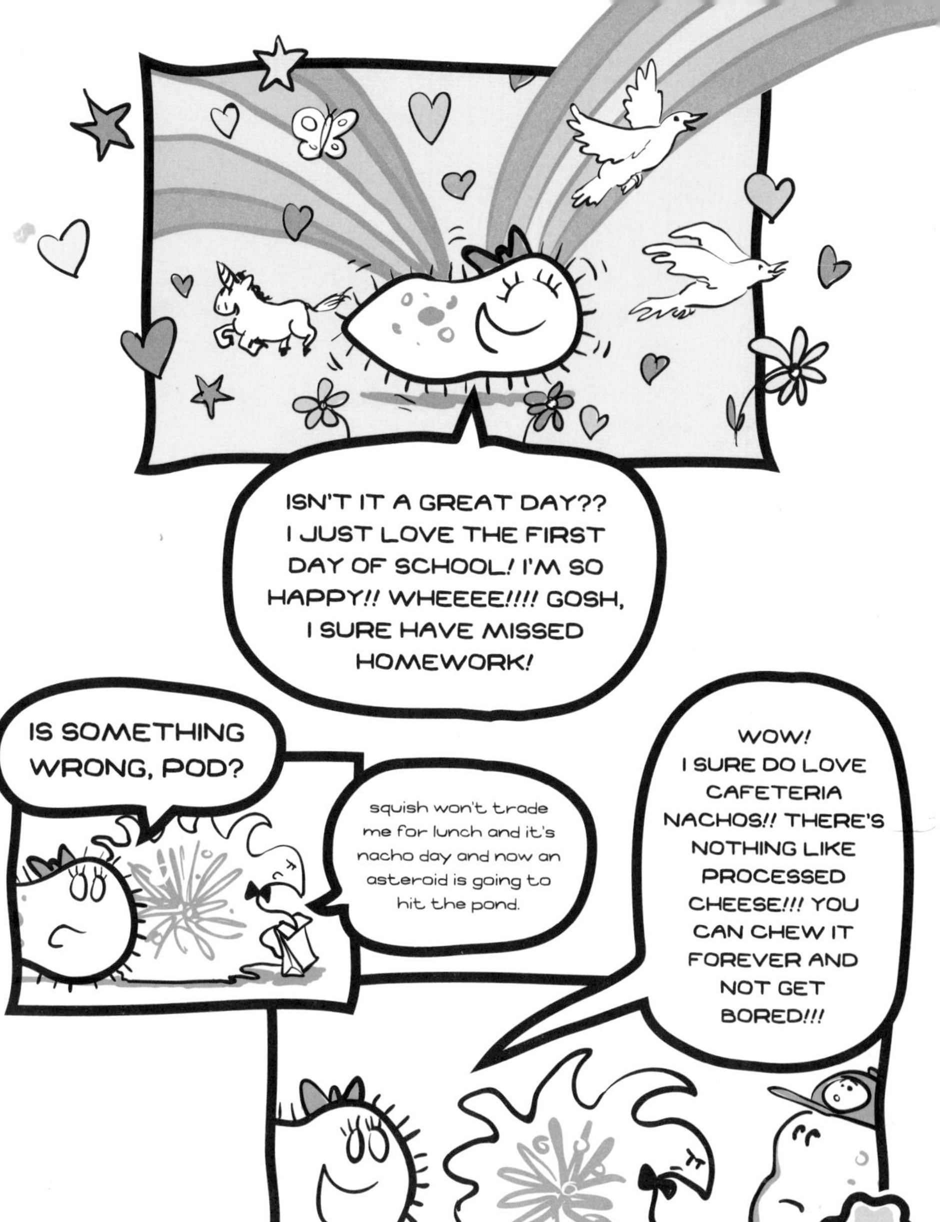
ISN'T IT A GREAT DAY?? I JUST LOVE THE FIRST DAY OF SCHOOL! I'M SO HAPPY!! WHEEEE!!!! GOSH, I SURE HAVE MISSED HOMEWORK!
IS SOMETHING WRONG, POD?
squish won't trade me for lunch and it's nacho day and now an asteroid is going to hit the pond.
WOW! I SURE DO LOVE CAFETERIA NACHOS!! THERE'S NOTHING LIKE PROCESSED CHEESE!!! YOU CAN CHEW IT FOREVER AND NOT GET BORED!!!

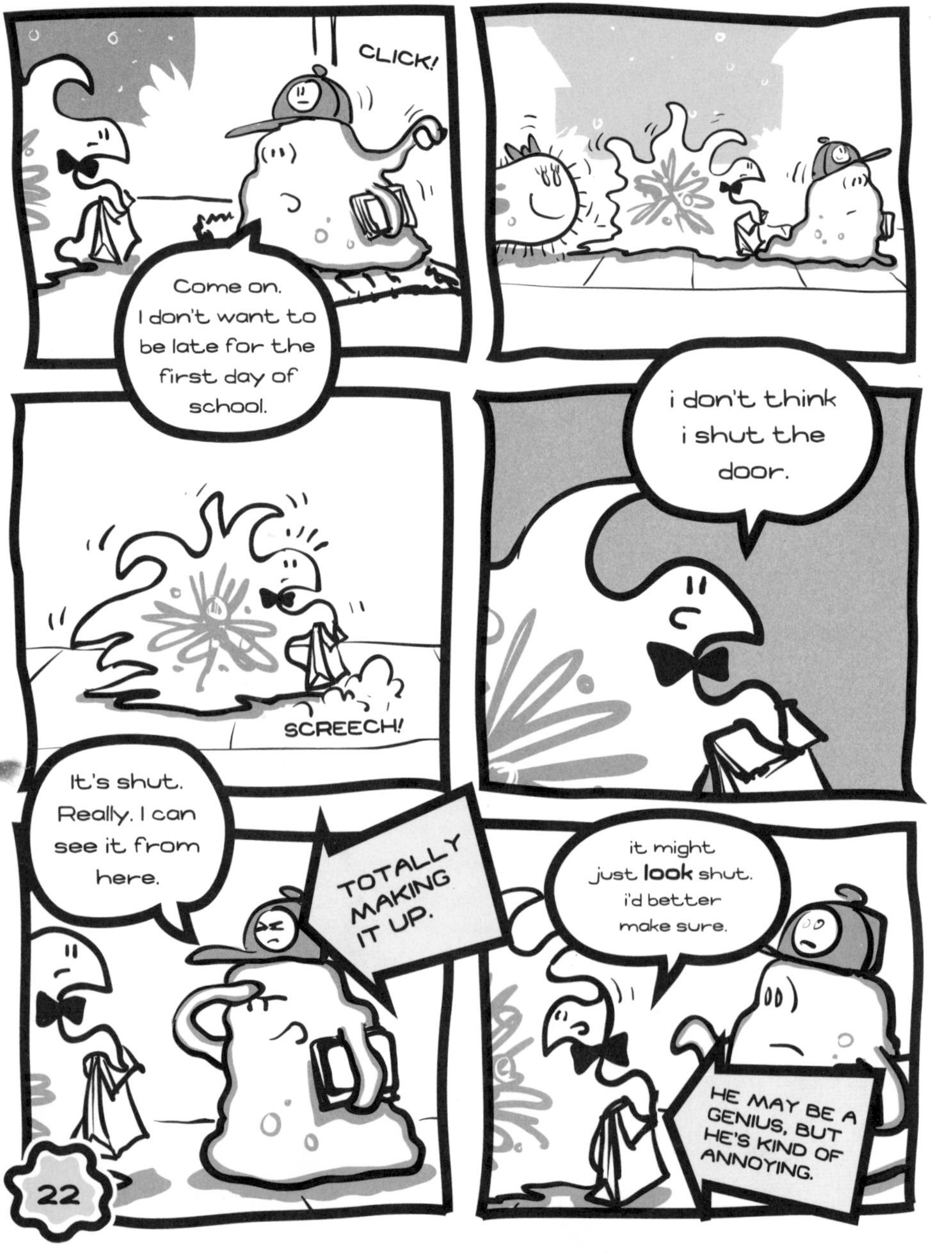
CLICK!
Come on. I don't want to be late for the first day of school.
SCREECH!
i don't think i shut the door.
It's shut. Really. I can see it from here.
TOTALLY MAKING IT UP.
it might just **look** shut. i'd better make sure.
HE MAY BE A GENIUS, BUT HE'S KIND OF ANNOYING.

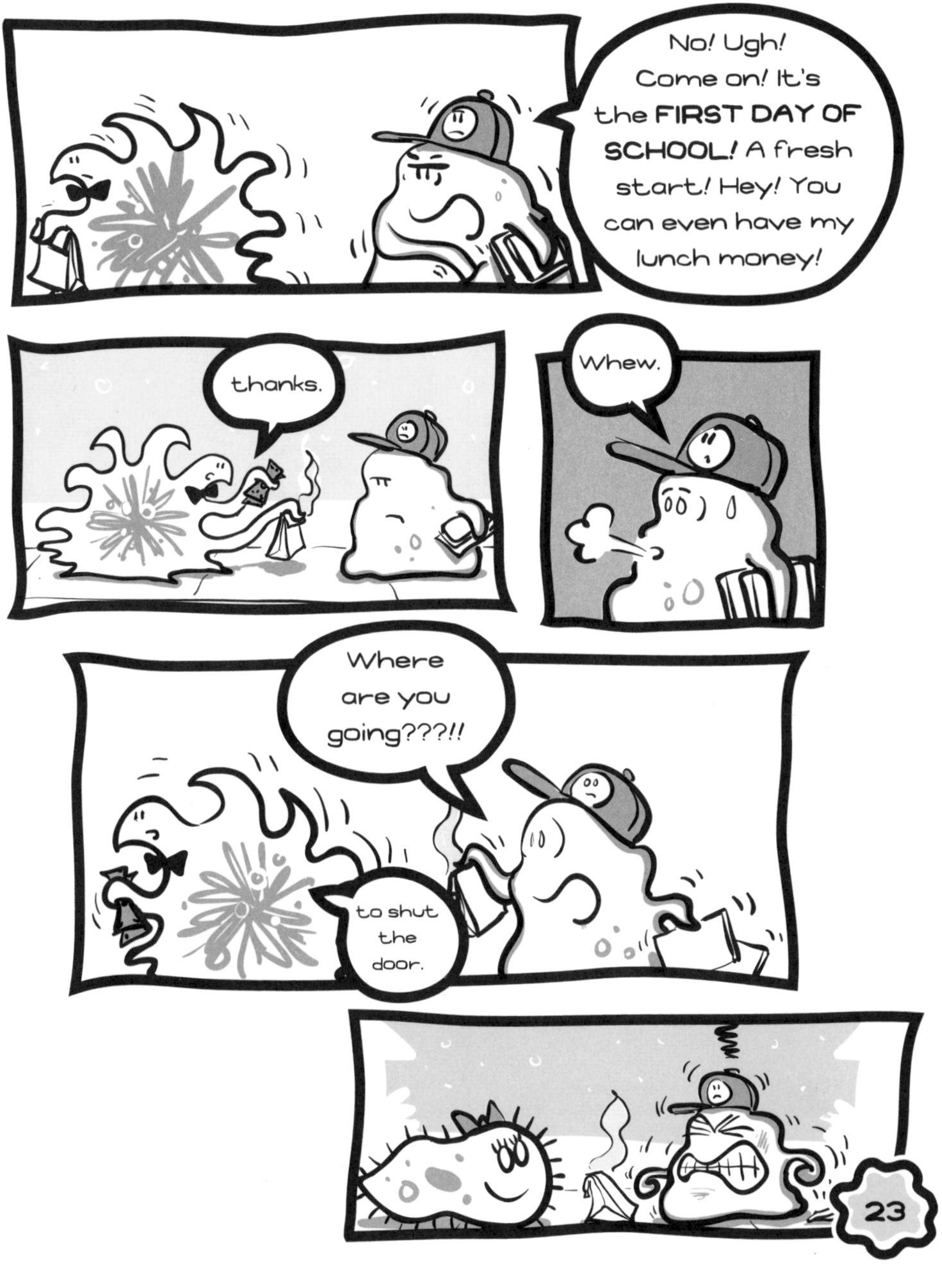
No! Ugh! Come on! It's the **FIRST DAY OF SCHOOL!** A fresh start! Hey! You can even have my lunch money!
thanks.
Whew.
Where are you going???!!
to shut the door.

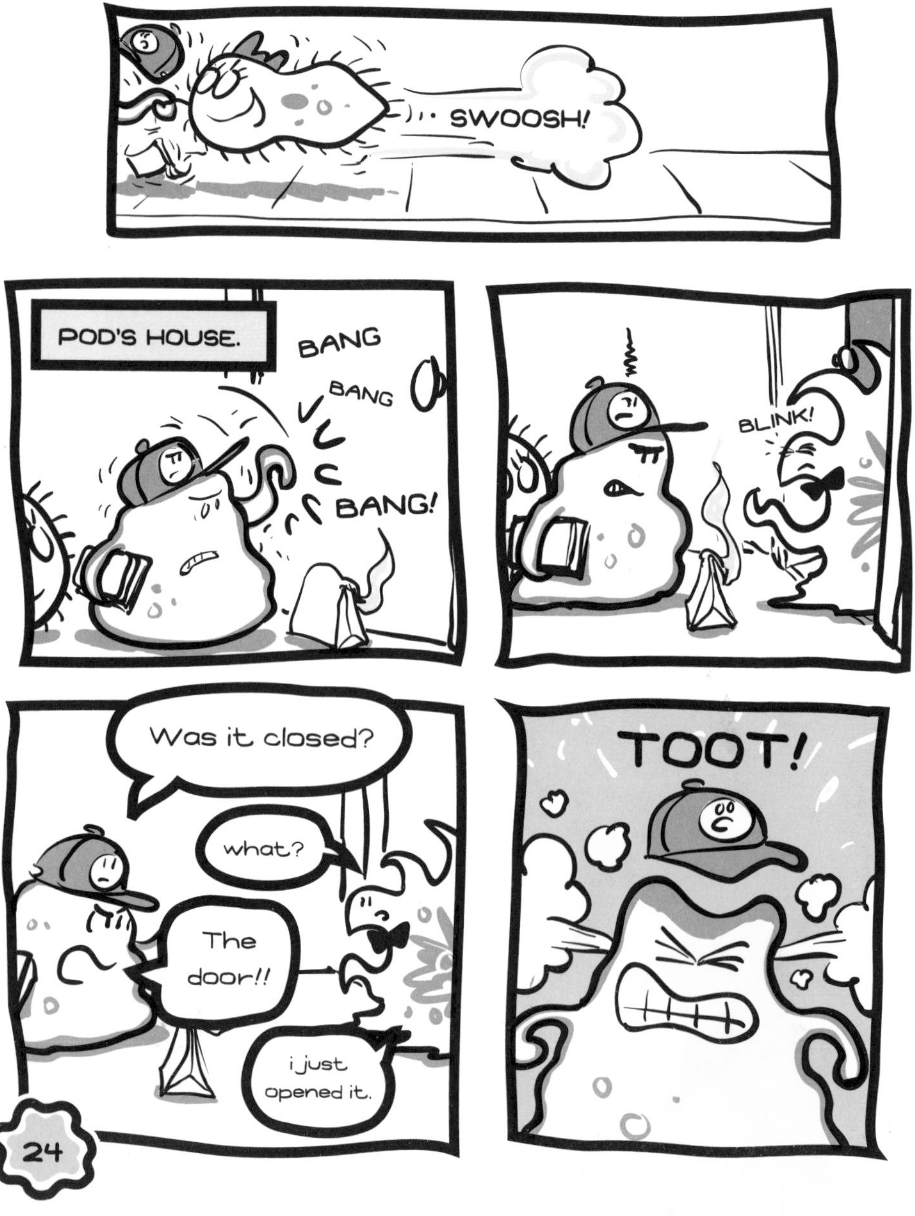
SWOOSH!
POD'S HOUSE.
BANG
BANG
BANG!
BLINK!
Was it closed?
what?
The door!!
i just opened it.
TOOT!

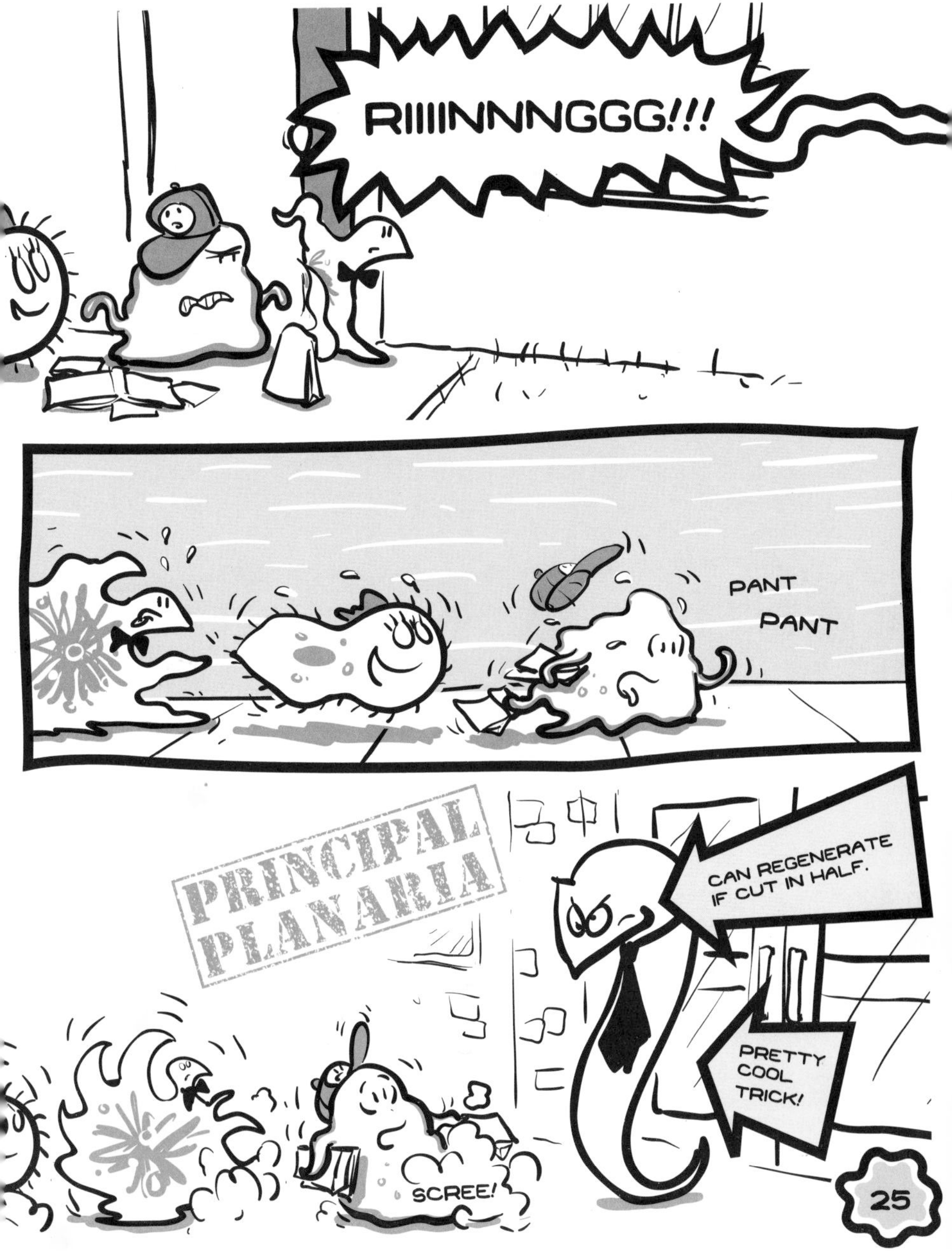
RIIIINNNGGG!!!
PANT
PANT
PRINCIPAL PLANARIA
CAN REGENERATE IF CUT IN HALF.
PRETTY COOL TRICK!
SCREE!

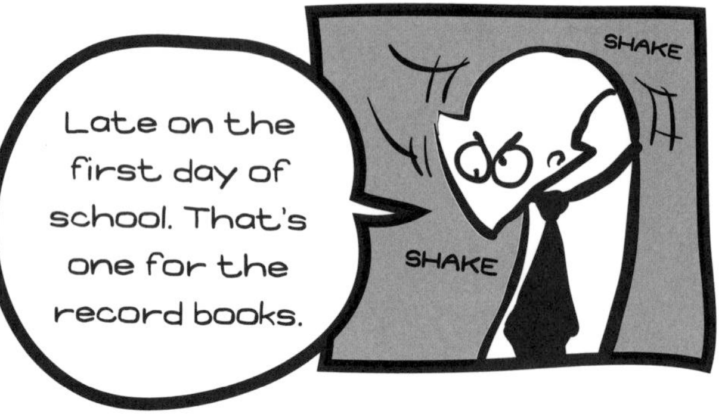
SHAKE
Late on the first day of school. That's one for the record books.
SHAKE

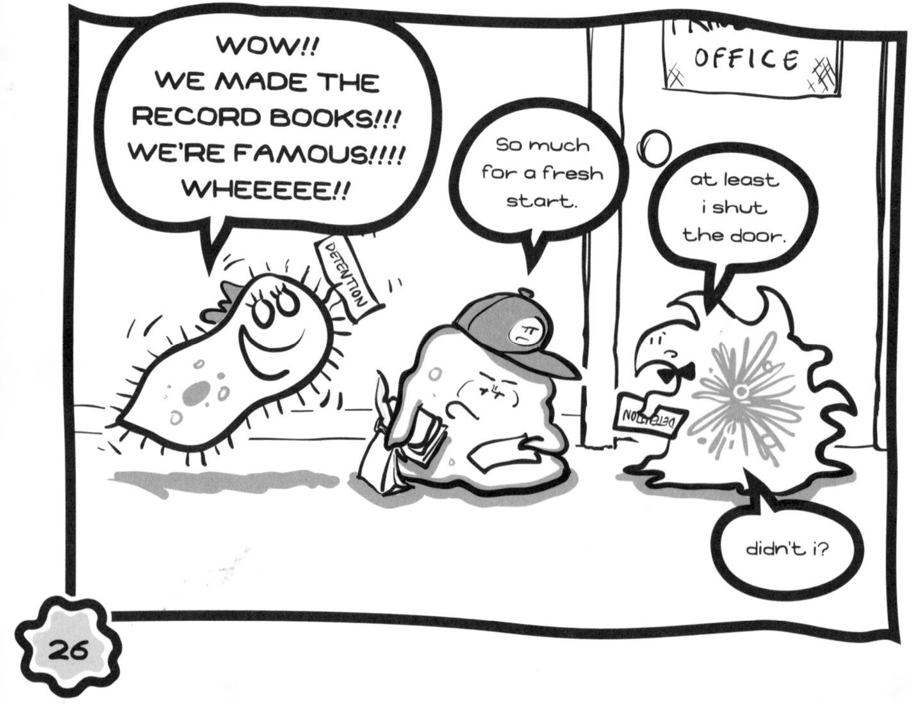
OFFICE
WOW!! WE MADE THE RECORD BOOKS!!! WE'RE FAMOUS!!!! WHEEEEE!!
DETENTION
So much for a fresh start.
at least i shut the door.
didn't i?

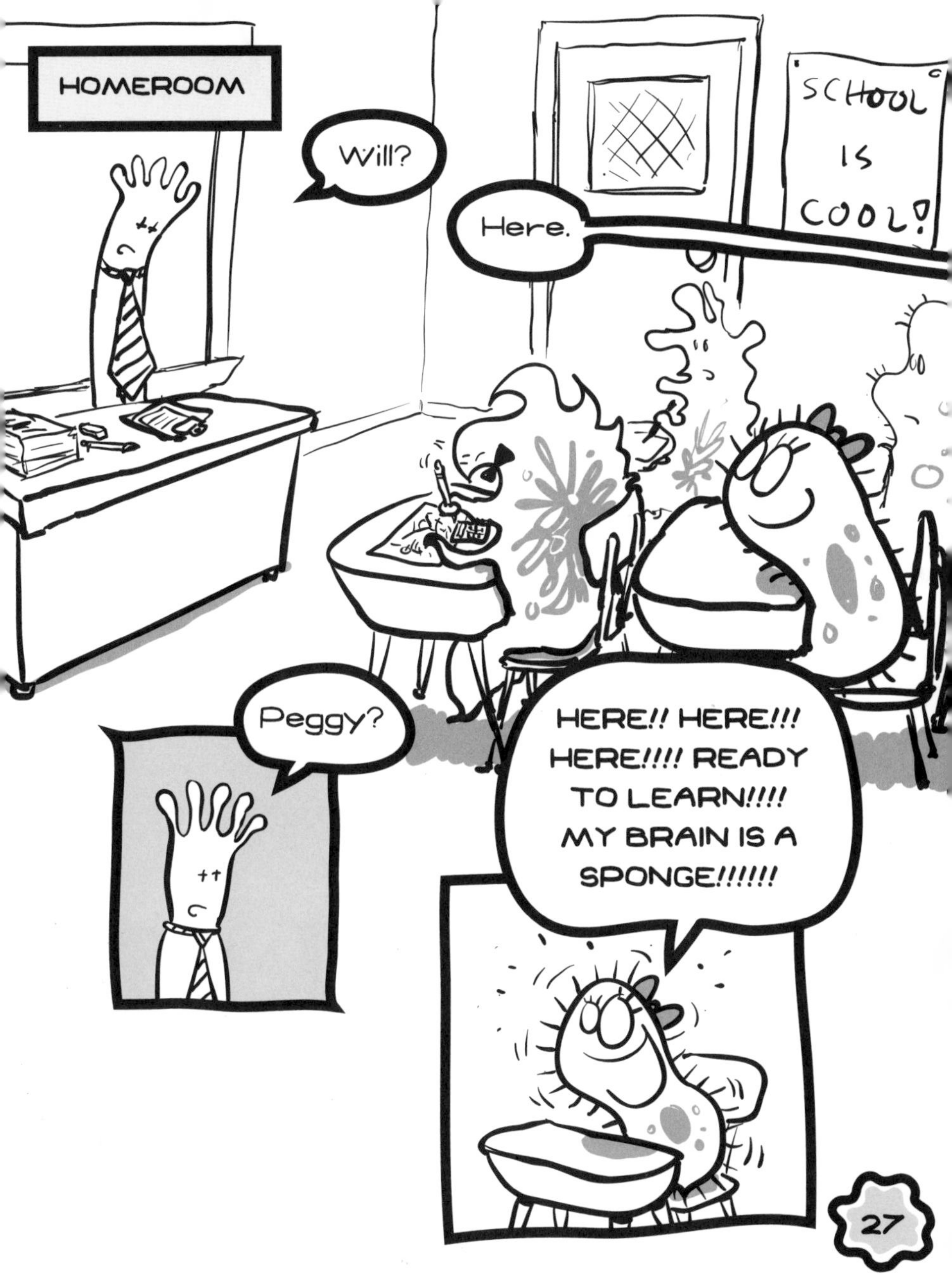

HOMEROOM
Will?
SCHOOL IS COOL!
Here.
Peggy?
HERE!! HERE!!! HERE!!!! READY TO LEARN!!!! MY BRAIN IS A SPONGE!!!!!!

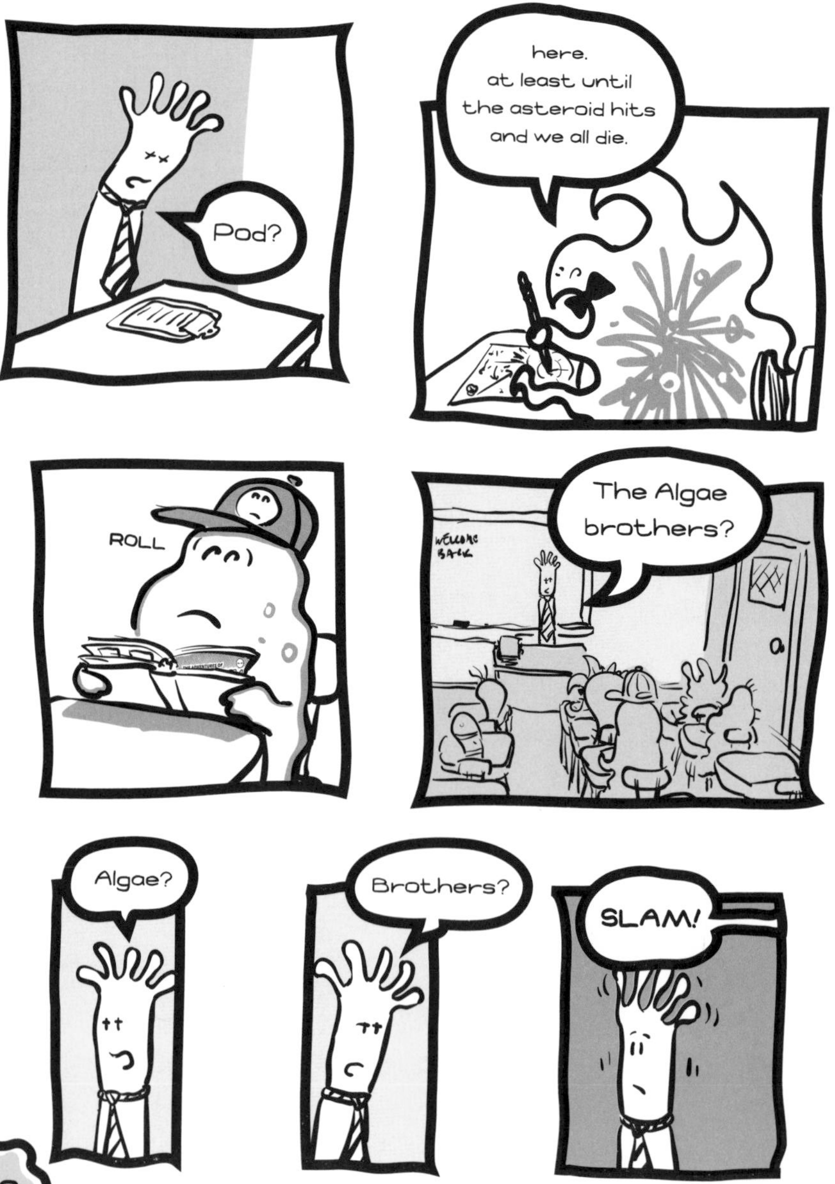
Pod?
here.
at least until
the asteroid hits
and we all die.
ROLL
The Algae
brothers?
Algae?
Brothers?
SLAM!

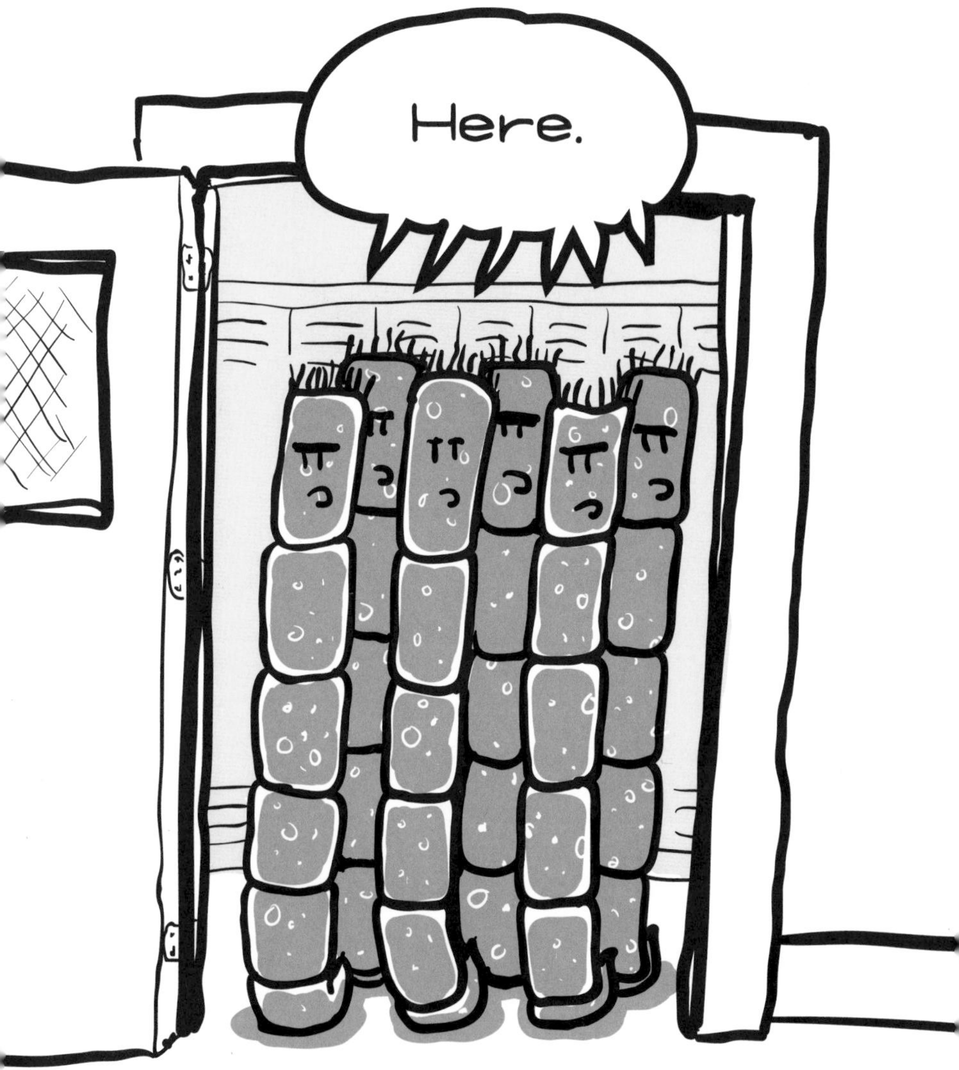
Here.

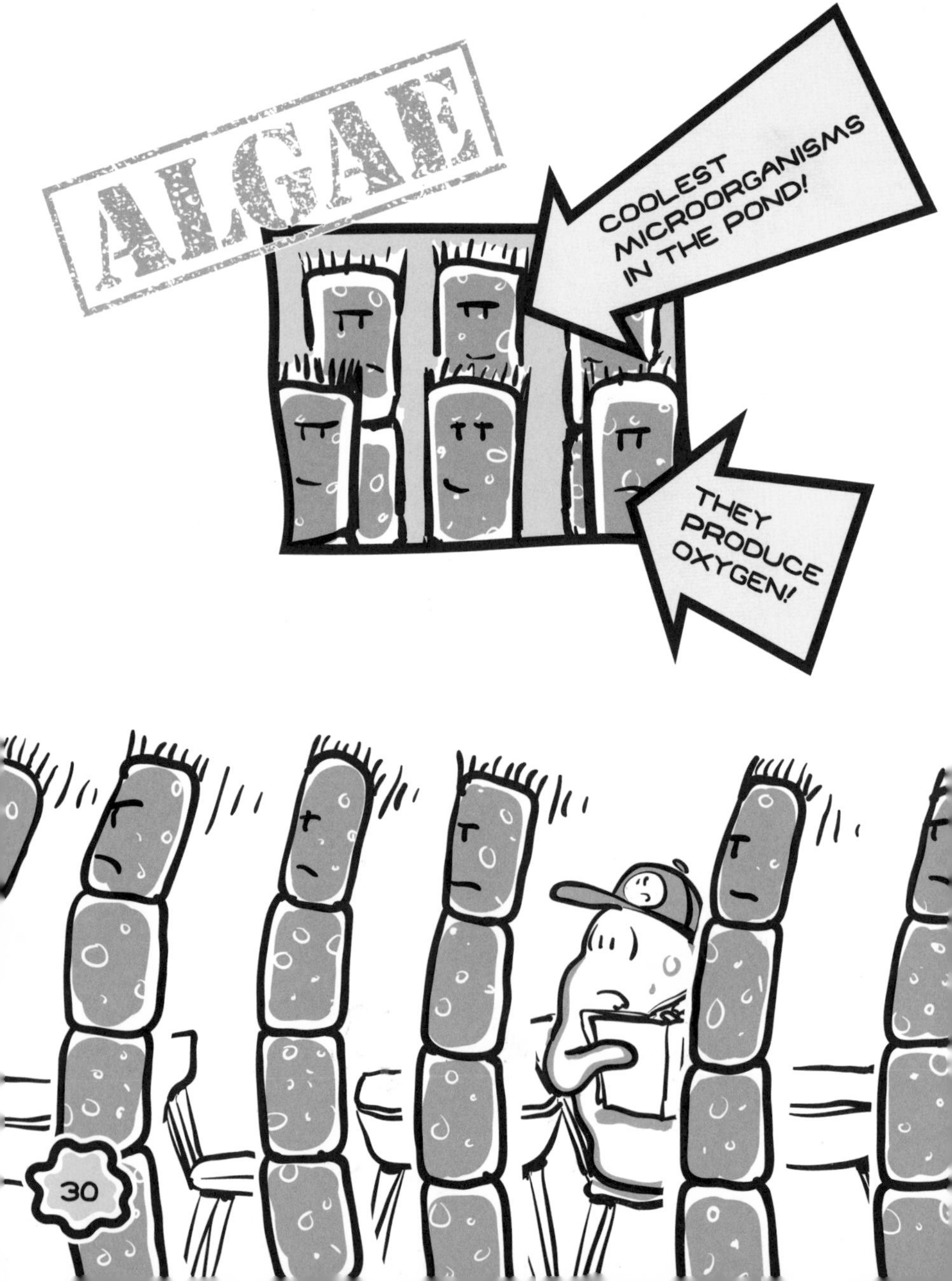
ALGAE
COOLEST MICROORGANISMS IN THE POND!
THEY PRODUCE OXYGEN!

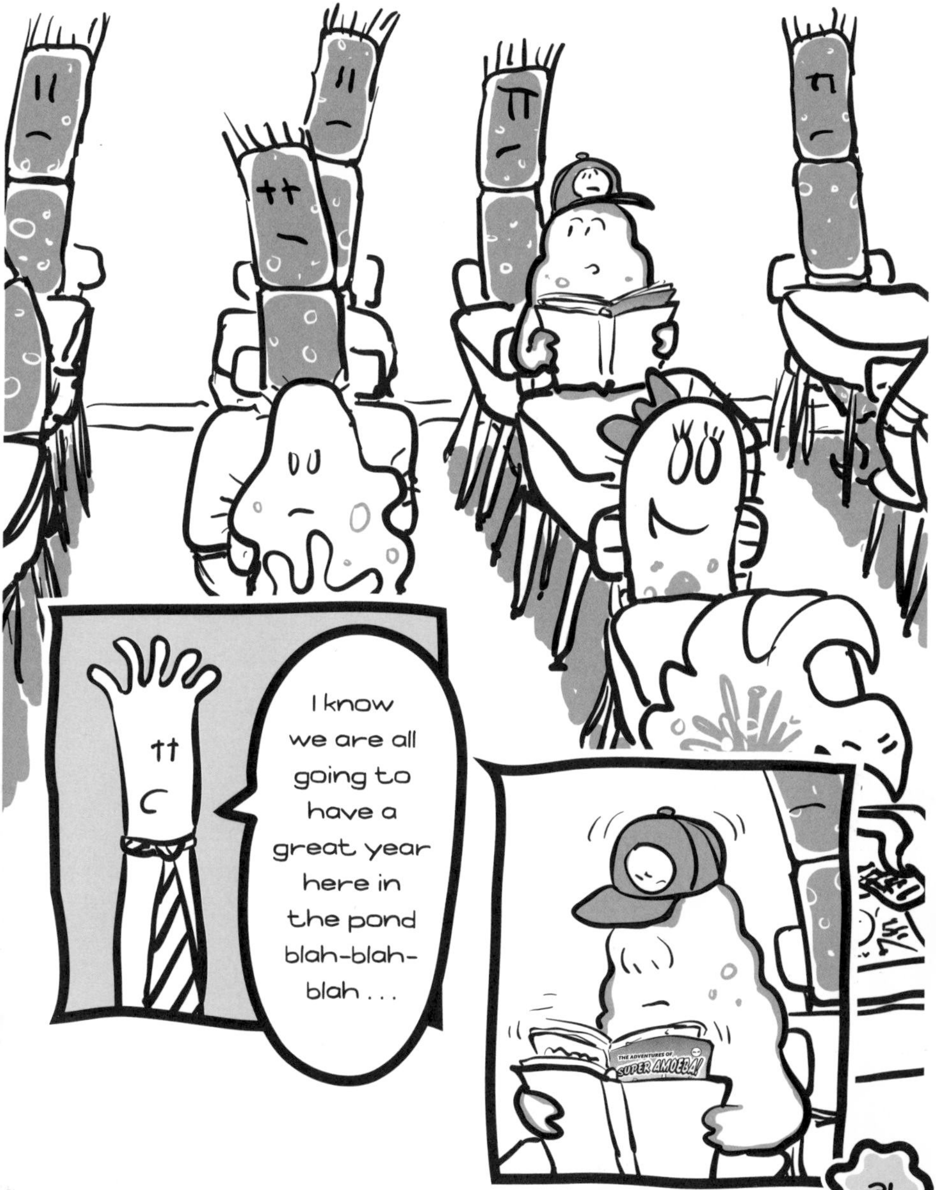
I know we are all going to have a great year here in the pond blah-blah-blah . . .
THE ADVENTURES OF
SUPER AMOEBA!

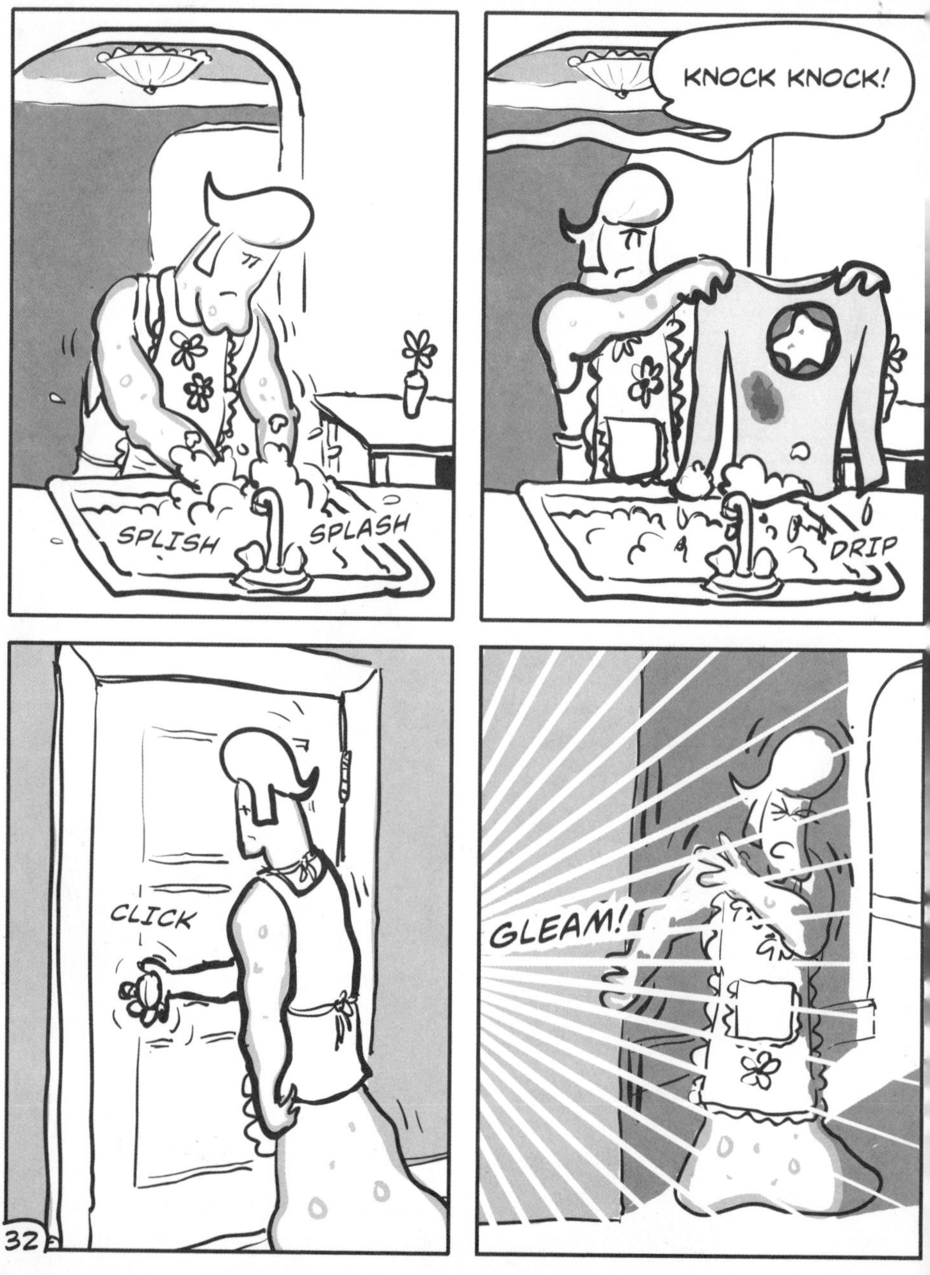
SPLISH
SPLASH
KNOCK KNOCK!
DRIP
CLICK
GLEAM!

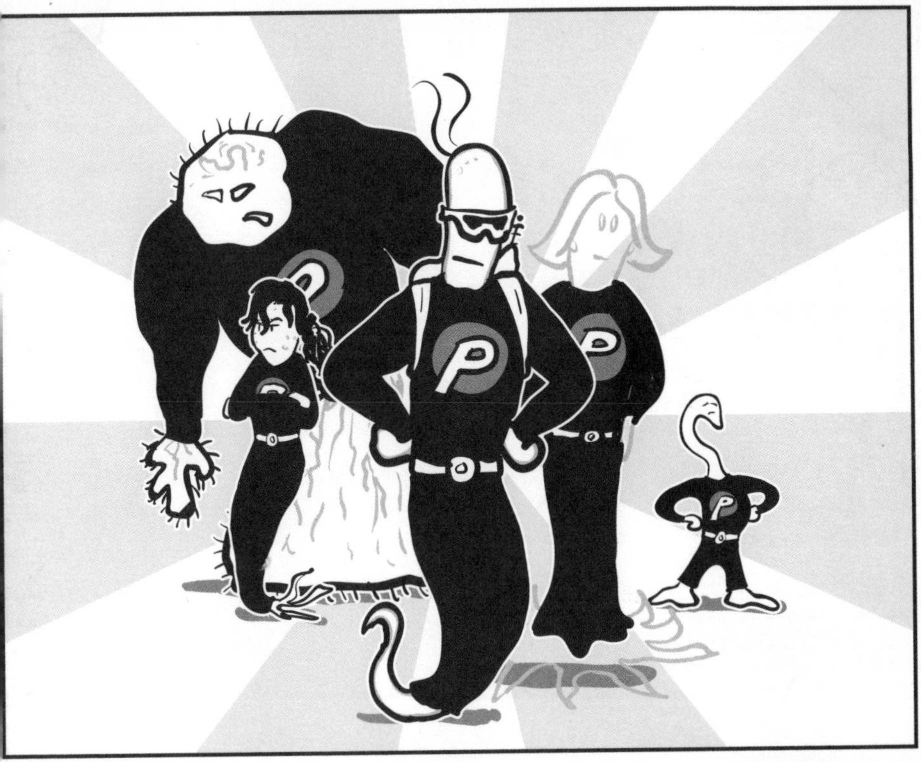

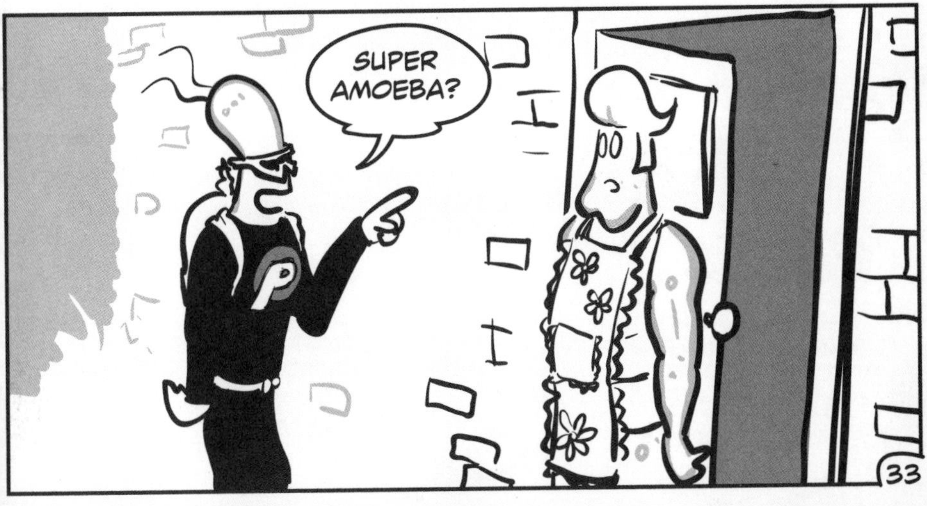
SUPER
AMOEBA?

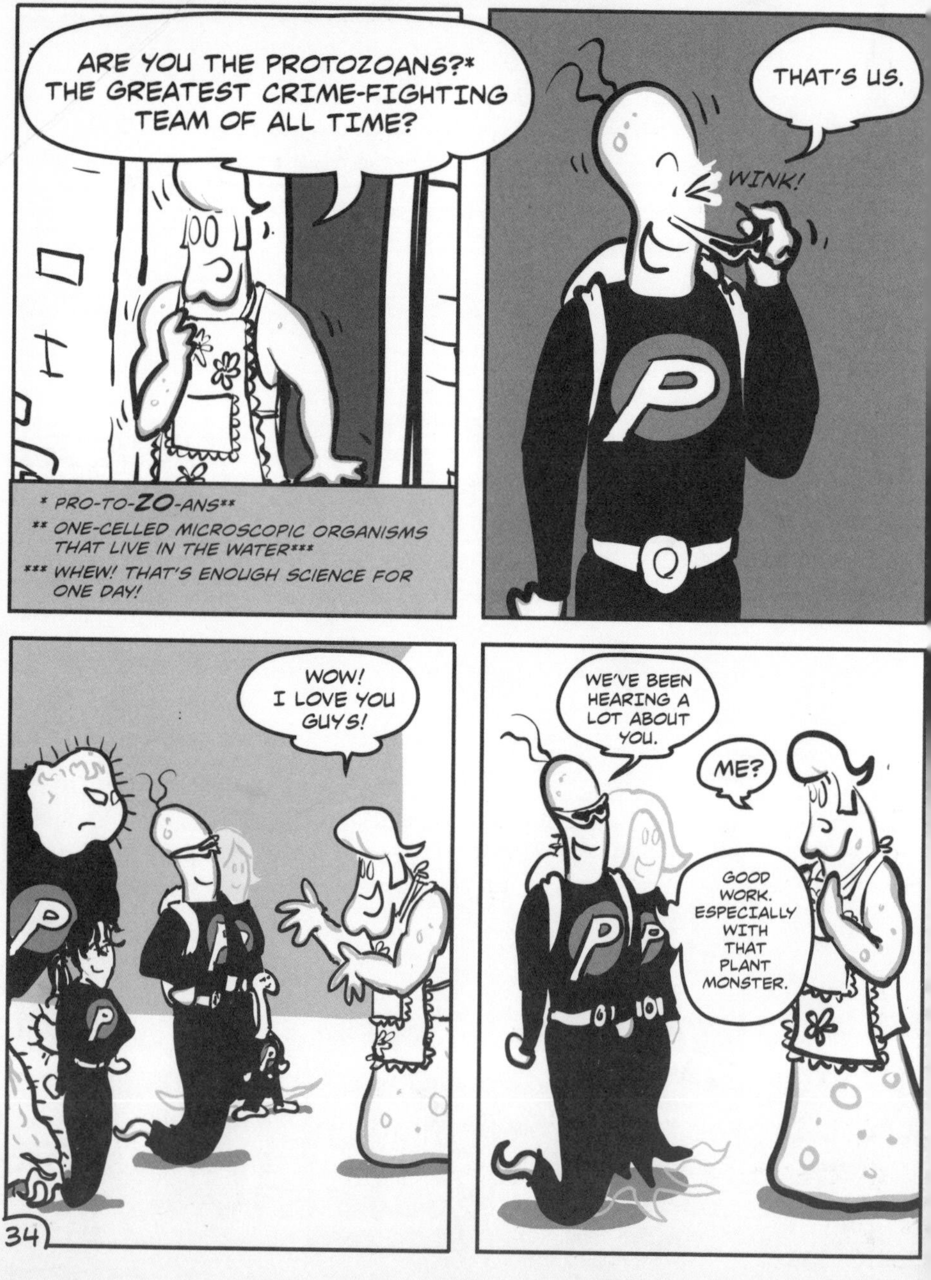
ARE YOU THE PROTOZOANS?* THE GREATEST CRIME-FIGHTING TEAM OF ALL TIME?
* PRO-TO-ZO-ANS**
** ONE-CELLED MICROSCOPIC ORGANISMS THAT LIVE IN THE WATER***
*** WHEW! THAT'S ENOUGH SCIENCE FOR ONE DAY!
THAT'S US.
WINK!
WOW! I LOVE YOU GUYS!
WE'VE BEEN HEARING A LOT ABOUT YOU.
ME?
GOOD WORK. ESPECIALLY WITH THAT PLANT MONSTER.

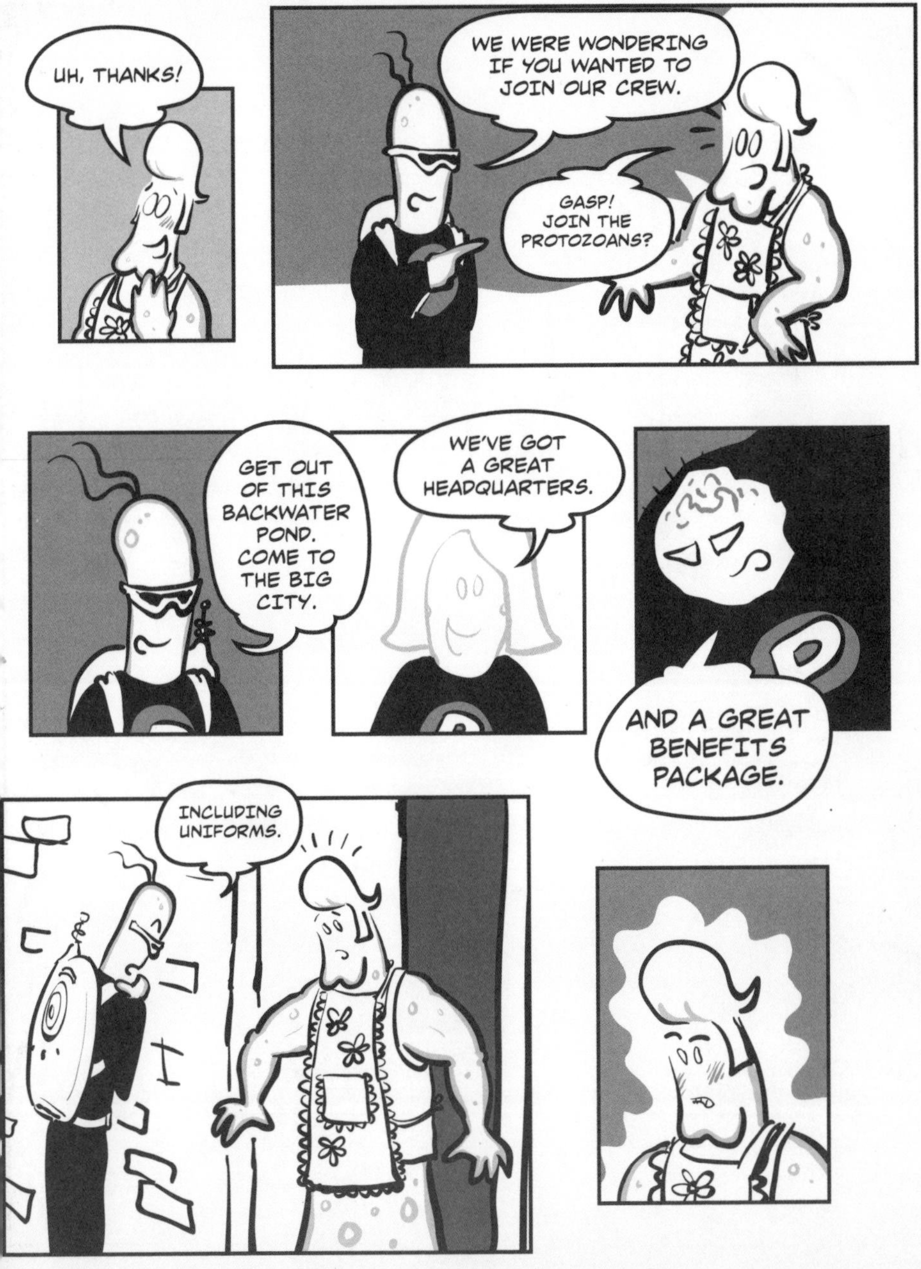
UH, THANKS!
WE WERE WONDERING IF YOU WANTED TO JOIN OUR CREW.
GASP! JOIN THE PROTOZOANS?
GET OUT OF THIS BACKWATER POND. COME TO THE BIG CITY.
WE'VE GOT A GREAT HEADQUARTERS.
AND A GREAT BENEFITS PACKAGE.
INCLUDING UNIFORMS.

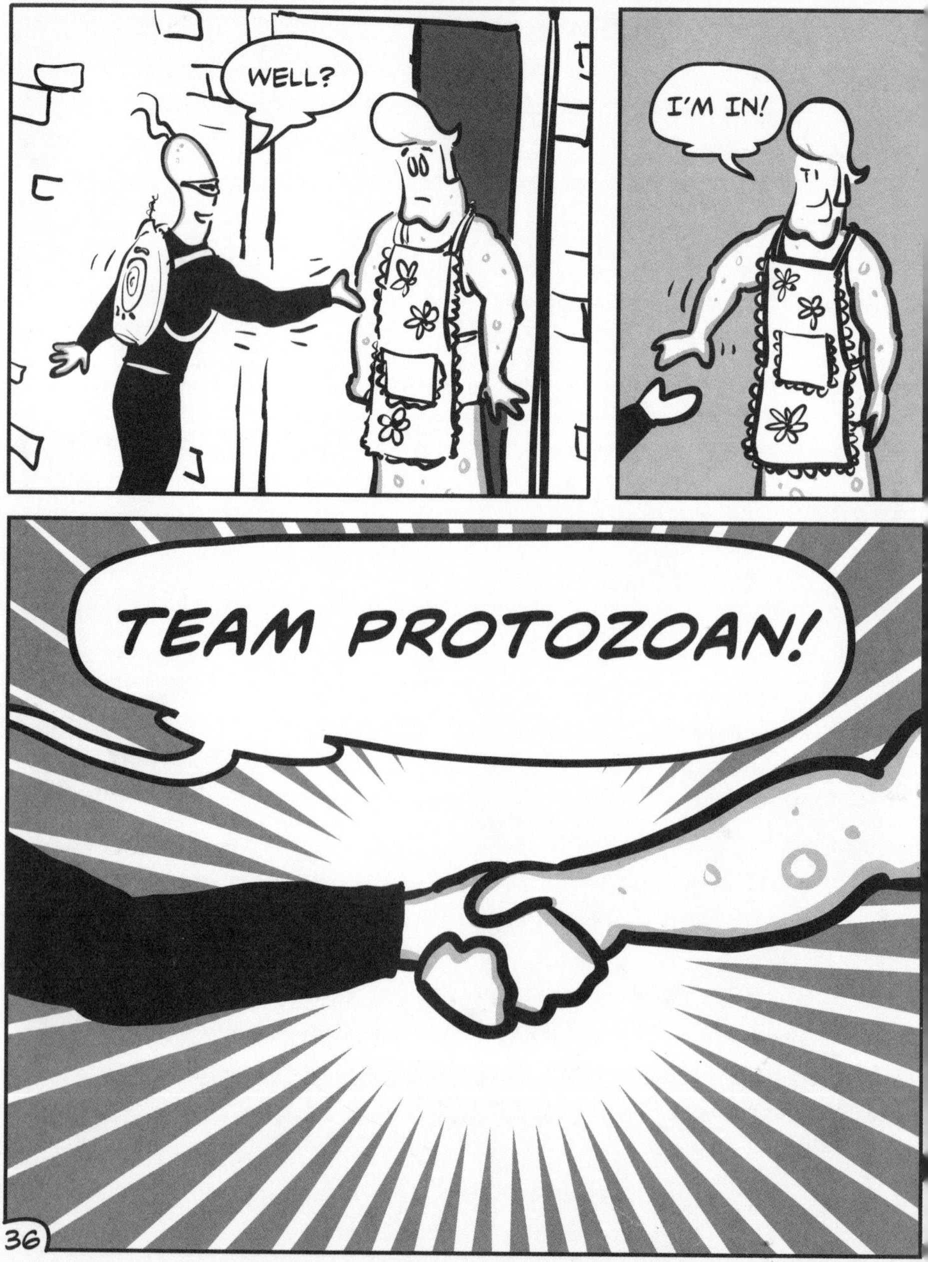
WELL?
I'M IN!
TEAM PROTOZOAN!

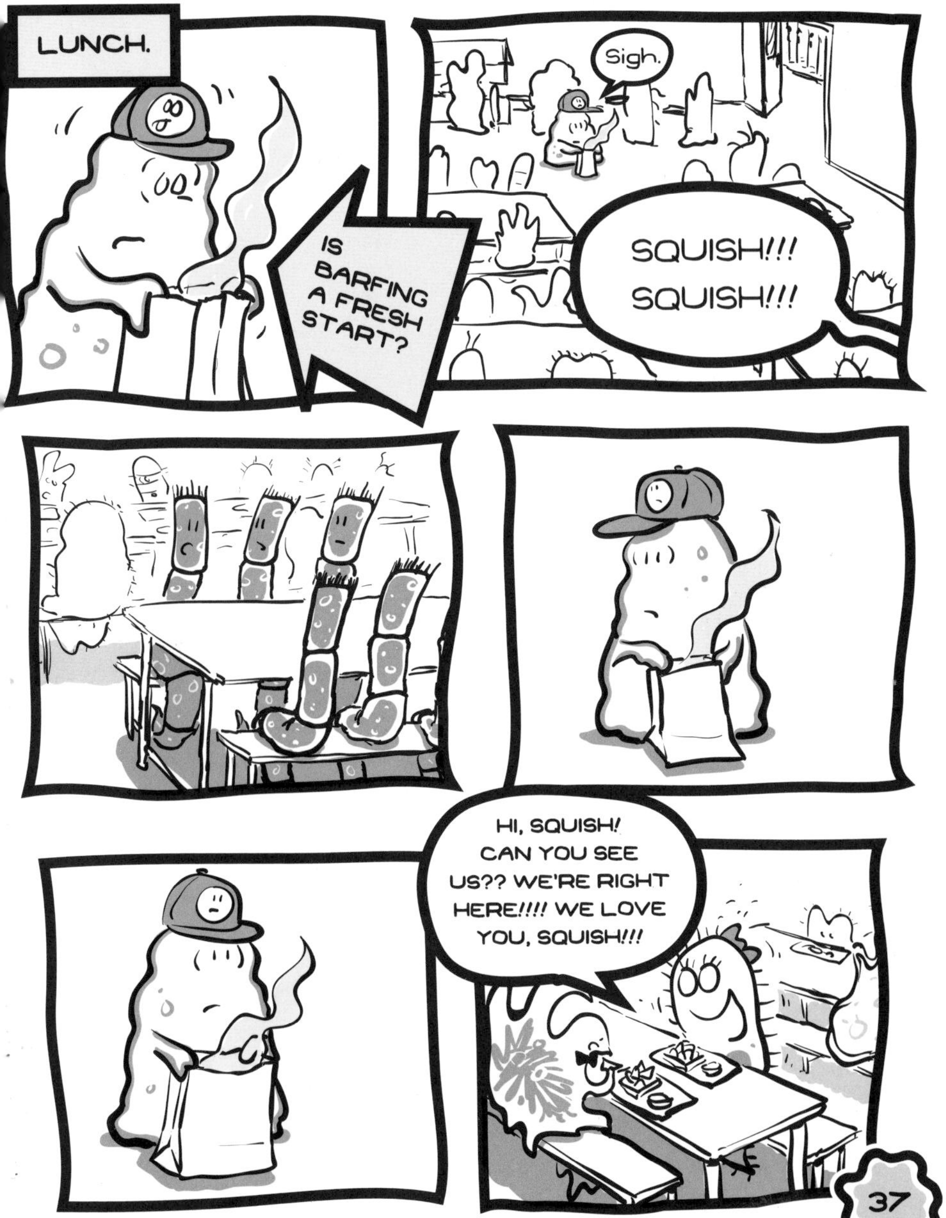
LUNCH.
IS BARFING A FRESH START?
Sigh.
SQUISH!!!
SQUISH!!!
HI, SQUISH! CAN YOU SEE US?? WE'RE RIGHT HERE!!!! WE LOVE YOU, SQUISH!!!

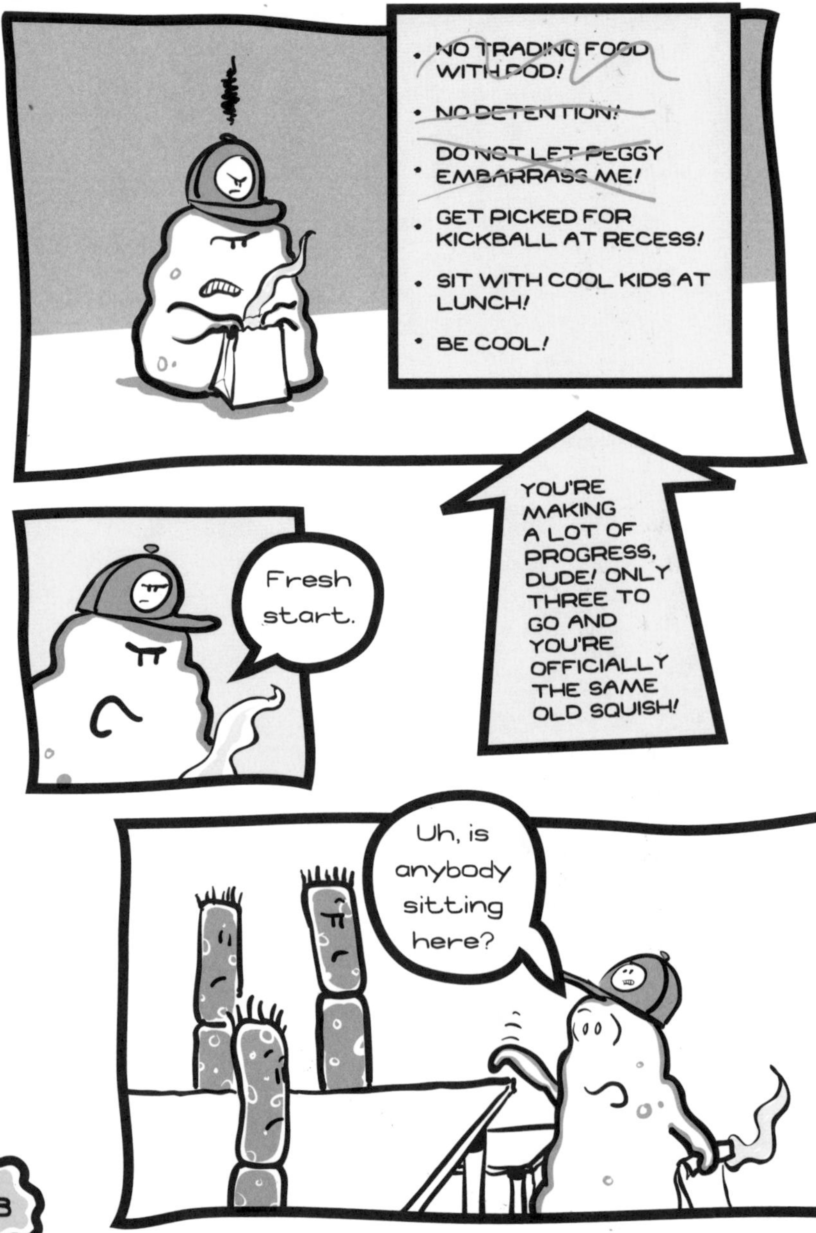

NO TRADING FOOD WITH POD!
NO DETENTION!
DO NOT LET PEGGY EMBARRASS ME!
GET PICKED FOR KICKBALL AT RECESS!
SIT WITH COOL KIDS AT LUNCH!
BE COOL!
Fresh start.
YOU'RE MAKING A LOT OF PROGRESS, DUDE! ONLY THREE TO GO AND YOU'RE OFFICIALLY THE SAME OLD SQUISH!
Uh, is anybody sitting here?

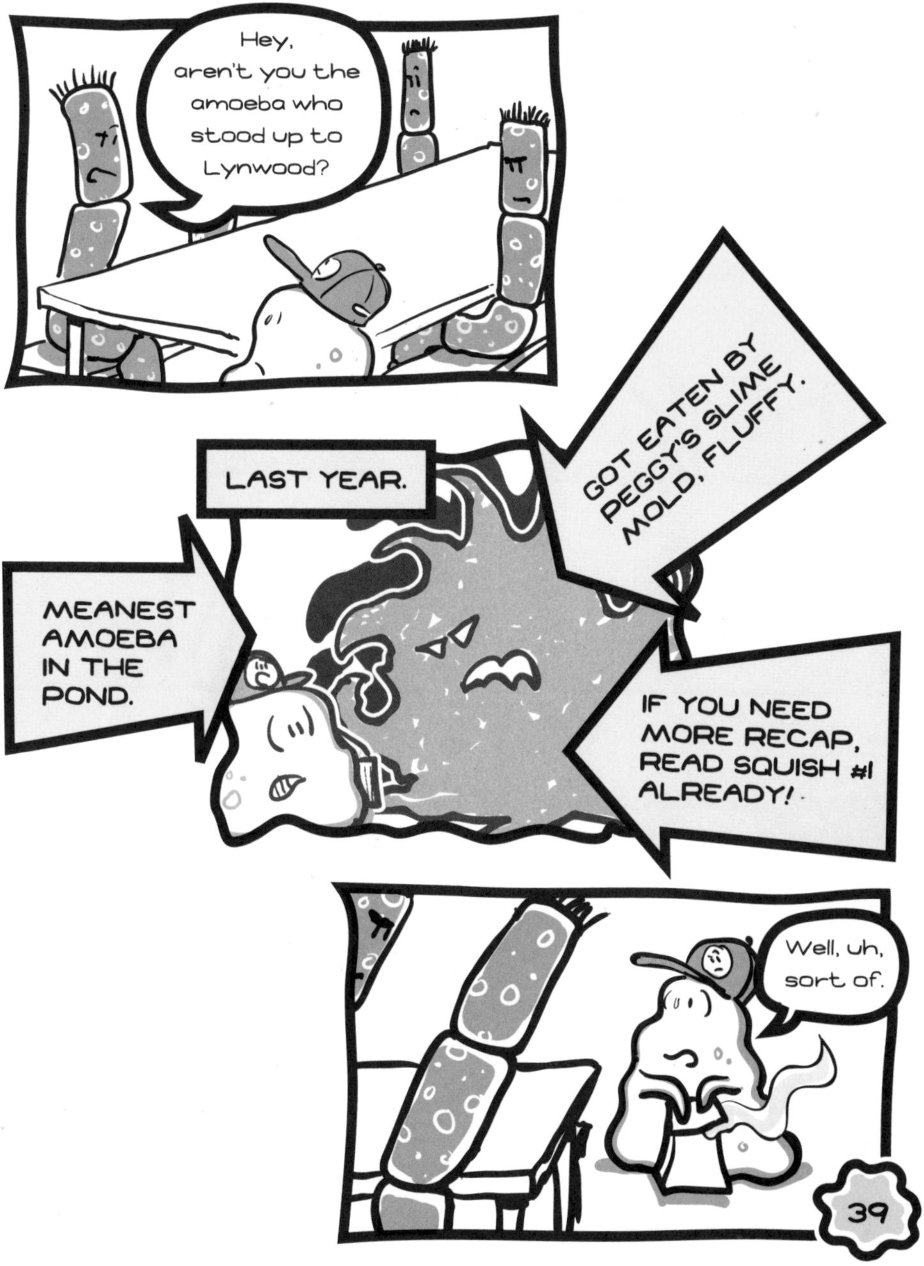
Hey, aren't you the amoeba who stood up to Lynwood?
LAST YEAR.
MEANEST AMOEBA IN THE POND.
GOT EATEN BY PEGGY'S SLIME MOLD, FLUFFY.
IF YOU NEED MORE RECAP, READ SQUISH #1 ALREADY!
Well, uh, sort of.

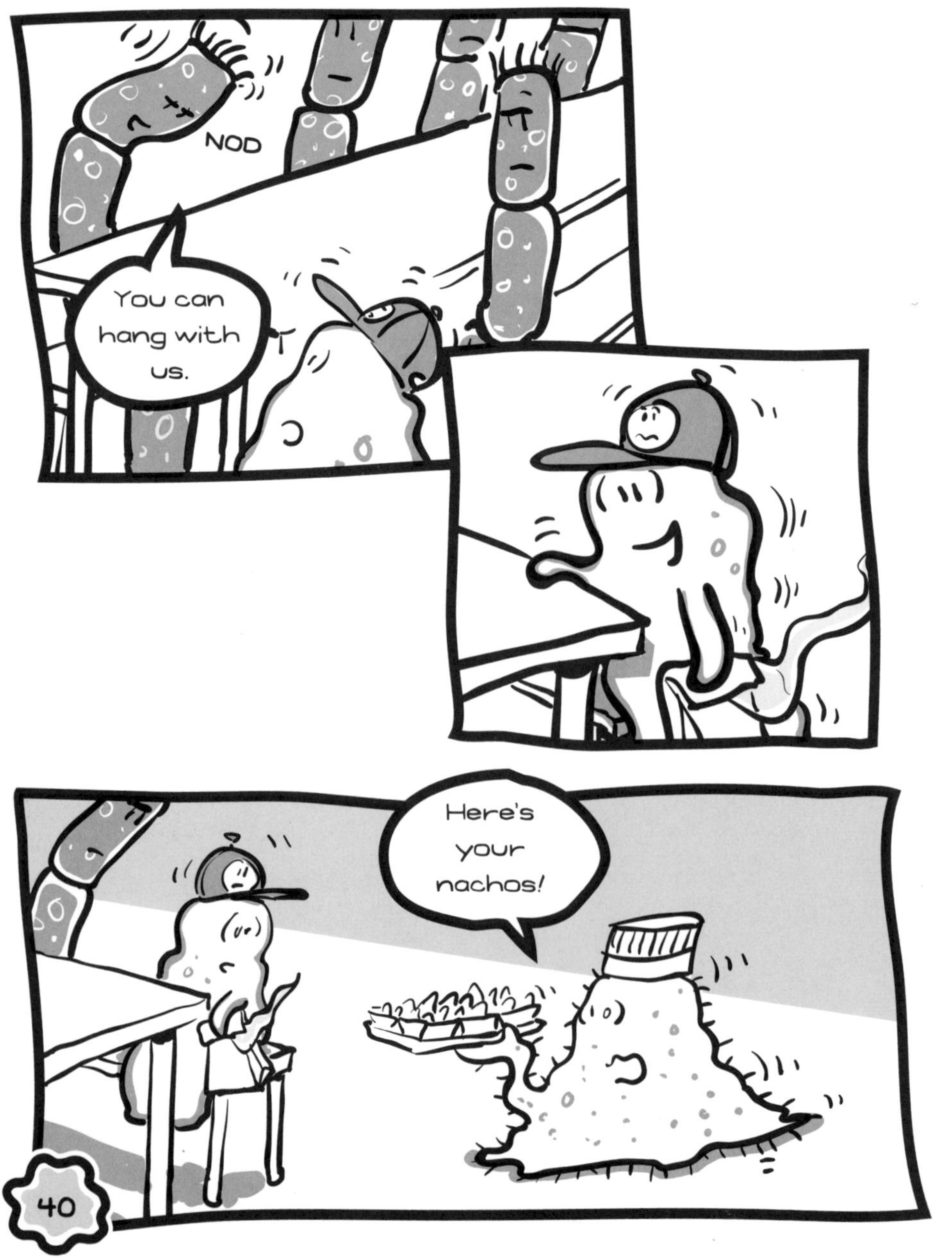
NOD
You can hang with us.
Here's your nachos!

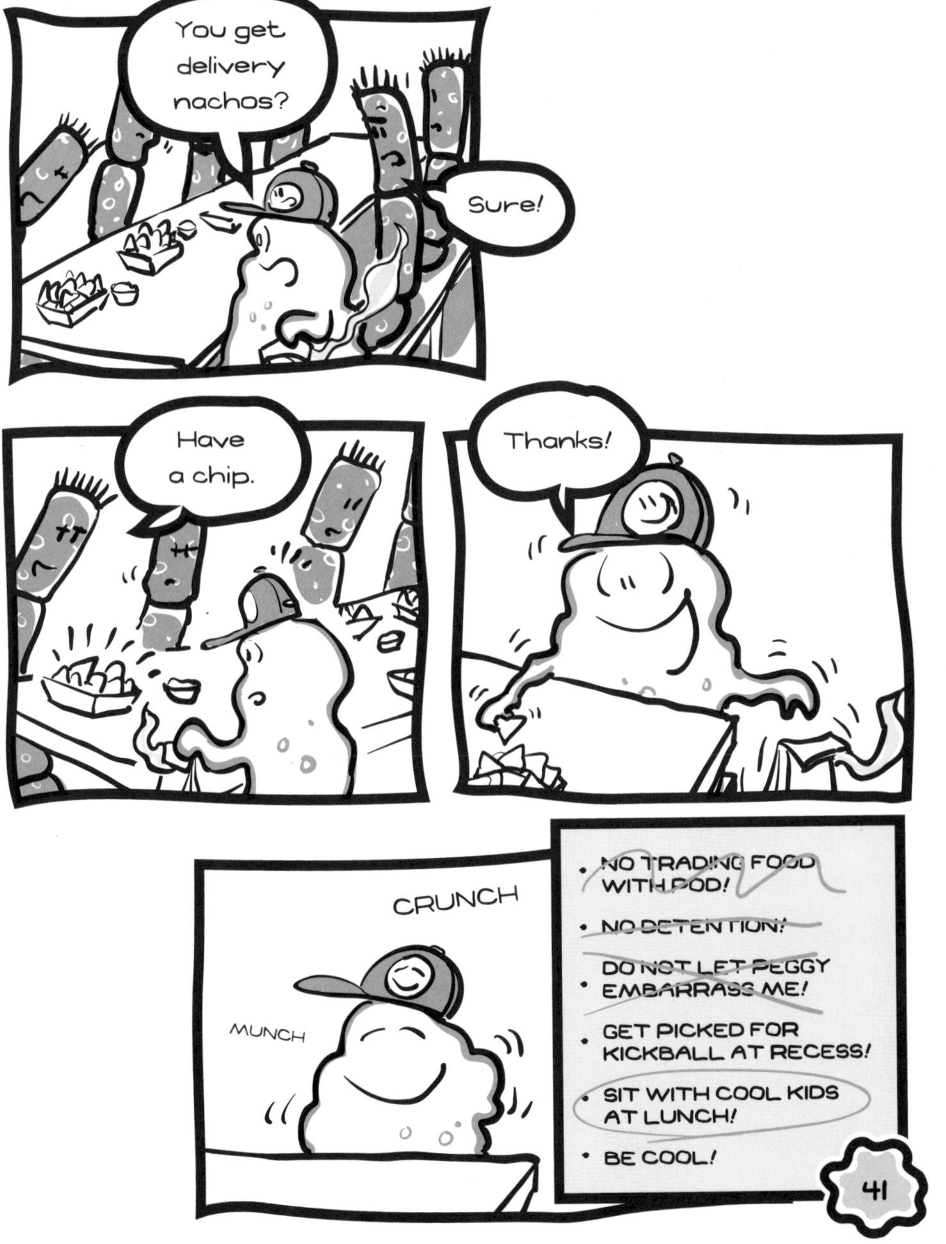
You get delivery nachos?
Sure!
Have a chip.
Thanks!
CRUNCH
MUNCH
• NO TRADING FOOD WITH POD!
• NO DETENTION!
• DO NOT LET PEGGY EMBARRASS ME!
• GET PICKED FOR KICKBALL AT RECESS!
• SIT WITH COOL KIDS AT LUNCH!
• BE COOL!

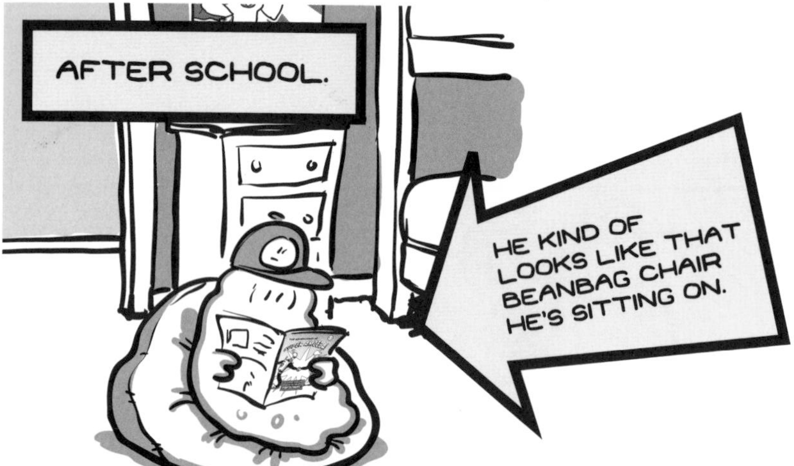
AFTER SCHOOL.
HE KIND OF LOOKS LIKE THAT BEANBAG CHAIR HE'S SITTING ON.

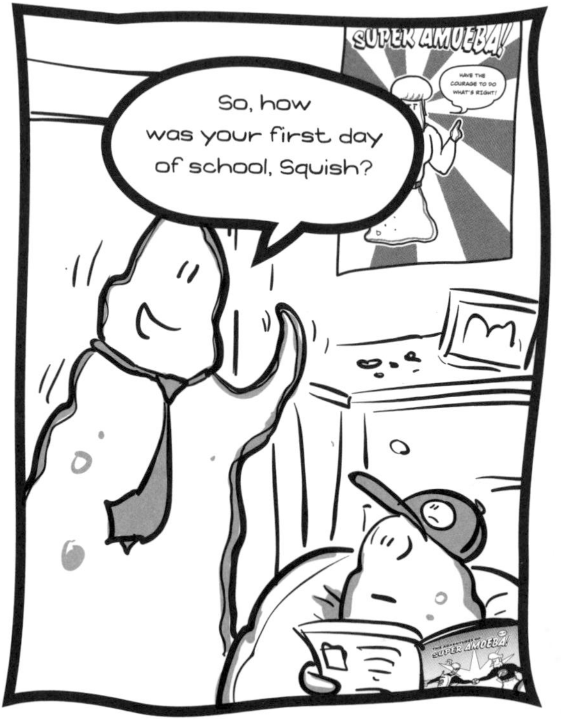
SUPER AMOEBA!
HAVE THE COURAGE TO DO WHAT'S RIGHT!
So, how was your first day of school, Squish?
THE ADVENTURES OF SUPER AMOEBA!

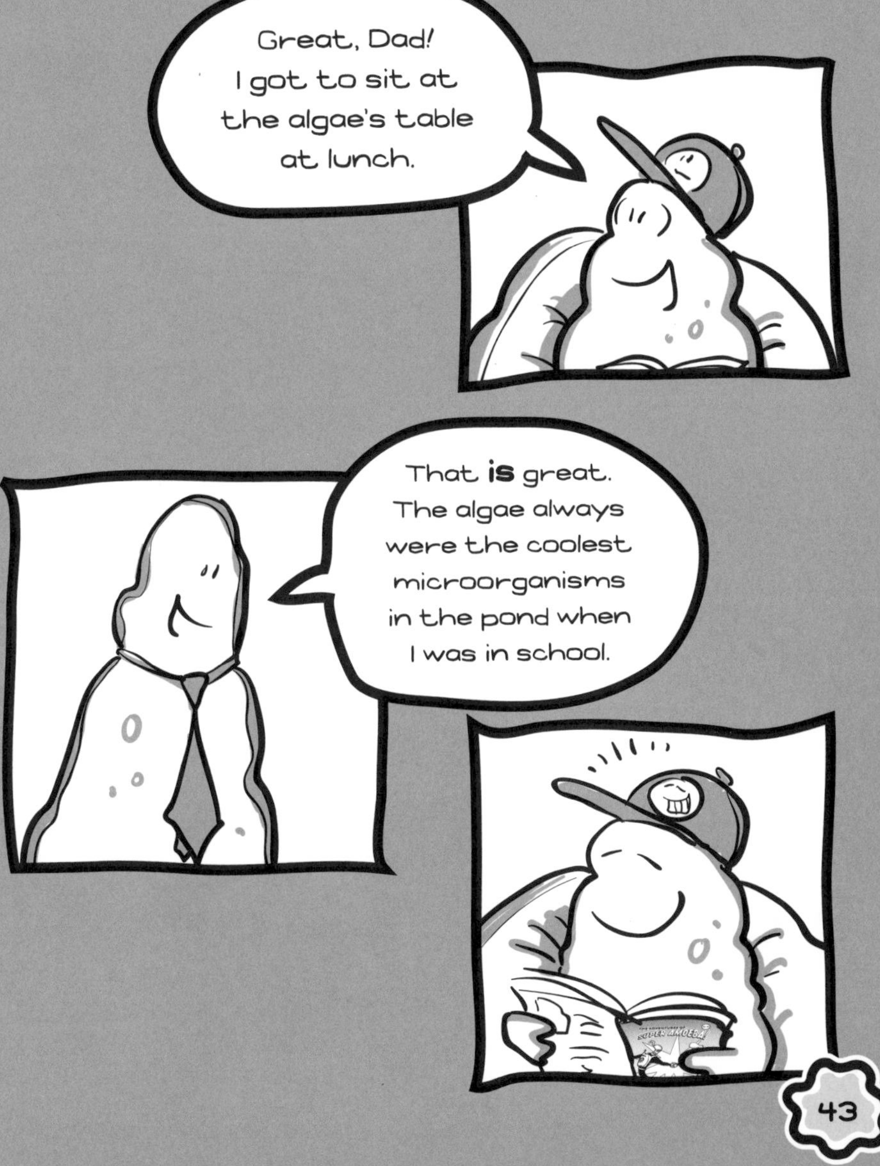
Great, Dad! I got to sit at the algae's table at lunch.
That **is** great. The algae always were the coolest microorganisms in the pond when I was in school.
SUPER AMOEBA!

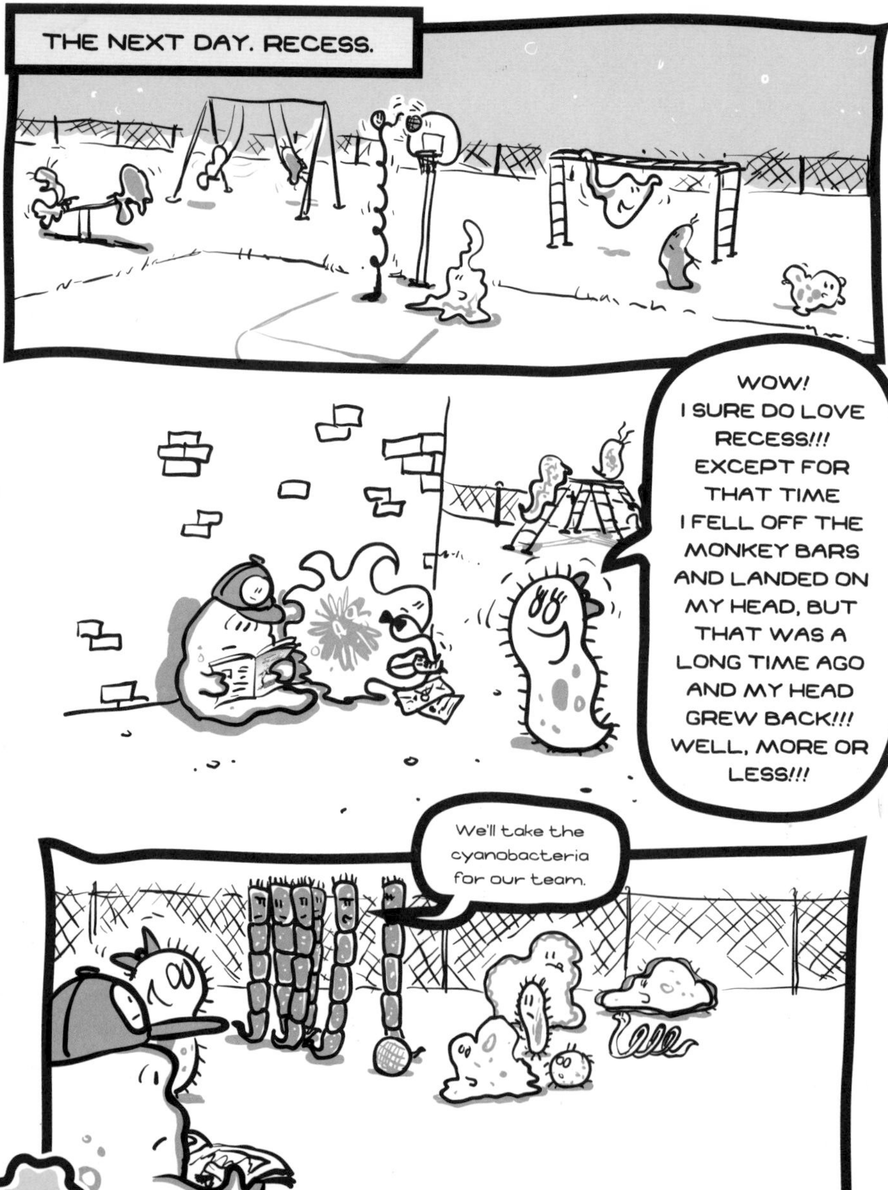
THE NEXT DAY. RECESS.
WOW! I SURE DO LOVE RECESS!!! EXCEPT FOR THAT TIME I FELL OFF THE MONKEY BARS AND LANDED ON MY HEAD, BUT THAT WAS A LONG TIME AGO AND MY HEAD GREW BACK!!! WELL, MORE OR LESS!!!
We'll take the cyanobacteria for our team.

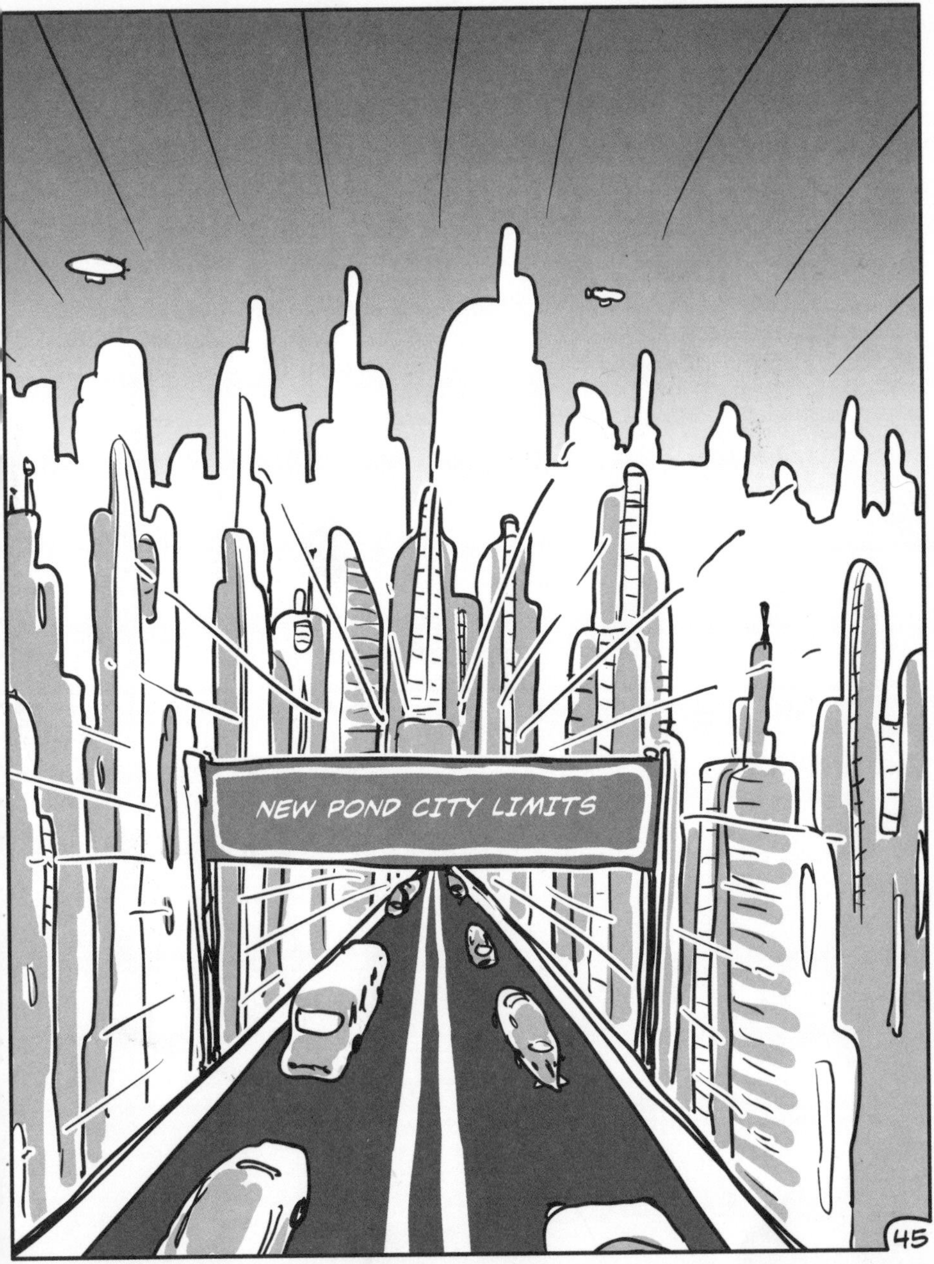
NEW POND CITY LIMITS

THE HALL OF THE PROTOZOANS

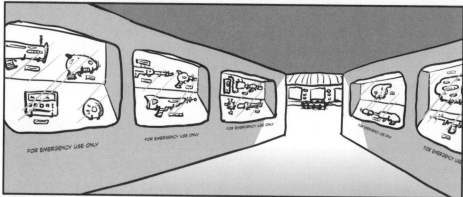

FOR EMERGENCY USE ONLY   FOR EMERGENCY USE ONLY   FOR EMERGENCY USE ONLY   FOR EMERGENCY USE ONLY   FOR EMERGENCY USE

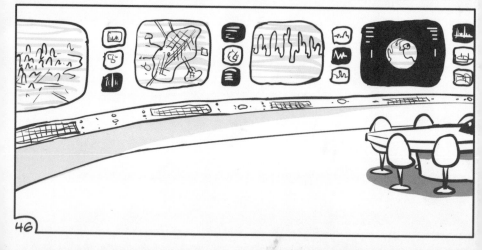

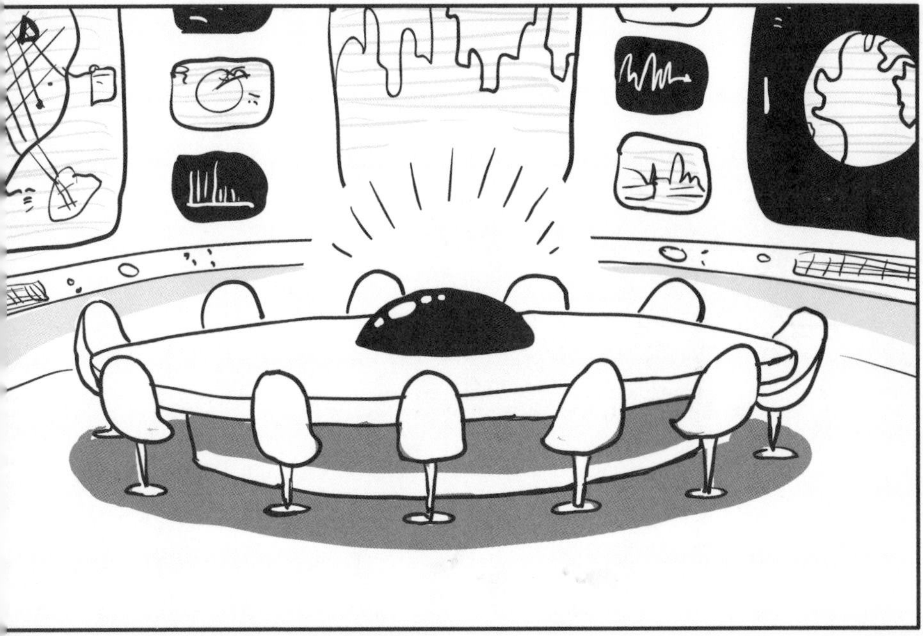

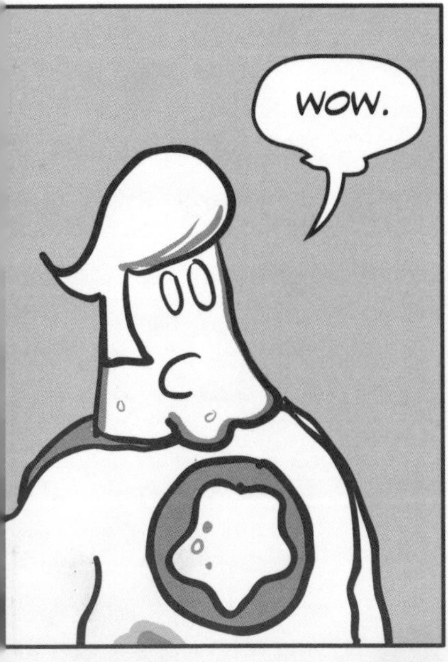
WOW.

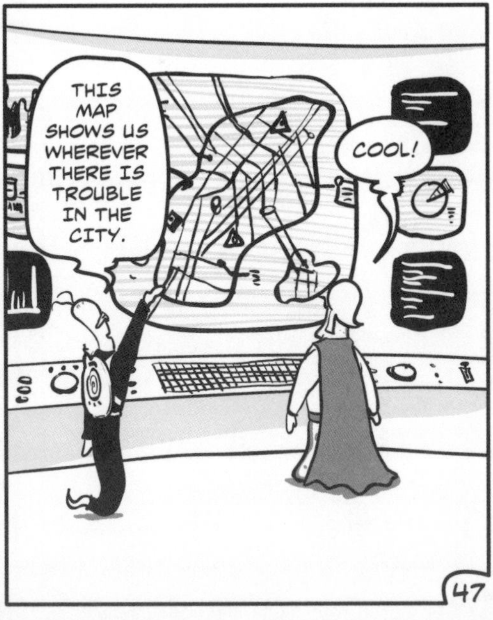
THIS MAP SHOWS US WHEREVER THERE IS TROUBLE IN THE CITY.
COOL!

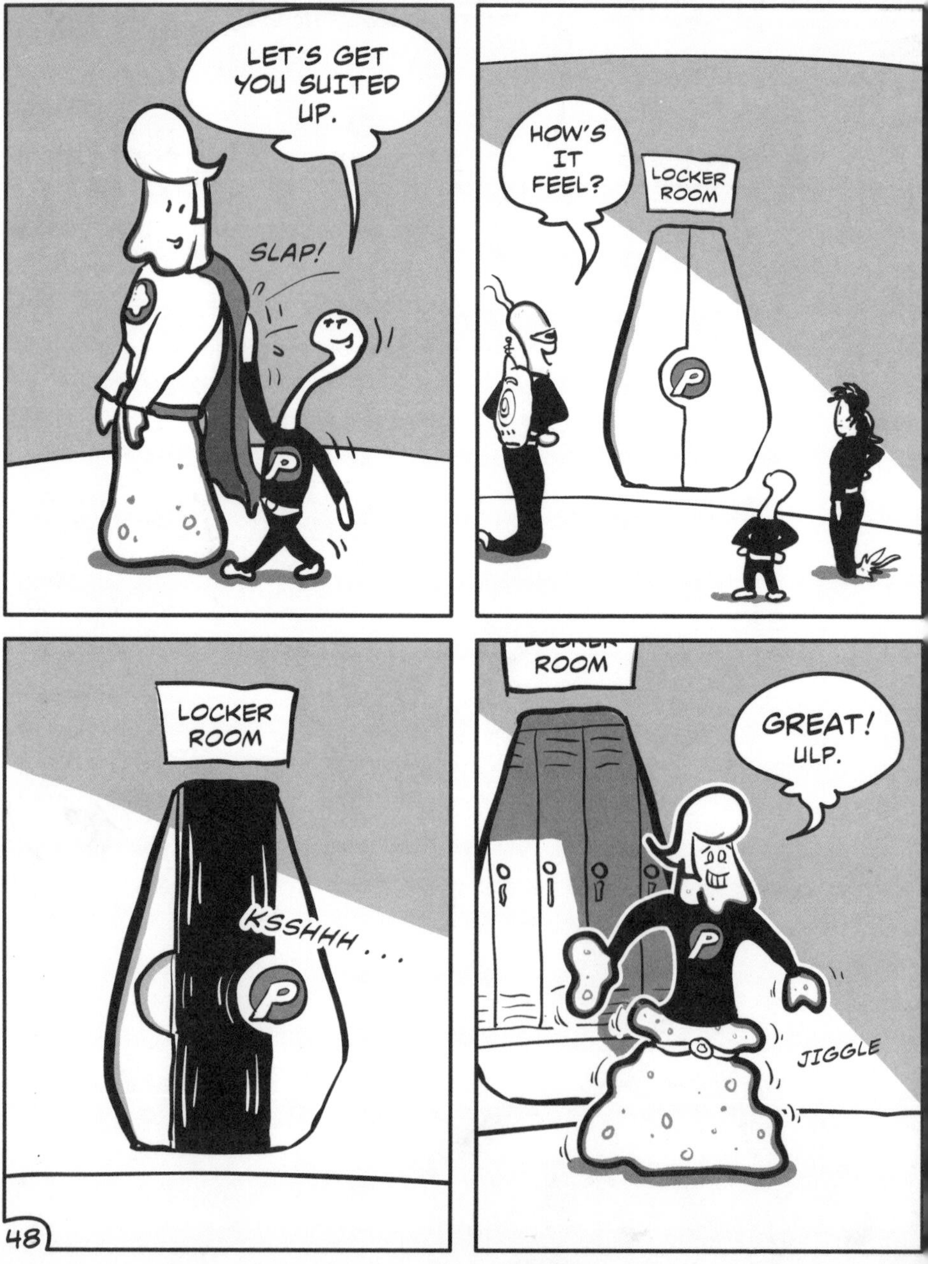
LET'S GET YOU SUITED UP.
SLAP!
HOW'S IT FEEL?
LOCKER ROOM
LOCKER ROOM
KSSHHH . . .
ROOM
GREAT! ULP.
JIGGLE

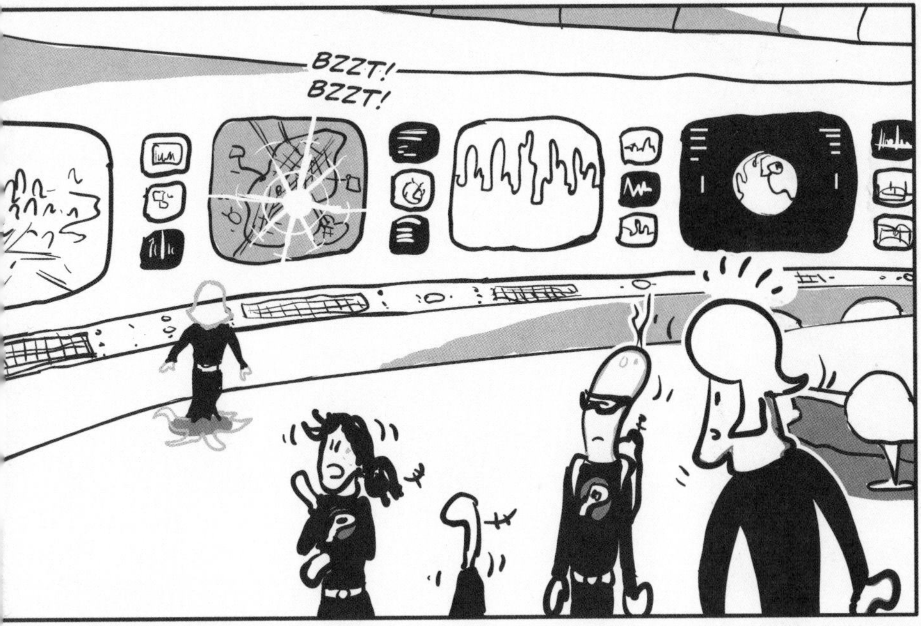
BZZT!
BZZT!

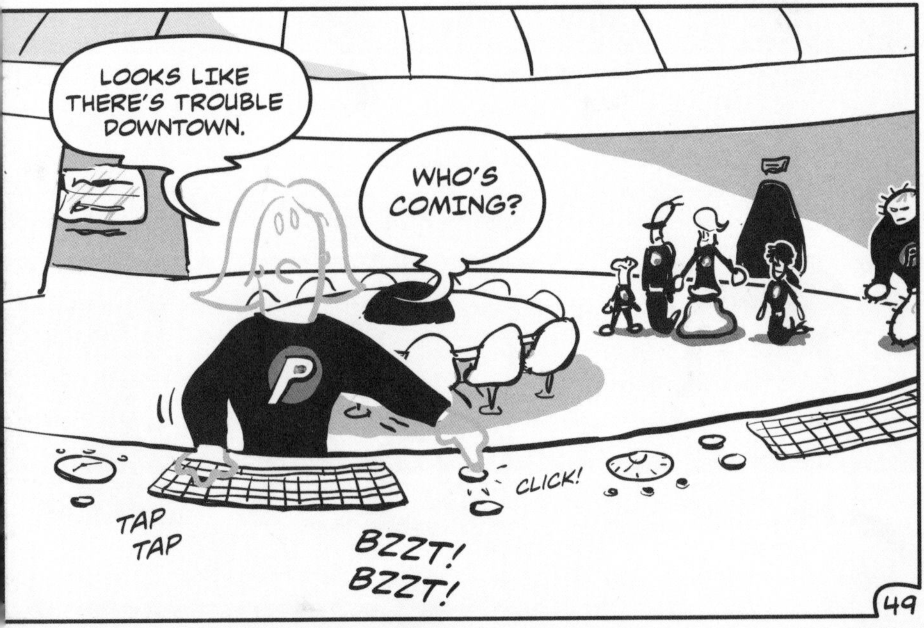
LOOKS LIKE THERE'S TROUBLE DOWNTOWN.
WHO'S COMING?
CLICK!
TAP
TAP
BZZT!
BZZT!

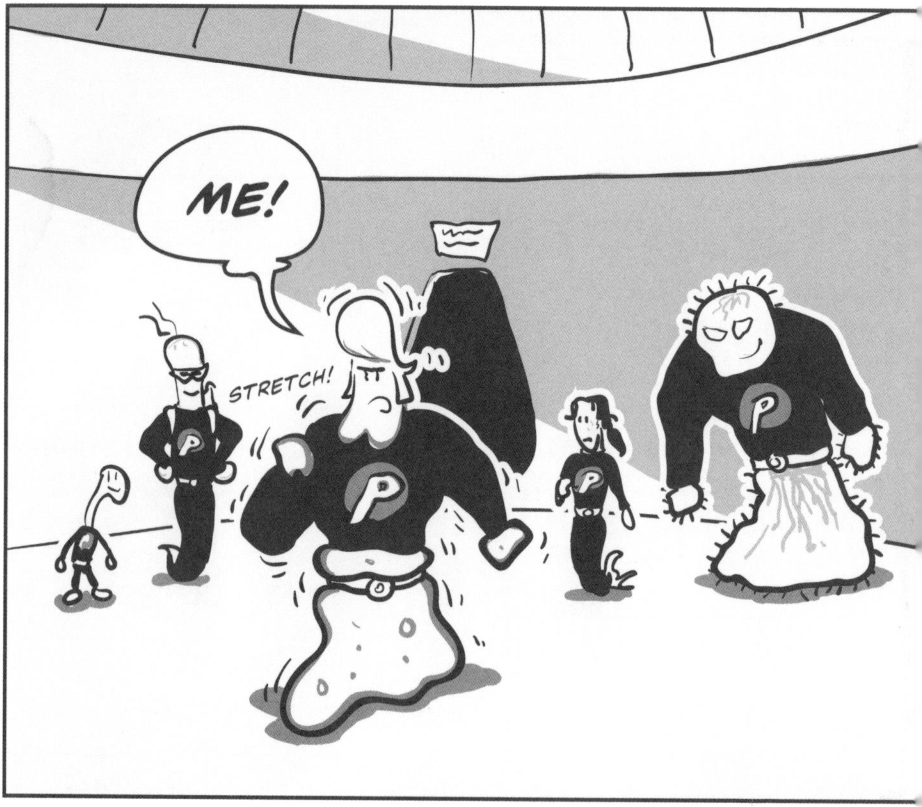
ME!
STRETCH!

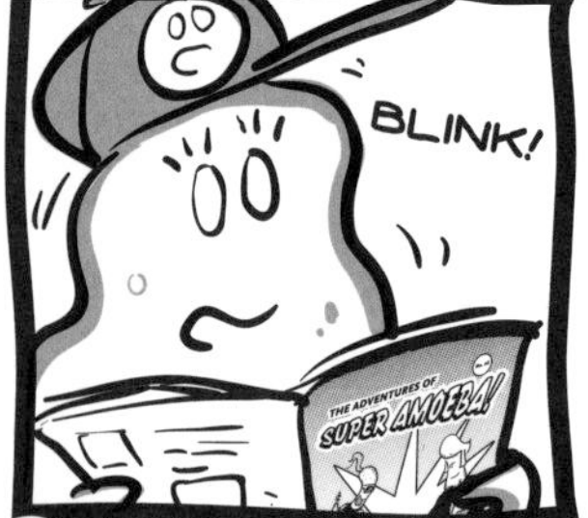
BLINK!
THE ADVENTURES OF SUPER AMOEBA!

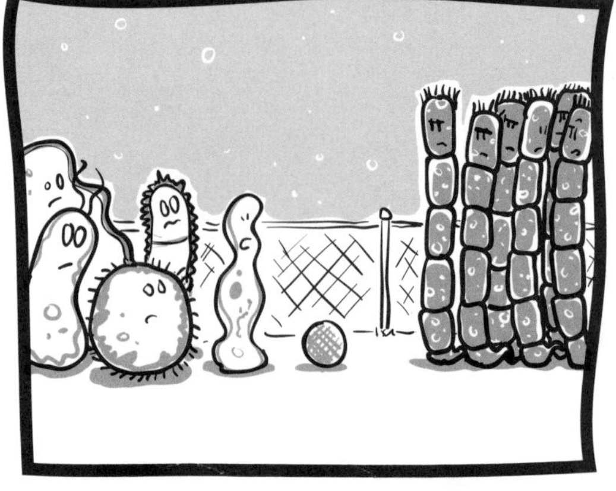

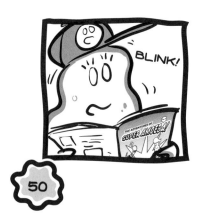

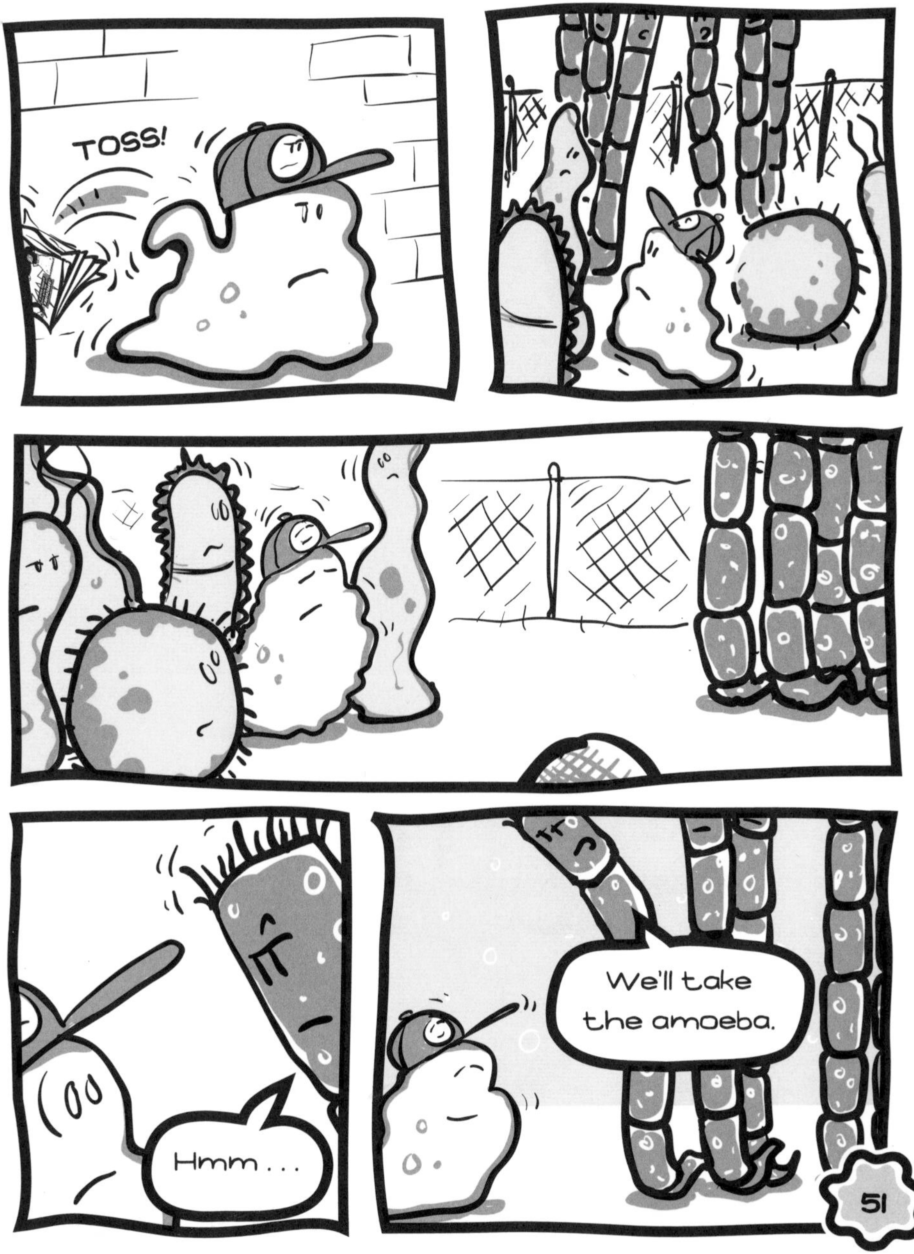
TOSS!
Hmm . . .
We'll take the amoeba.

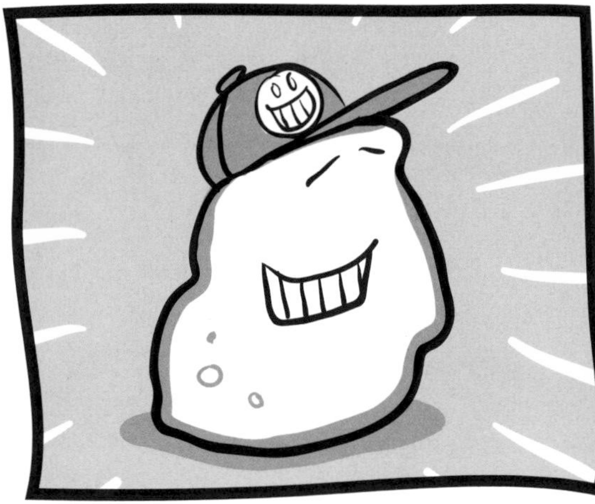

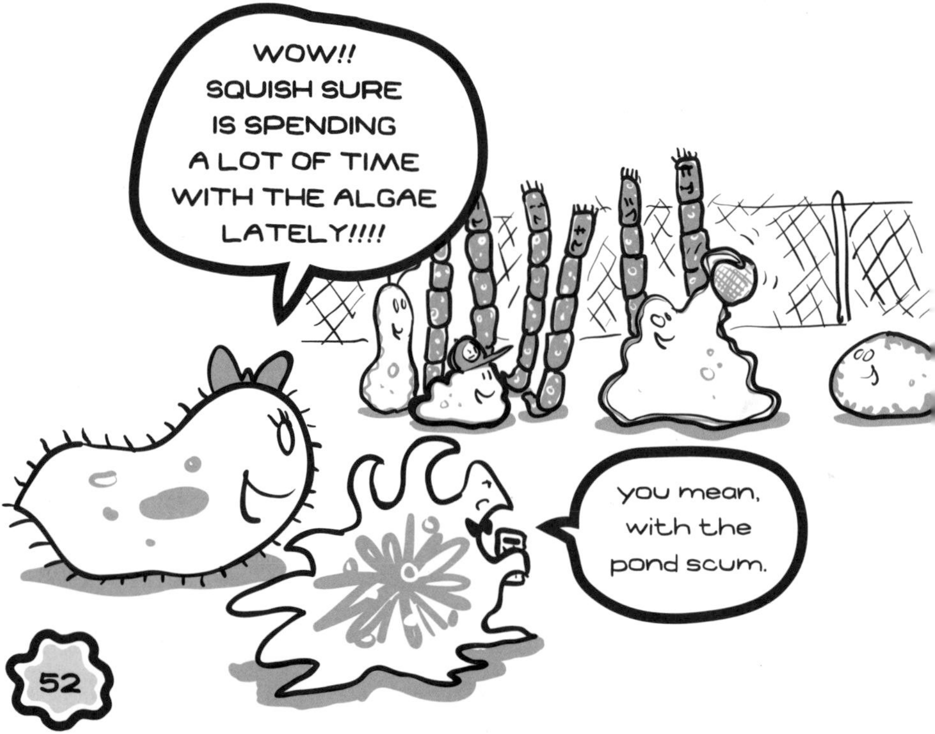
WOW!!
SQUISH SURE IS SPENDING A LOT OF TIME WITH THE ALGAE LATELY!!!!
you mean, with the pond scum.

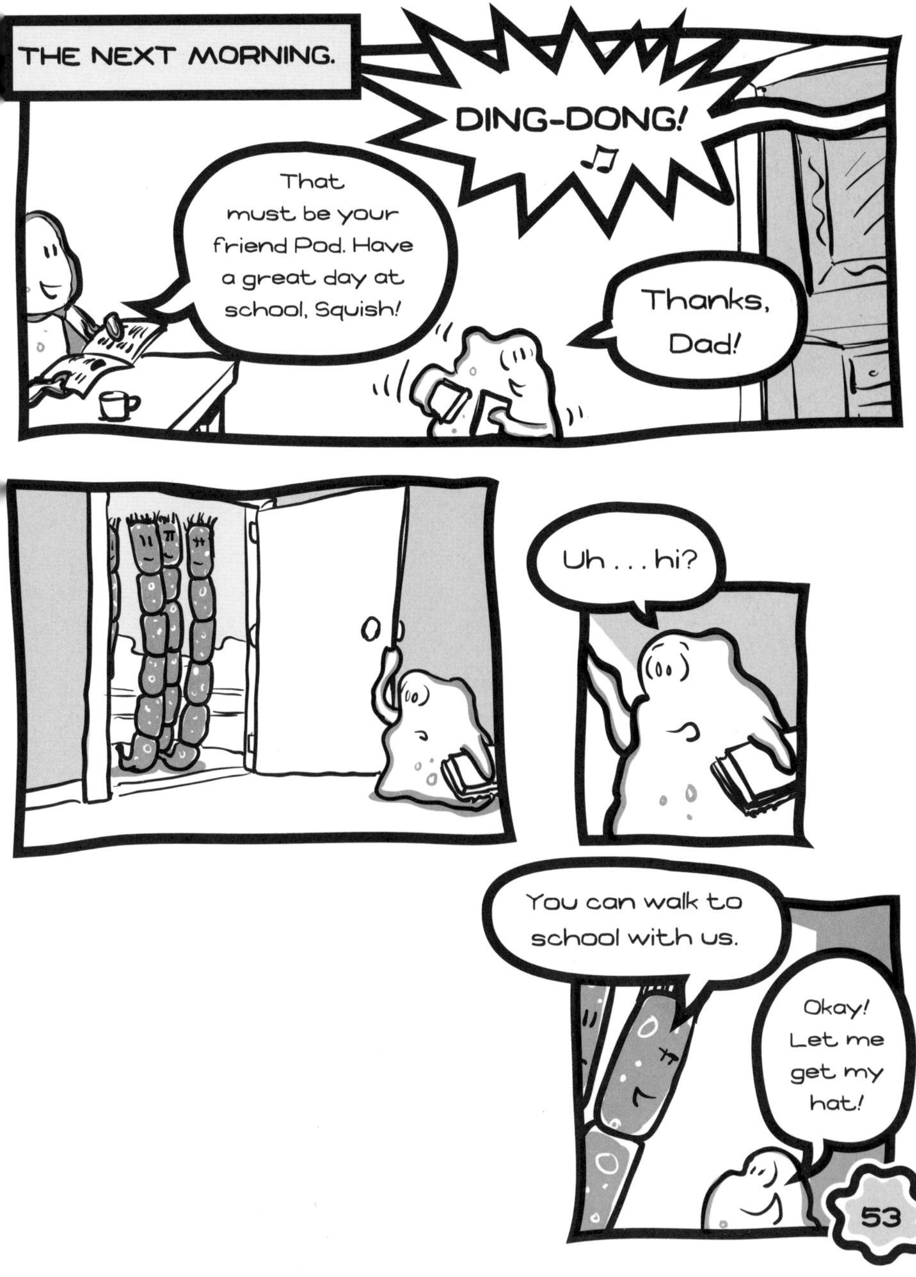
THE NEXT MORNING.
DING-DONG!
That must be your friend Pod. Have a great day at school, Squish!
Thanks, Dad!
Uh . . . hi?
You can walk to school with us.
Okay! Let me get my hat!

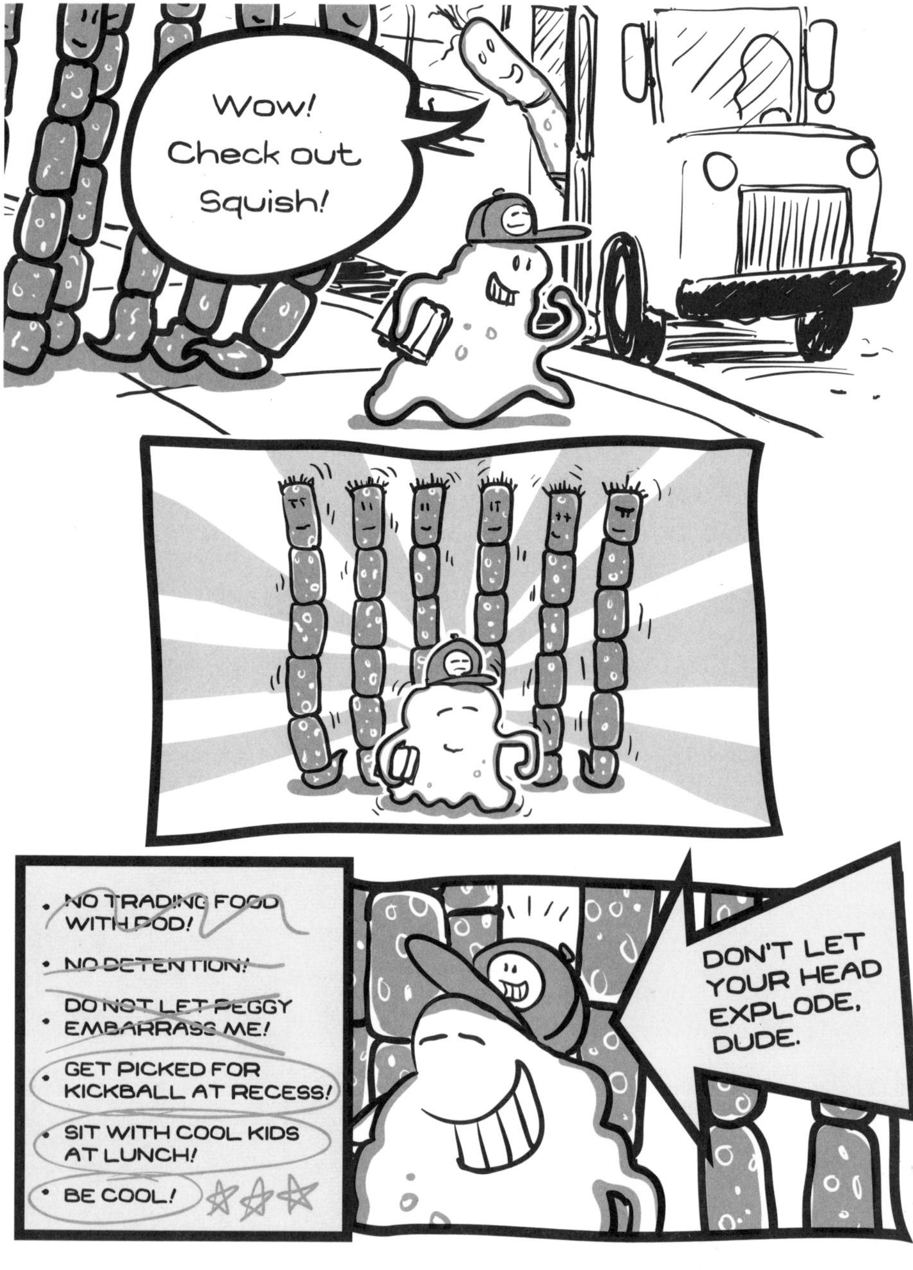
Wow! Check out Squish!
NO TRADING FOOD WITH POD!
NO DETENTION!
DO NOT LET PEGGY EMBARRASS ME!
GET PICKED FOR KICKBALL AT RECESS!
SIT WITH COOL KIDS AT LUNCH!
BE COOL!
DON'T LET YOUR HEAD EXPLODE, DUDE.

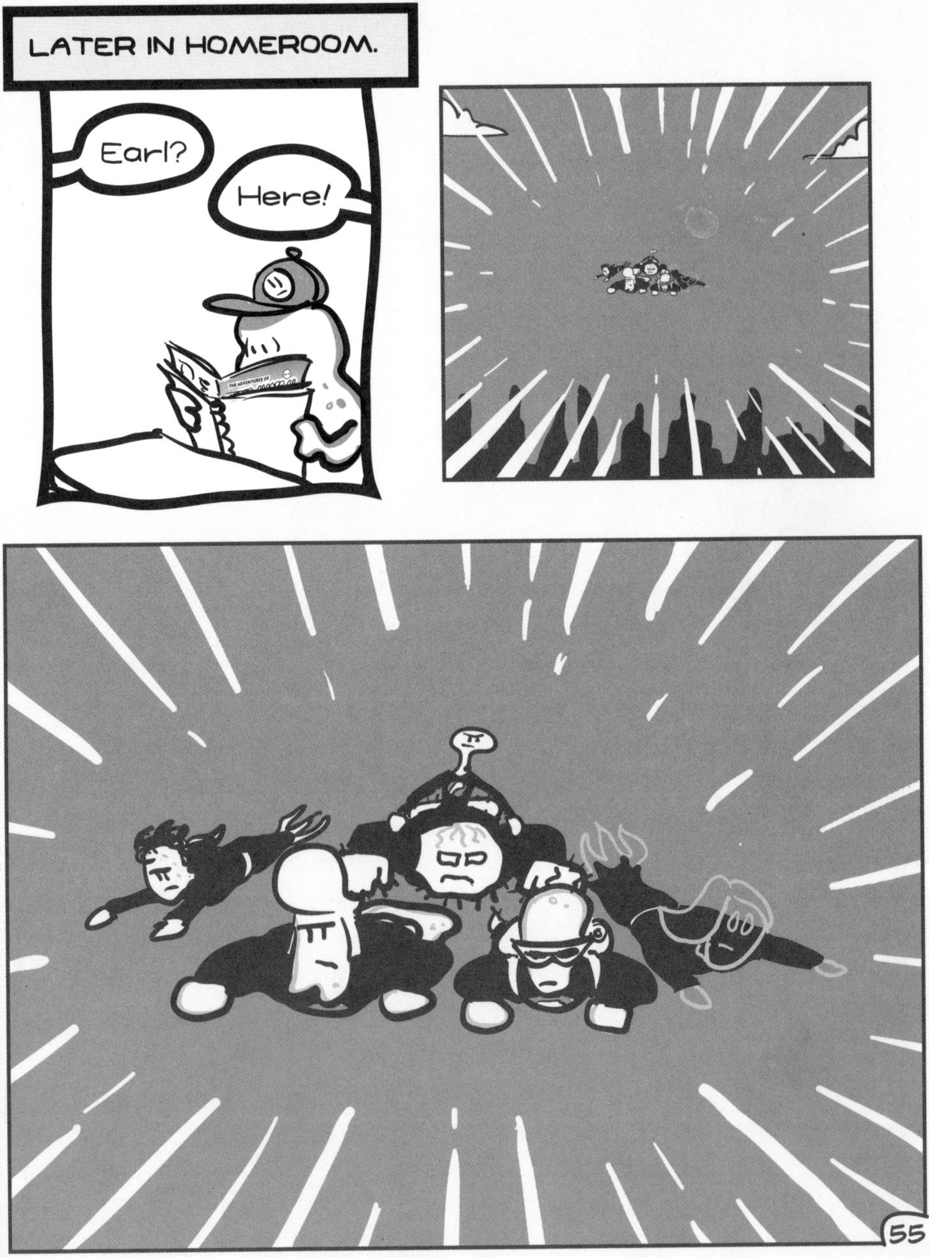
LATER IN HOMEROOM.
Earl?
Here!
THE ADVENTURES OF

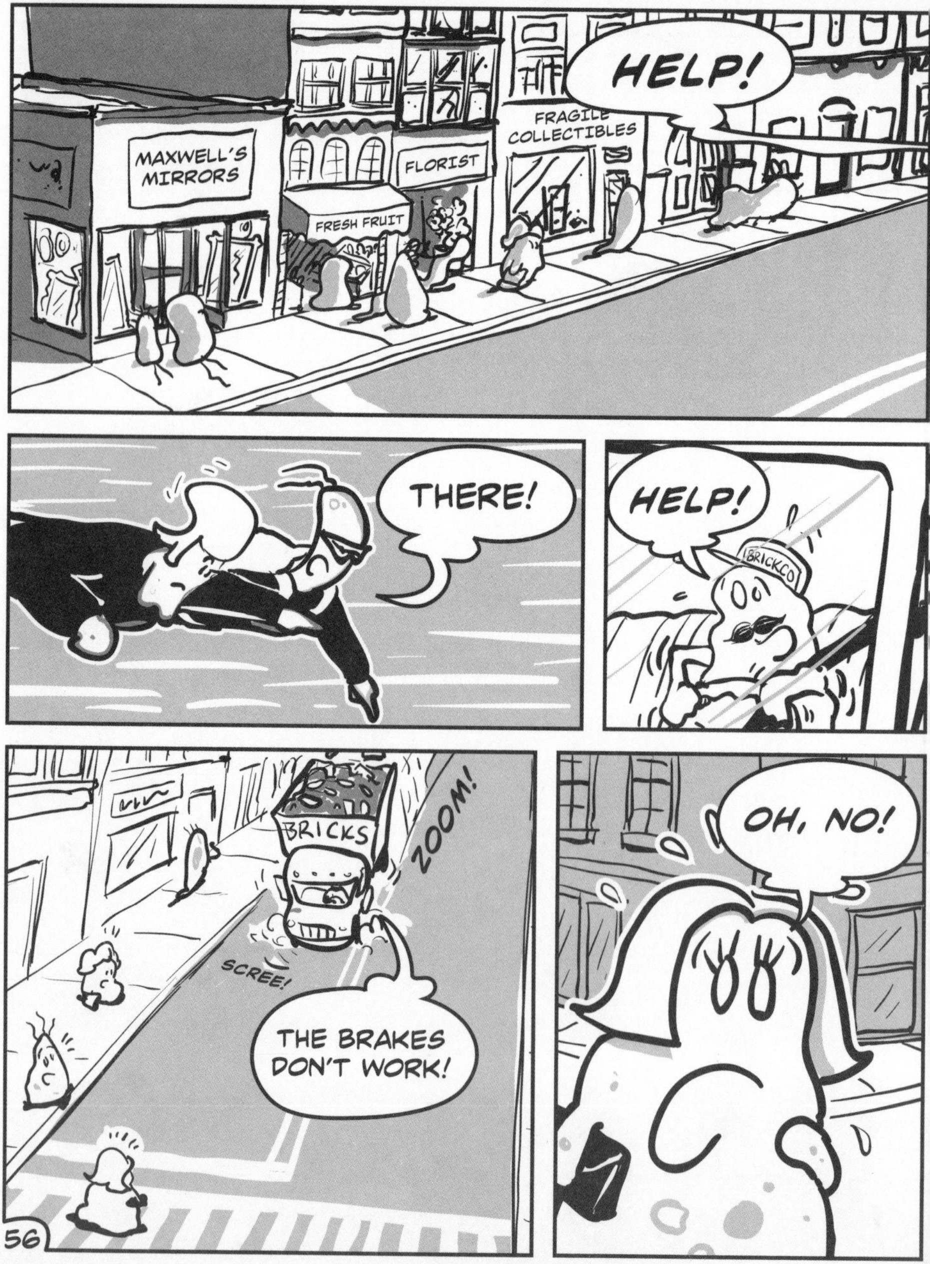
MAXWELL'S MIRRORS
FRESH FRUIT
FLORIST
FRAGILE COLLECTIBLES
HELP!
THERE!
HELP!
BRICKCO
BRICKS
ZOOM!
SCREE!
THE BRAKES DON'T WORK!
OH, NO!

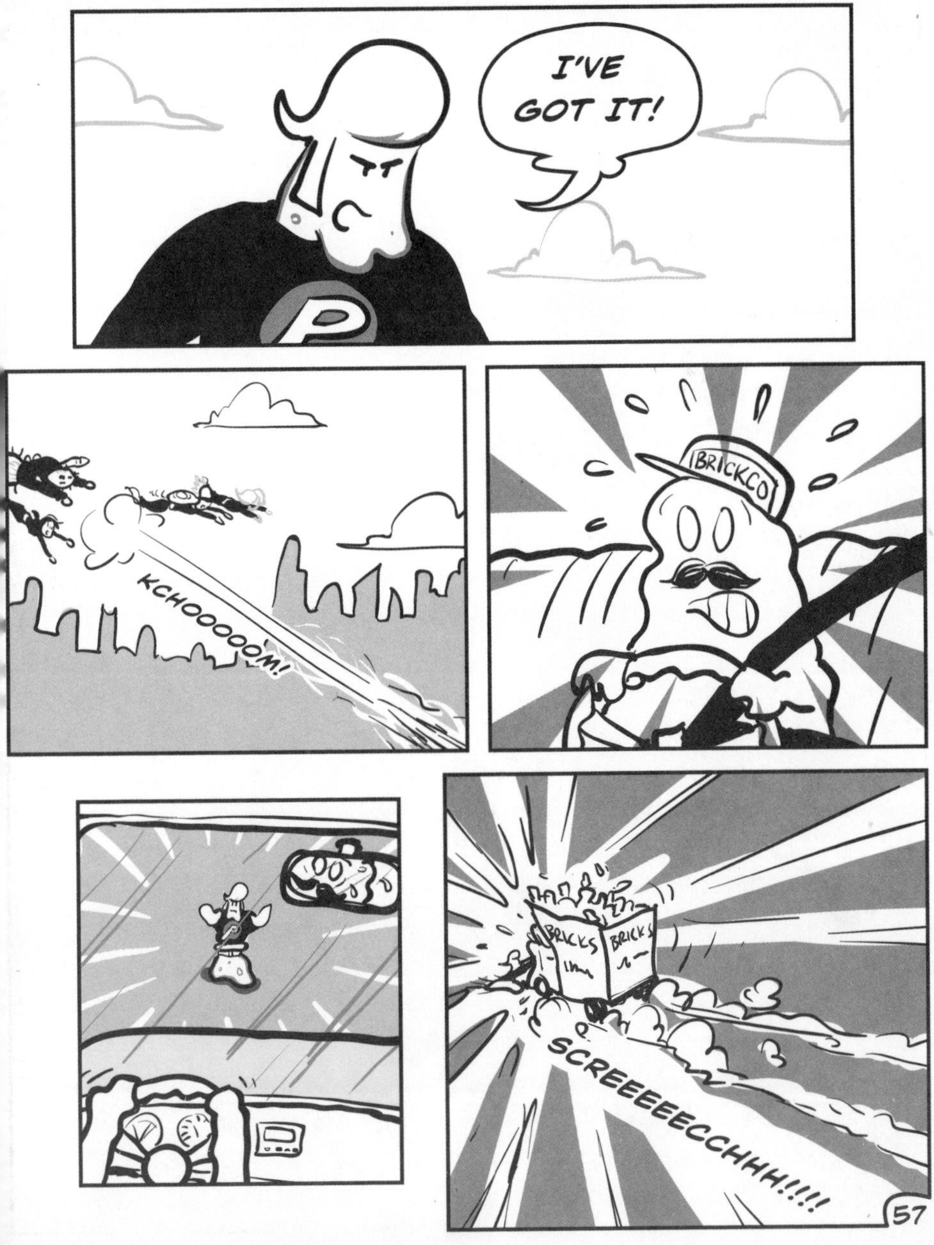

I'VE GOT IT!
KCHOOOOOOM!
BRICKCO
BRICKS
BRICKS
SCREEEEEEECCHHHH!!!!!

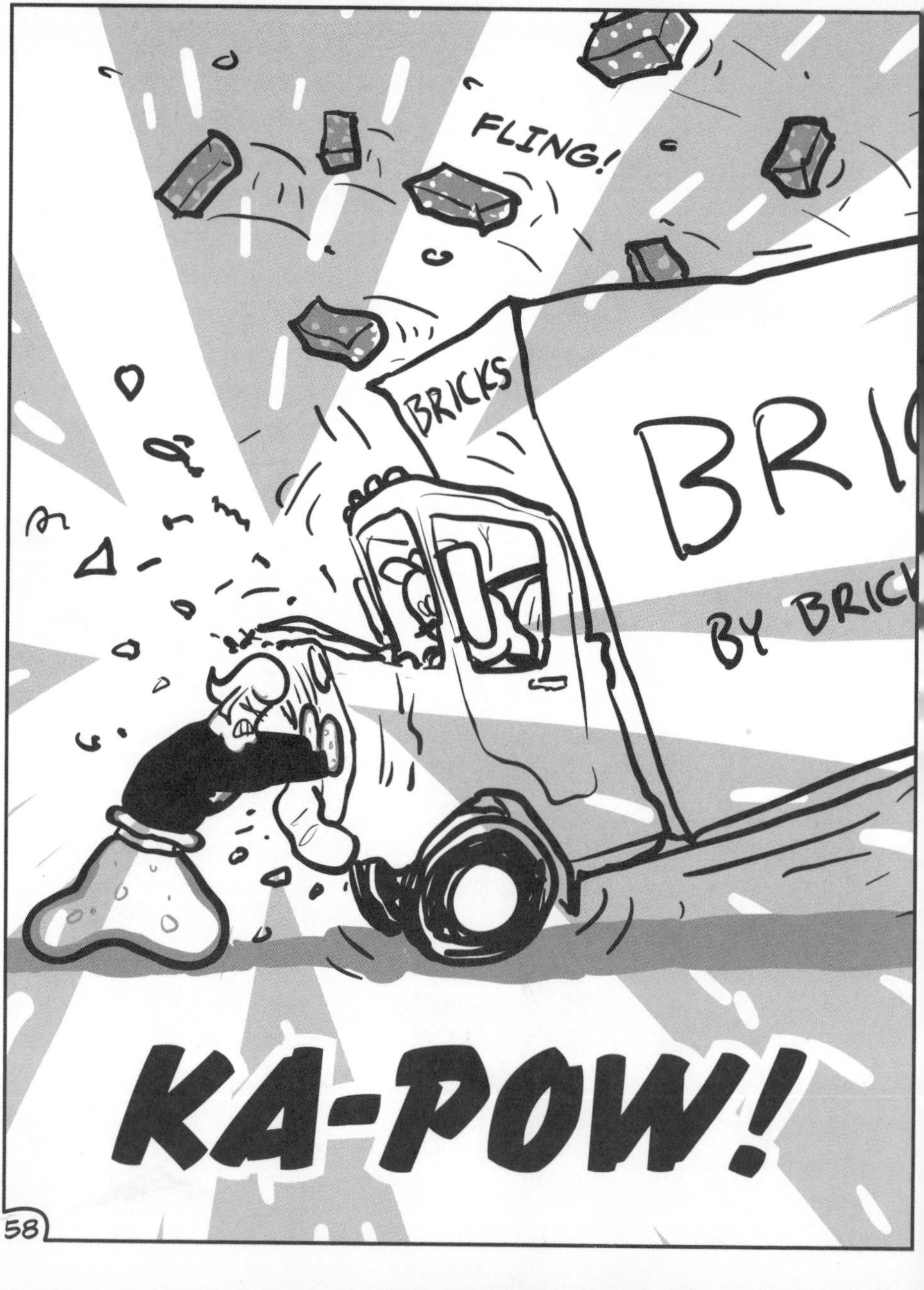
FLING!
BRICKS
BRI
BY BRIC
KA-POW!

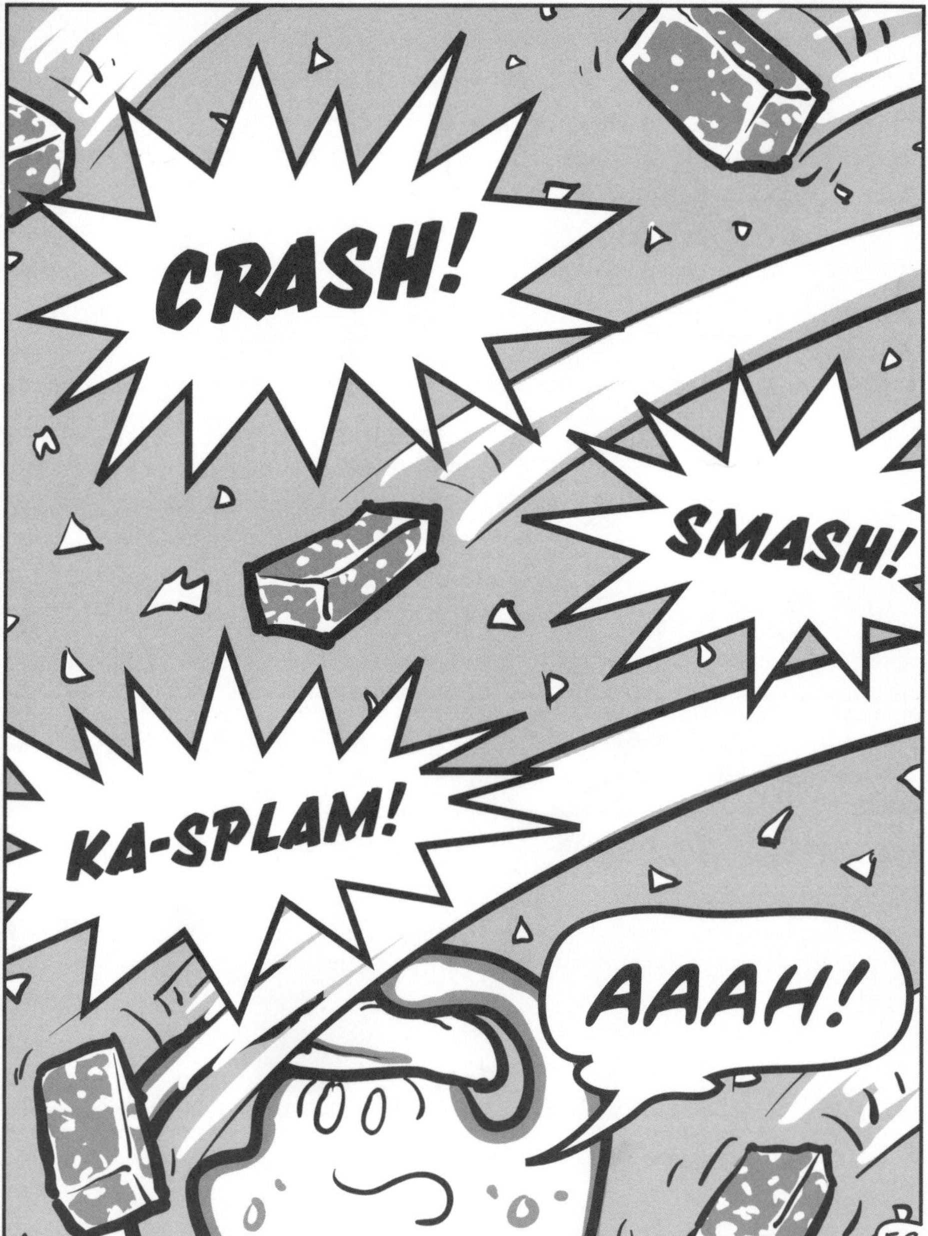
CRASH!
SMASH!
KA-SPLAM!
AAAH!

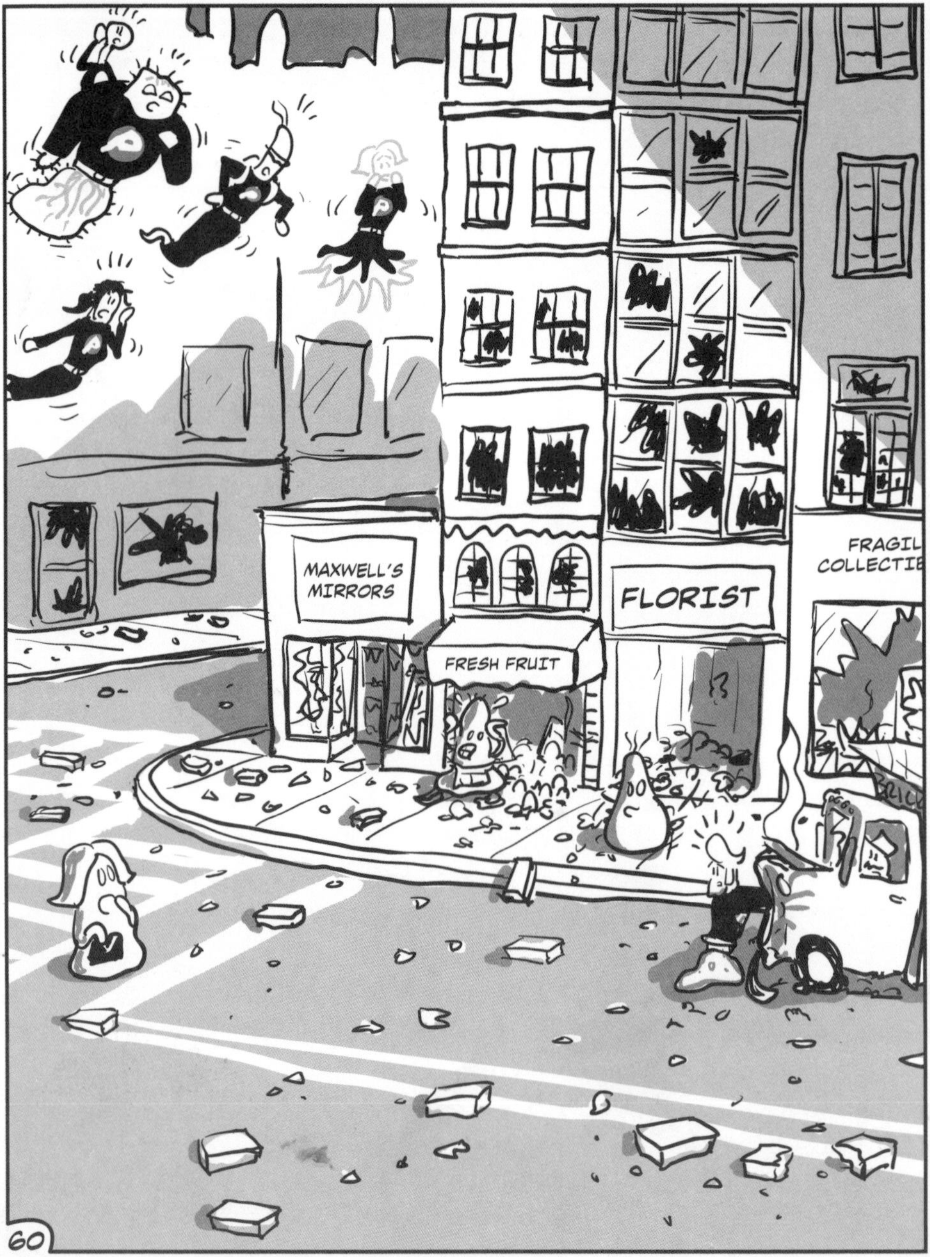
MAXWELL'S MIRRORS
FRESH FRUIT
FLORIST
FRAGIL
COLLECTIE

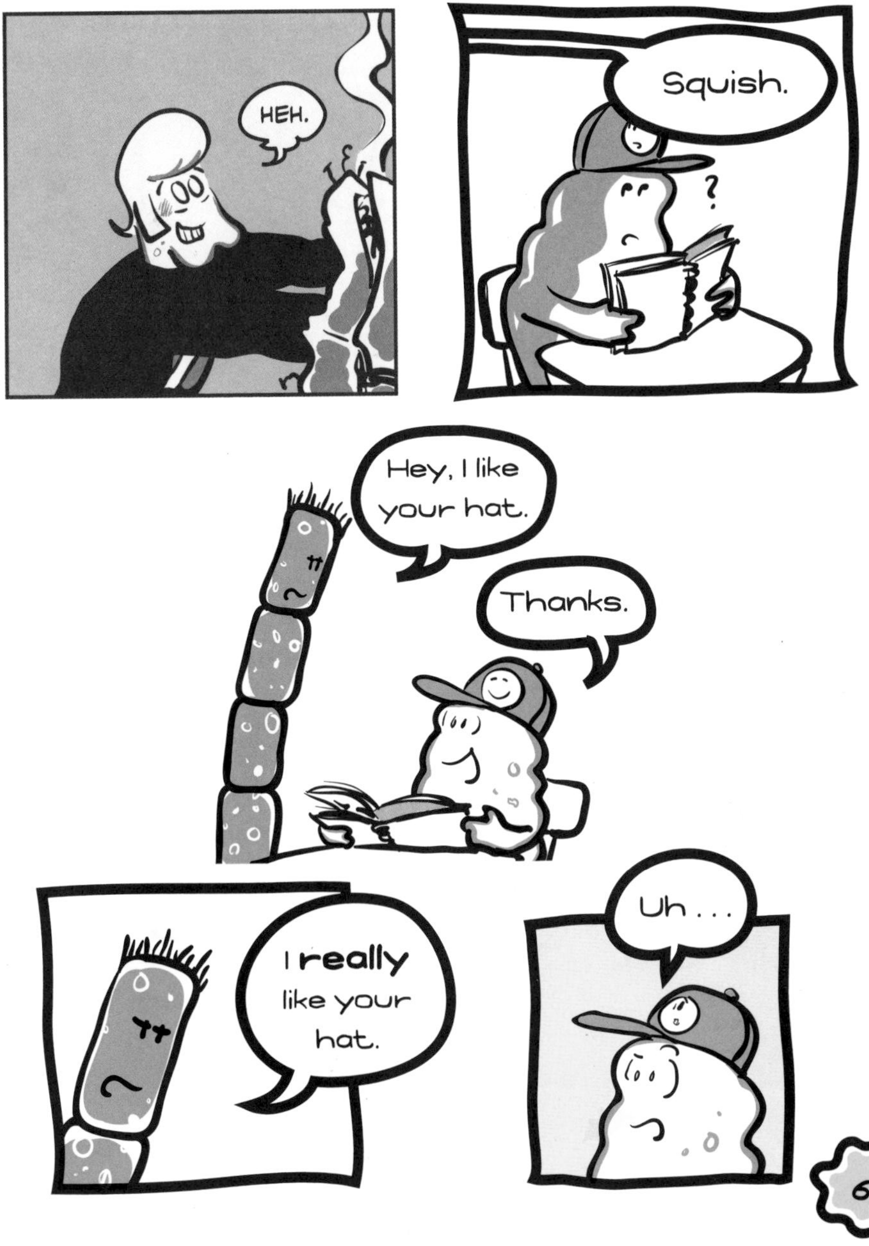
HEH.
Squish.
?
Hey, I like your hat.
Thanks.
I **really** like your hat.
Uh . . .

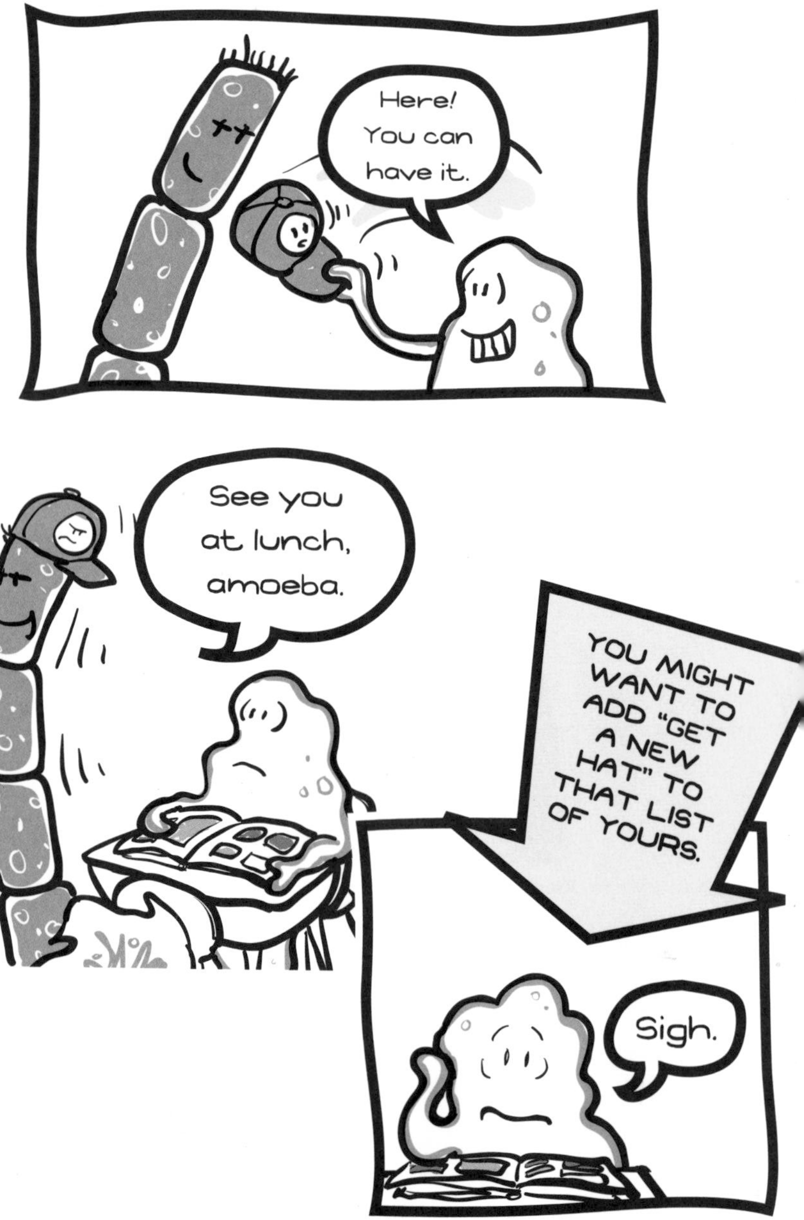
Here! You can have it.
See you at lunch, amoeba.
YOU MIGHT WANT TO ADD "GET A NEW HAT" TO THAT LIST OF YOURS.
Sigh.

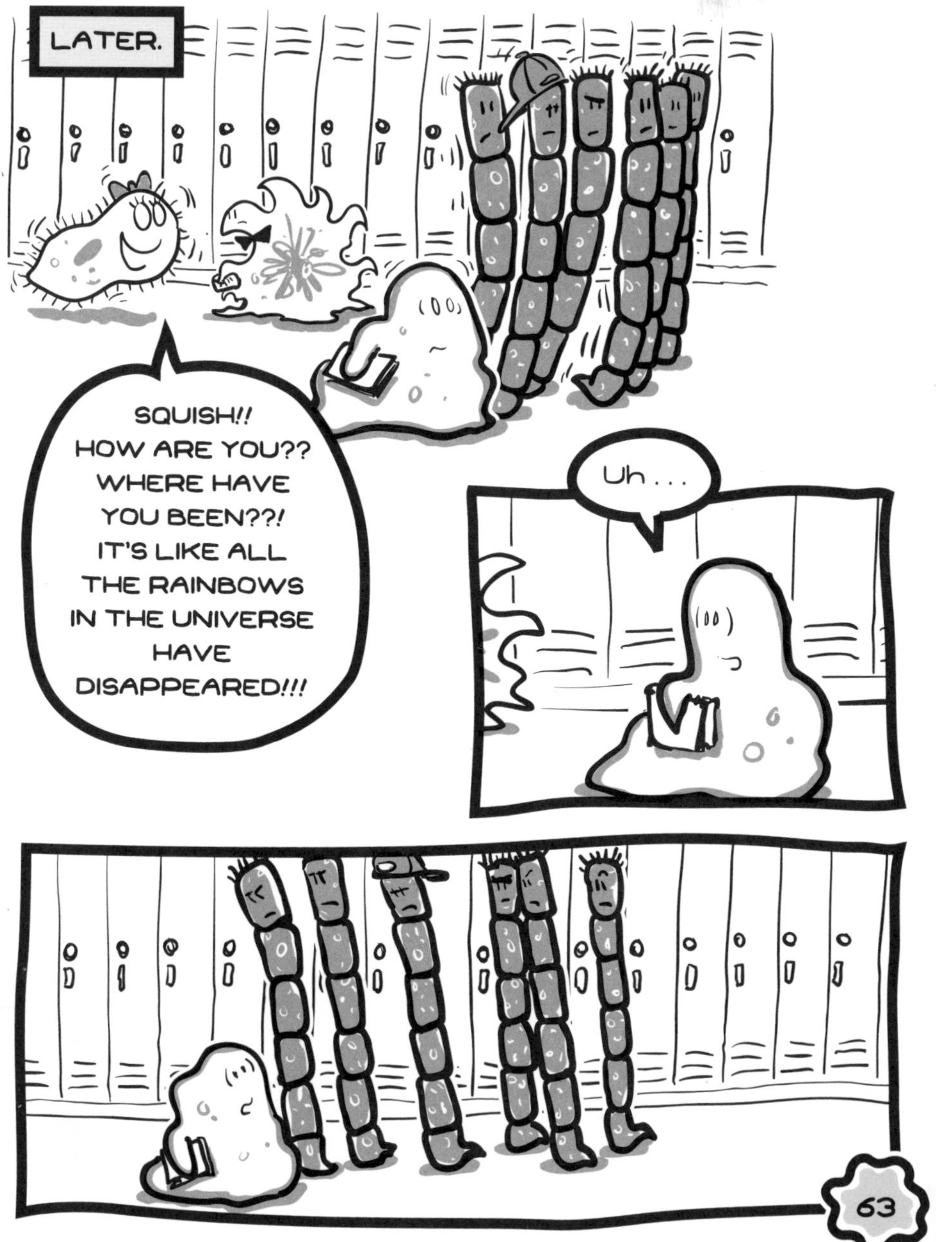
LATER.
SQUISH!! HOW ARE YOU?? WHERE HAVE YOU BEEN??! IT'S LIKE ALL THE RAINBOWS IN THE UNIVERSE HAVE DISAPPEARED!!!
Uh . . .

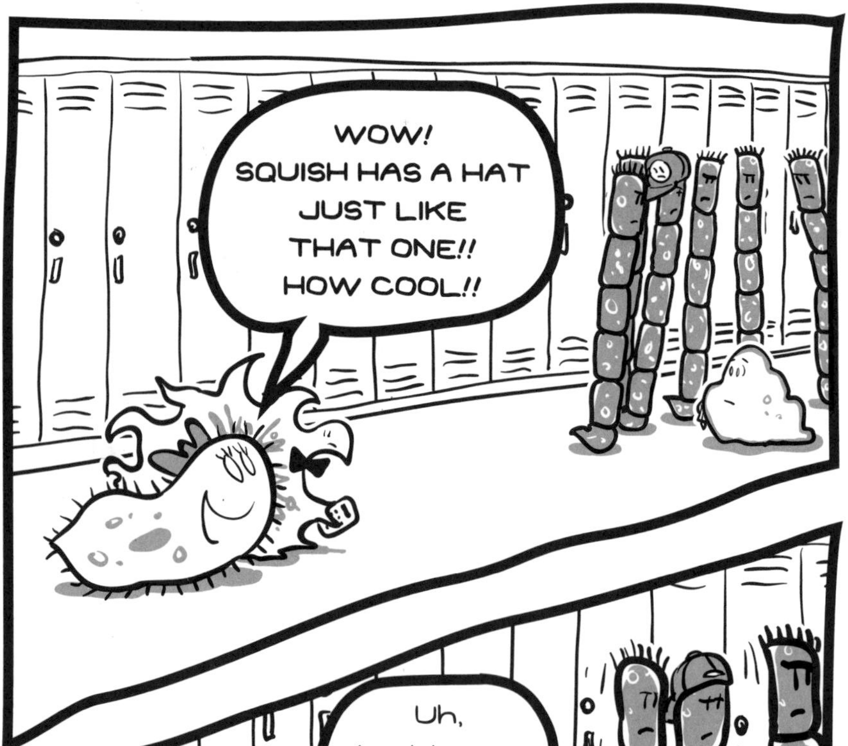
WOW! SQUISH HAS A HAT JUST LIKE THAT ONE!! HOW COOL!!

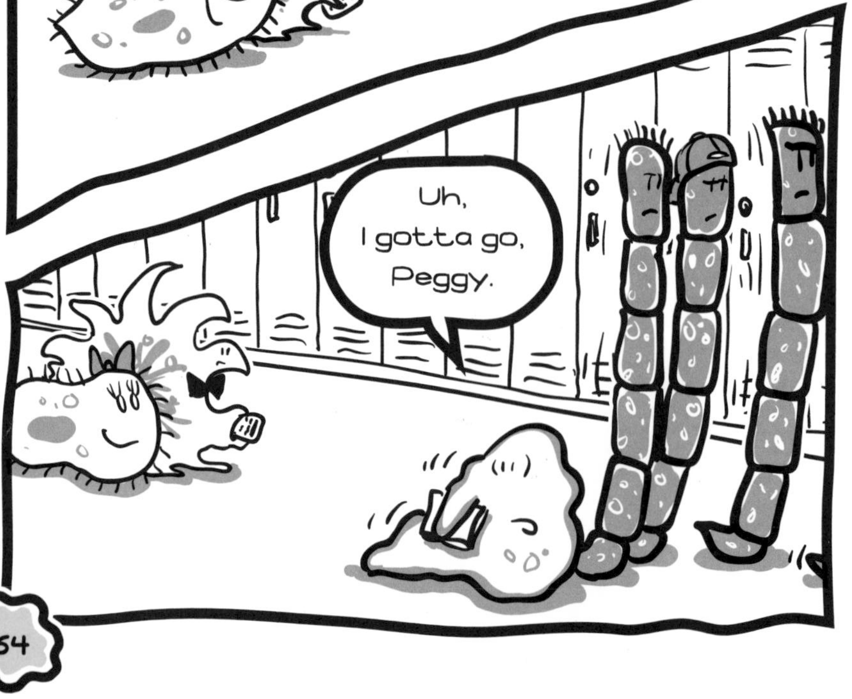
Uh, I gotta go, Peggy.

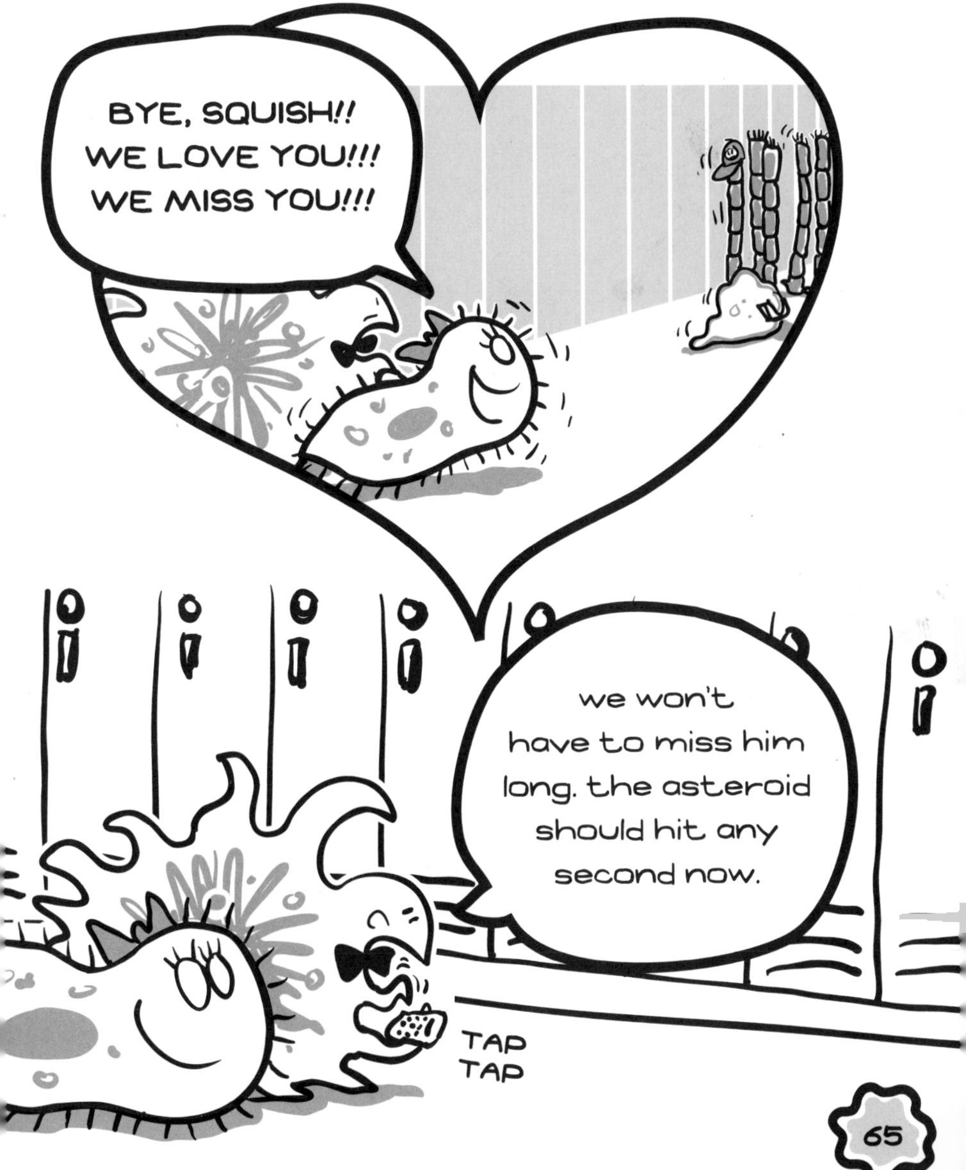
BYE, SQUISH!! WE LOVE YOU!!! WE MISS YOU!!!
we won't have to miss him long. the asteroid should hit any second now.
TAP TAP

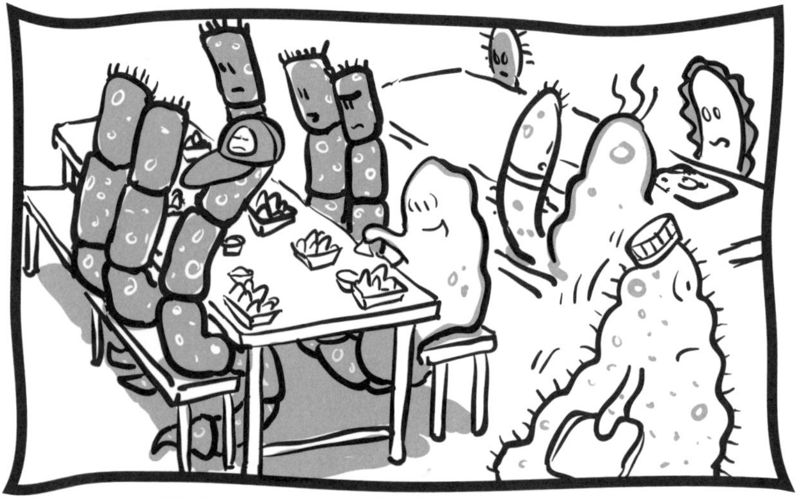

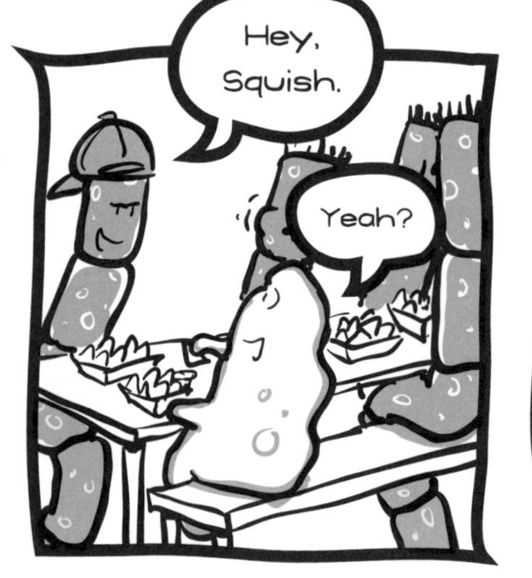
Hey, Squish.
Yeah?

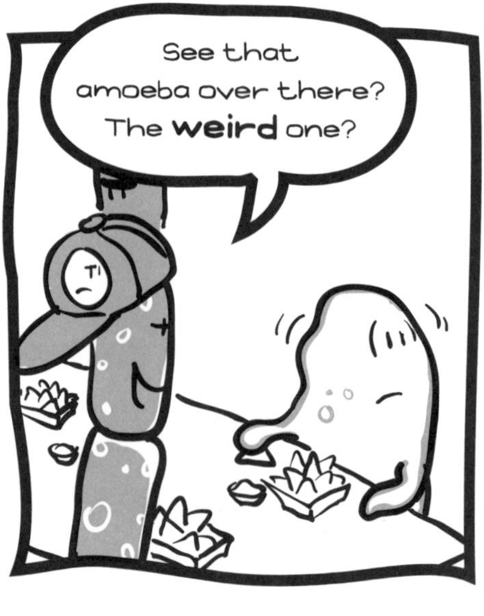
See that amoeba over there? The **weird** one?

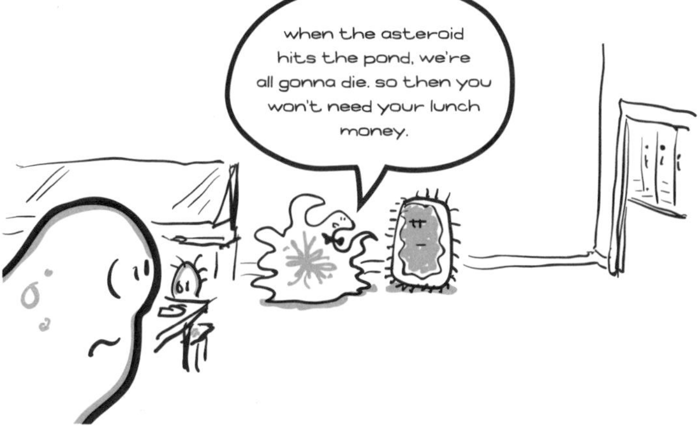
when the asteroid hits the pond, we're all gonna die. so then you won't need your lunch money.

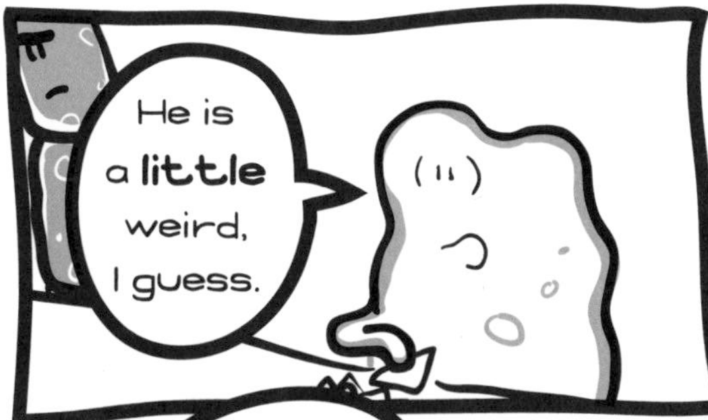
He is a **little** weird, I guess.

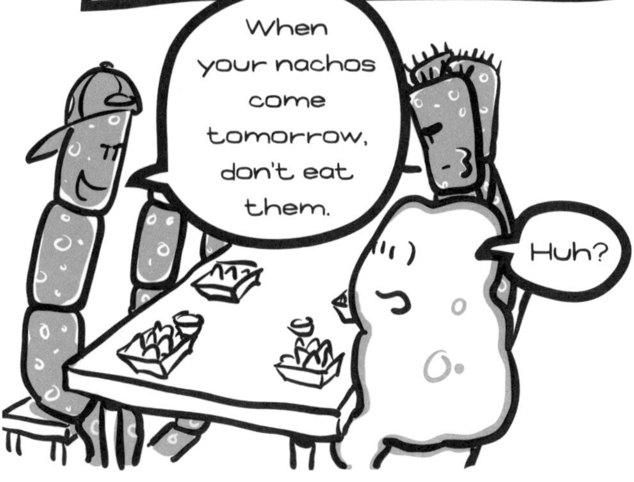
When your nachos come tomorrow, don't eat them.
Huh?

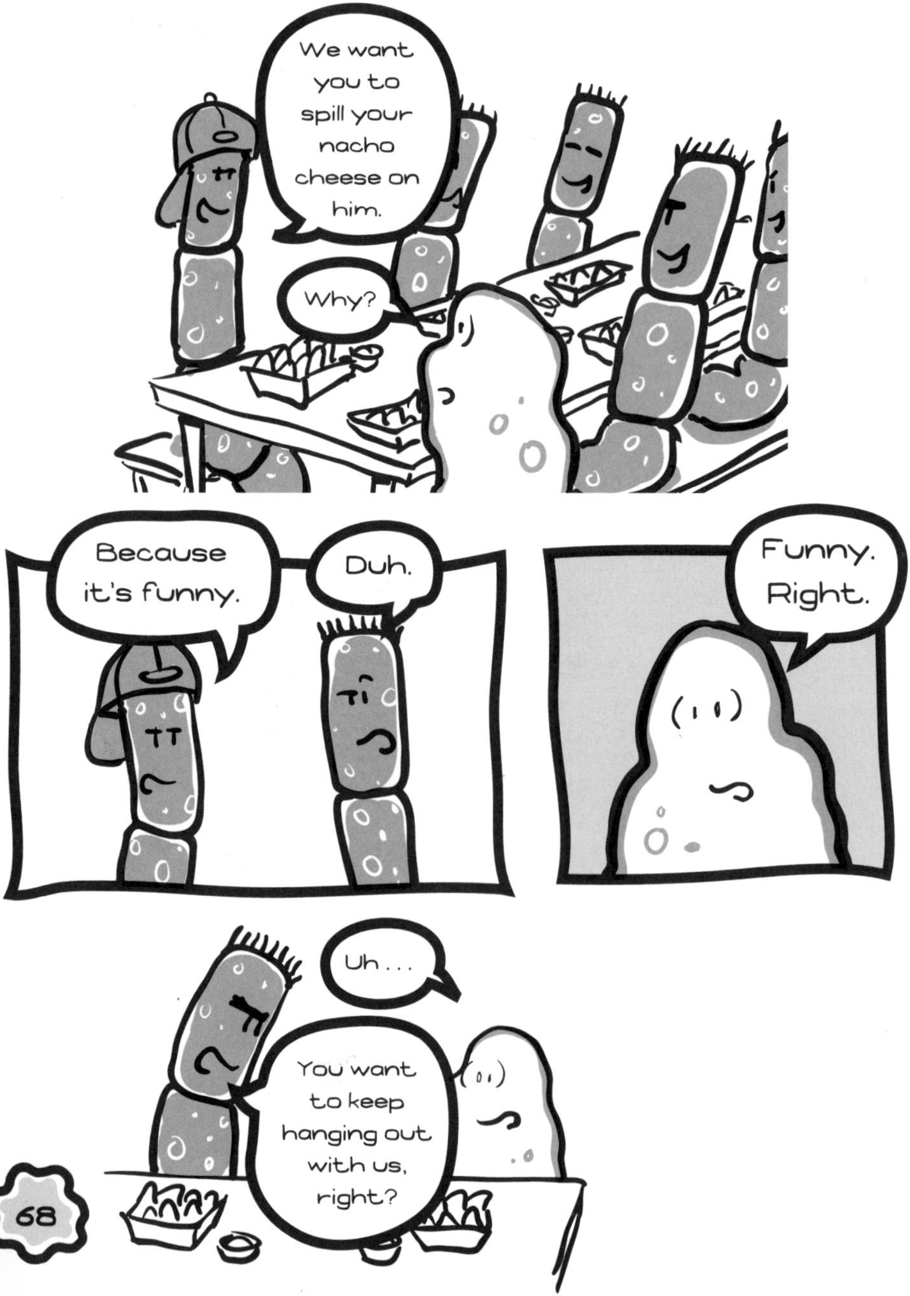
We want you to spill your nacho cheese on him.
Why?
Because it's funny.
Duh.
Funny. Right.
Uh . . .
You want to keep hanging out with us, right?

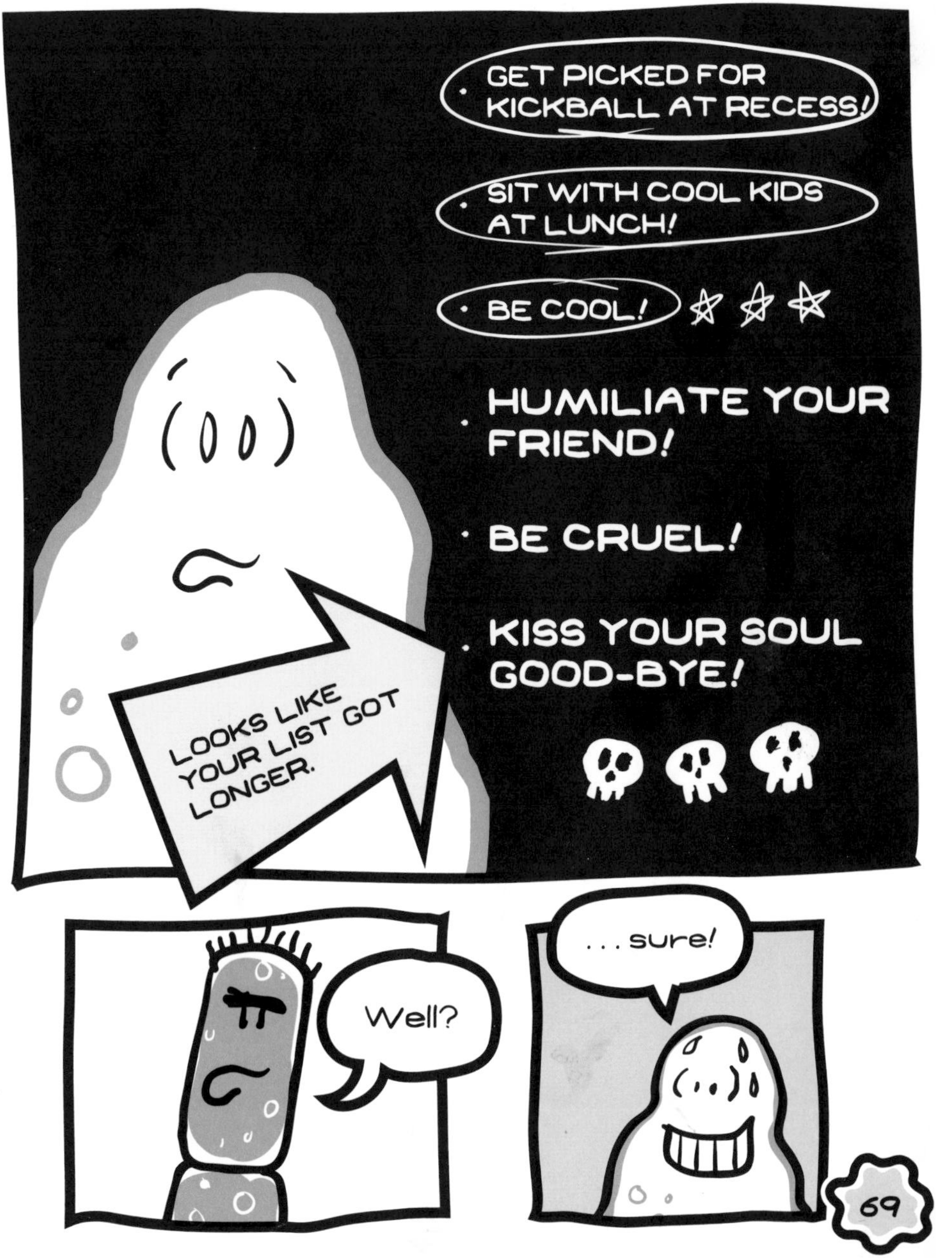
GET PICKED FOR KICKBALL AT RECESS!
SIT WITH COOL KIDS AT LUNCH!
BE COOL!
HUMILIATE YOUR FRIEND!
BE CRUEL!
KISS YOUR SOUL GOOD-BYE!
LOOKS LIKE YOUR LIST GOT LONGER.
Well?
. . . sure!

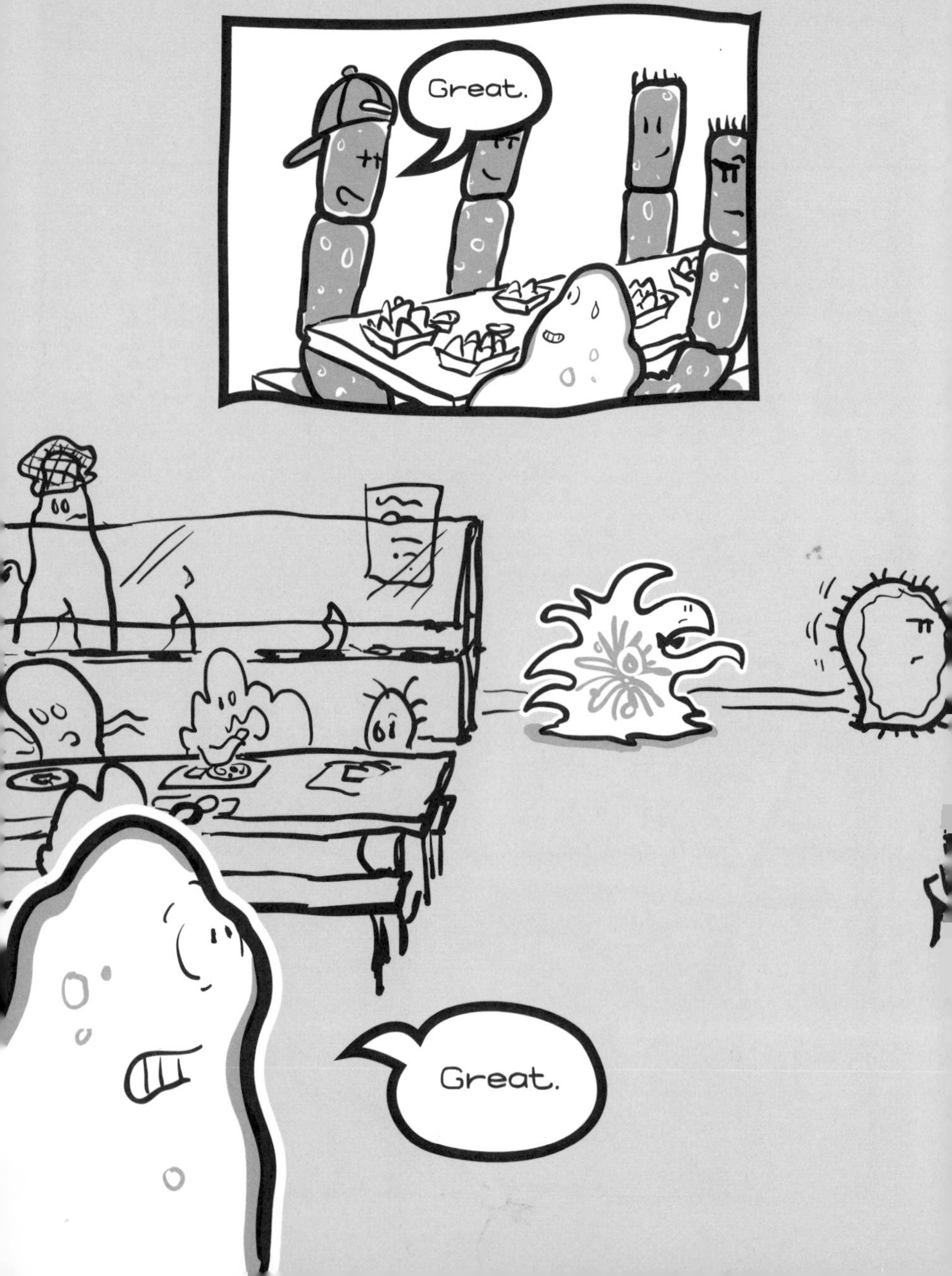
Great.
Great.

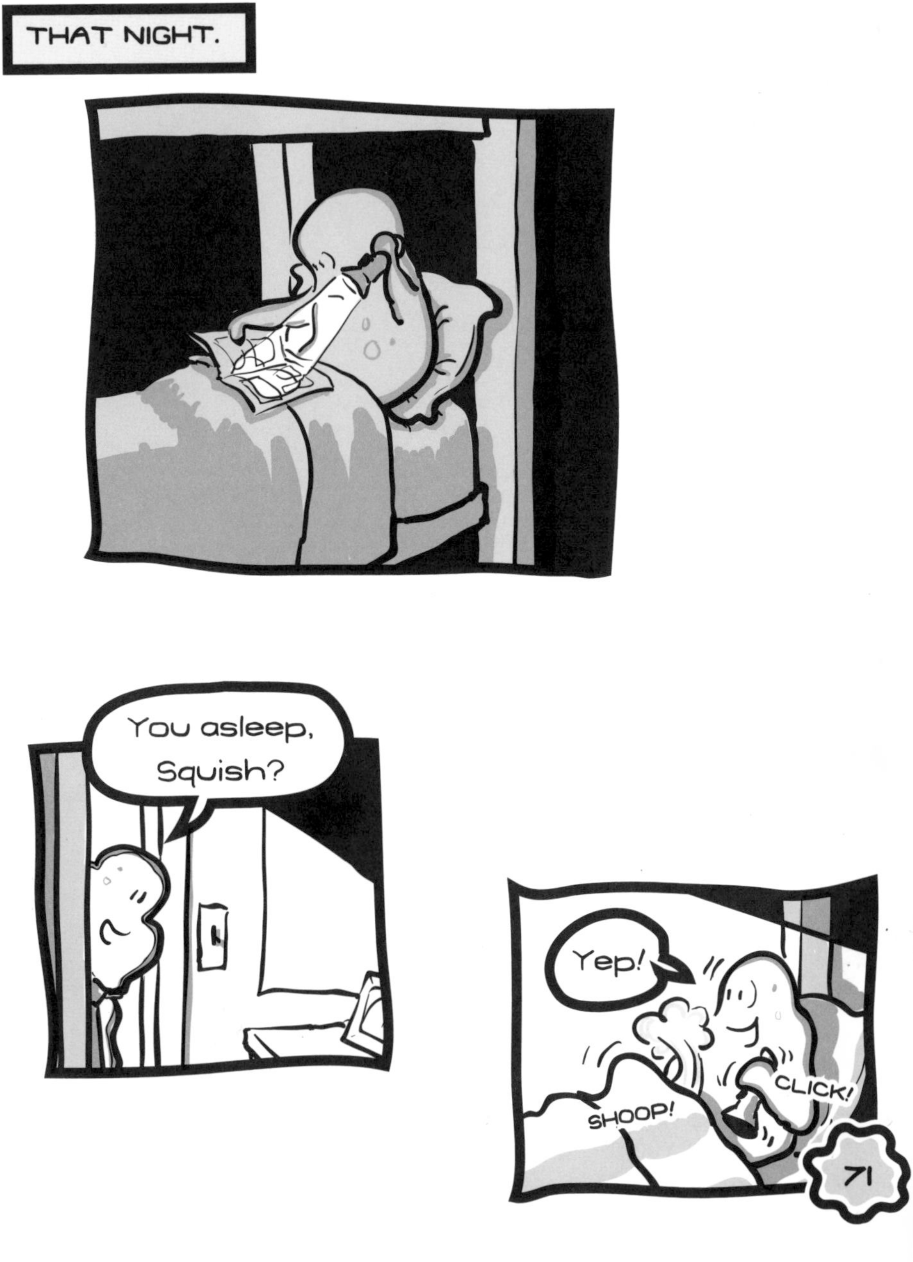
THAT NIGHT.
You asleep, Squish?
Yep!
SHOOP!
CLICK!

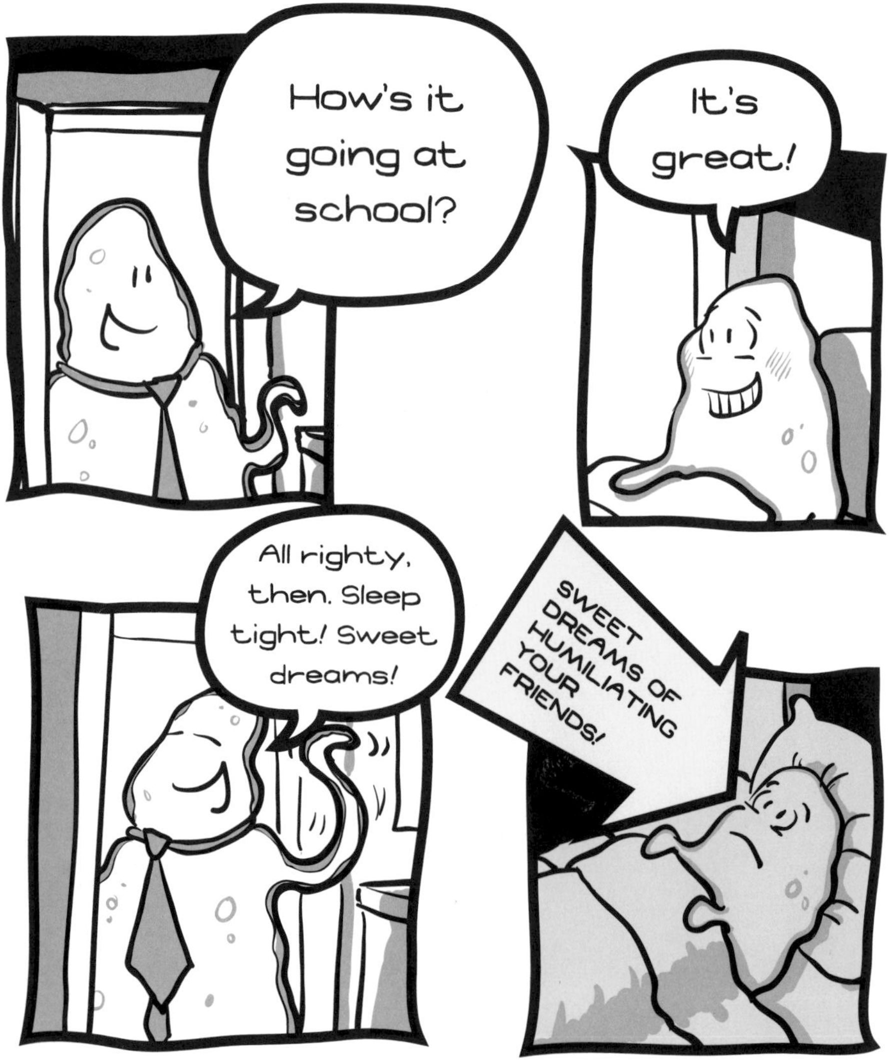
How's it going at school?
It's great!
All righty, then. Sleep tight! Sweet dreams!
SWEET DREAMS OF HUMILIATING YOUR FRIENDS!

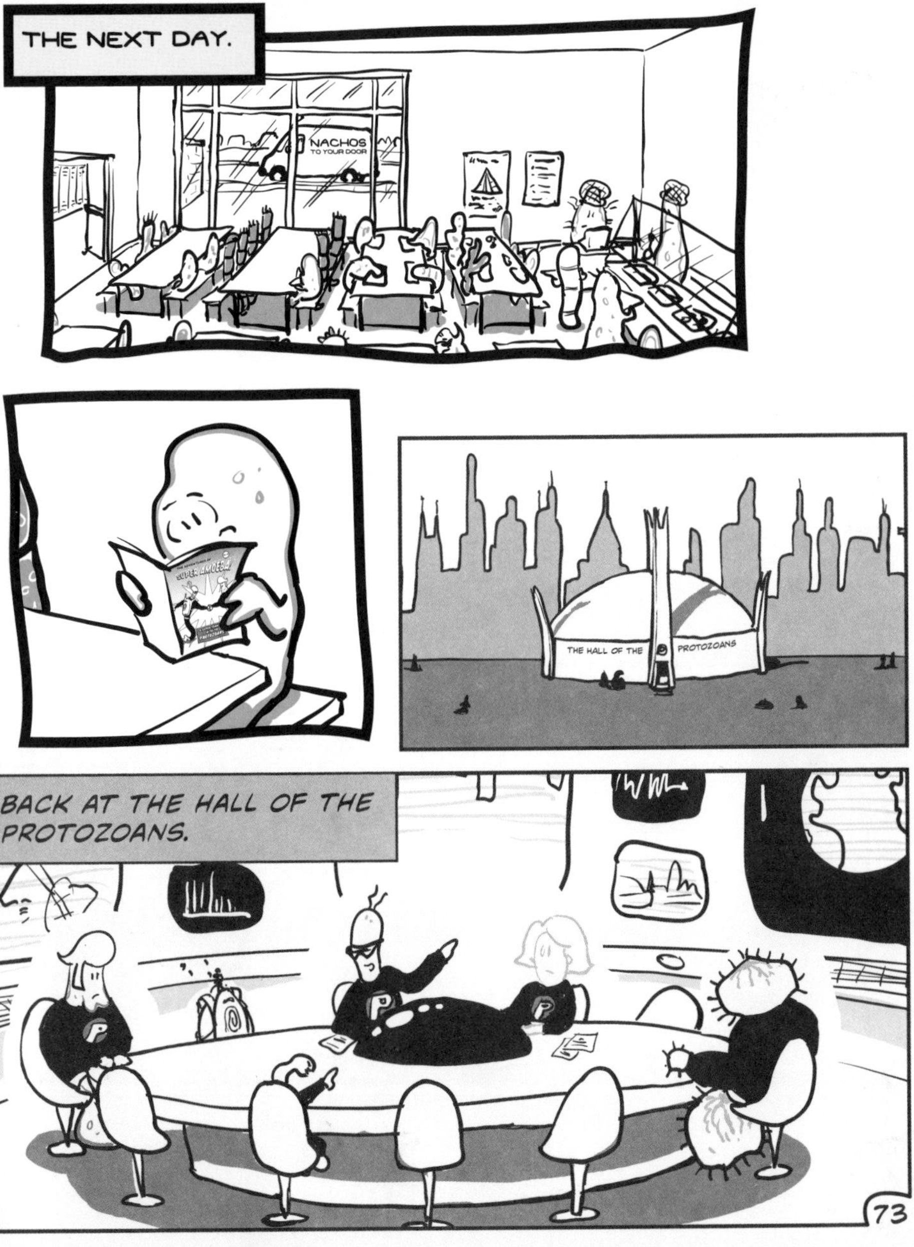
THE NEXT DAY.
NACHOS
TO YOUR DOOR
SUPER AMOEBA!
THE HALL OF THE PROTOZOANS
BACK AT THE HALL OF THE PROTOZOANS.

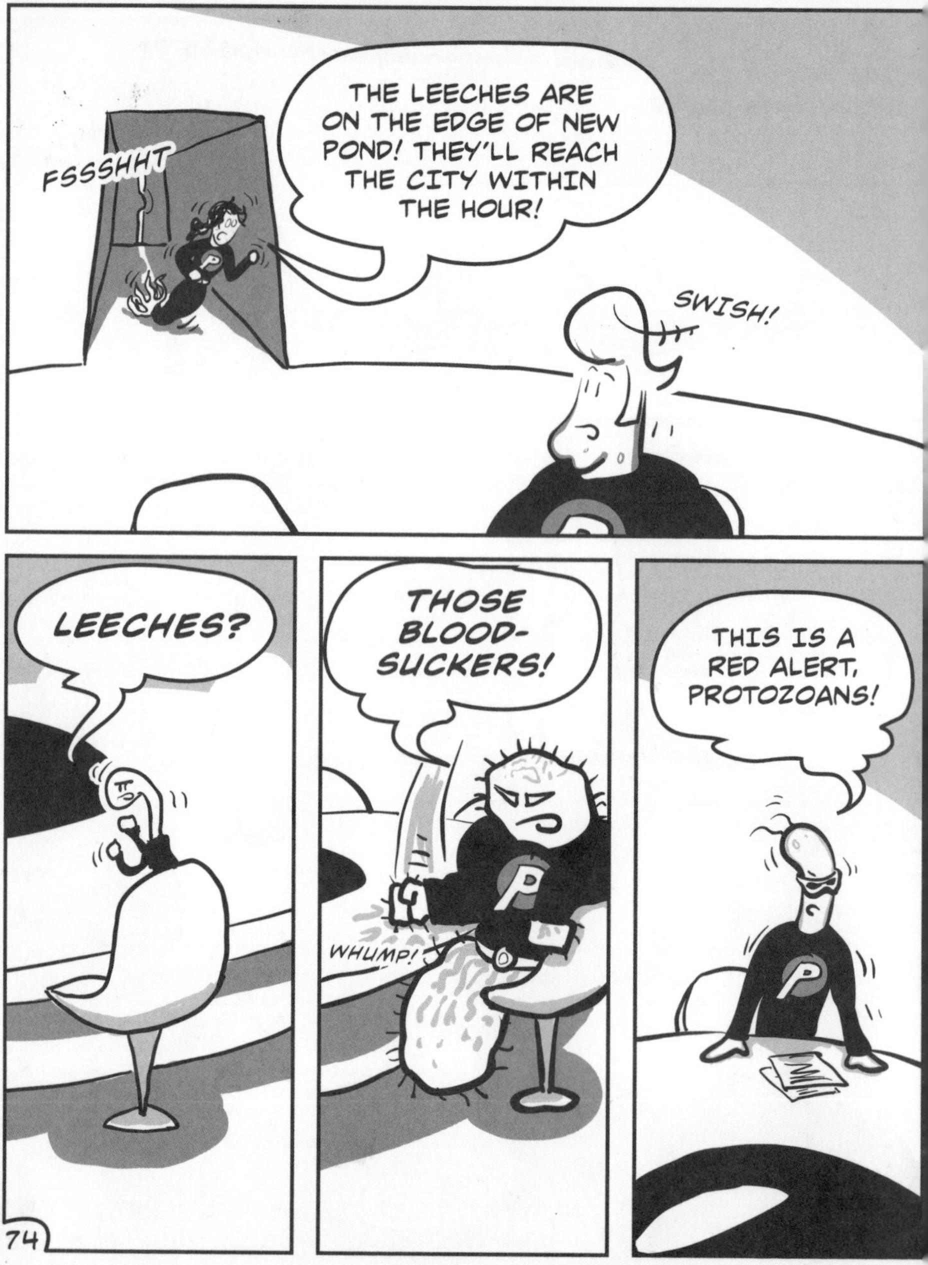
FSSSHHT
THE LEECHES ARE ON THE EDGE OF NEW POND! THEY'LL REACH THE CITY WITHIN THE HOUR!
SWISH!
LEECHES?
THOSE BLOOD-SUCKERS!
WHUMP!
THIS IS A RED ALERT, PROTOZOANS!

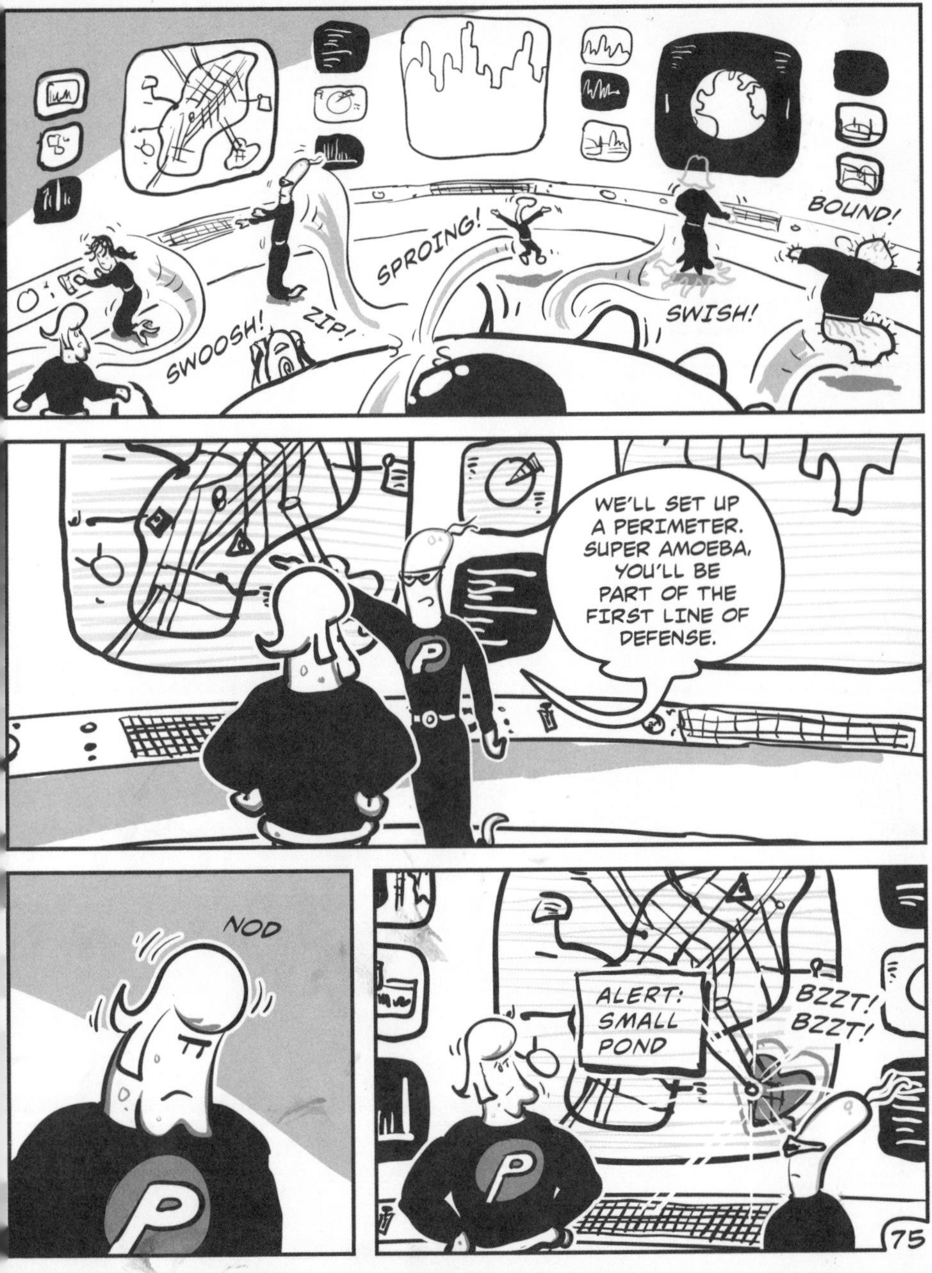
SPROING!
BOUND!
SWOOSH!
ZIP!
SWISH!
WE'LL SET UP A PERIMETER. SUPER AMOEBA, YOU'LL BE PART OF THE FIRST LINE OF DEFENSE.
NOD
ALERT: SMALL POND
BZZT! BZZT!

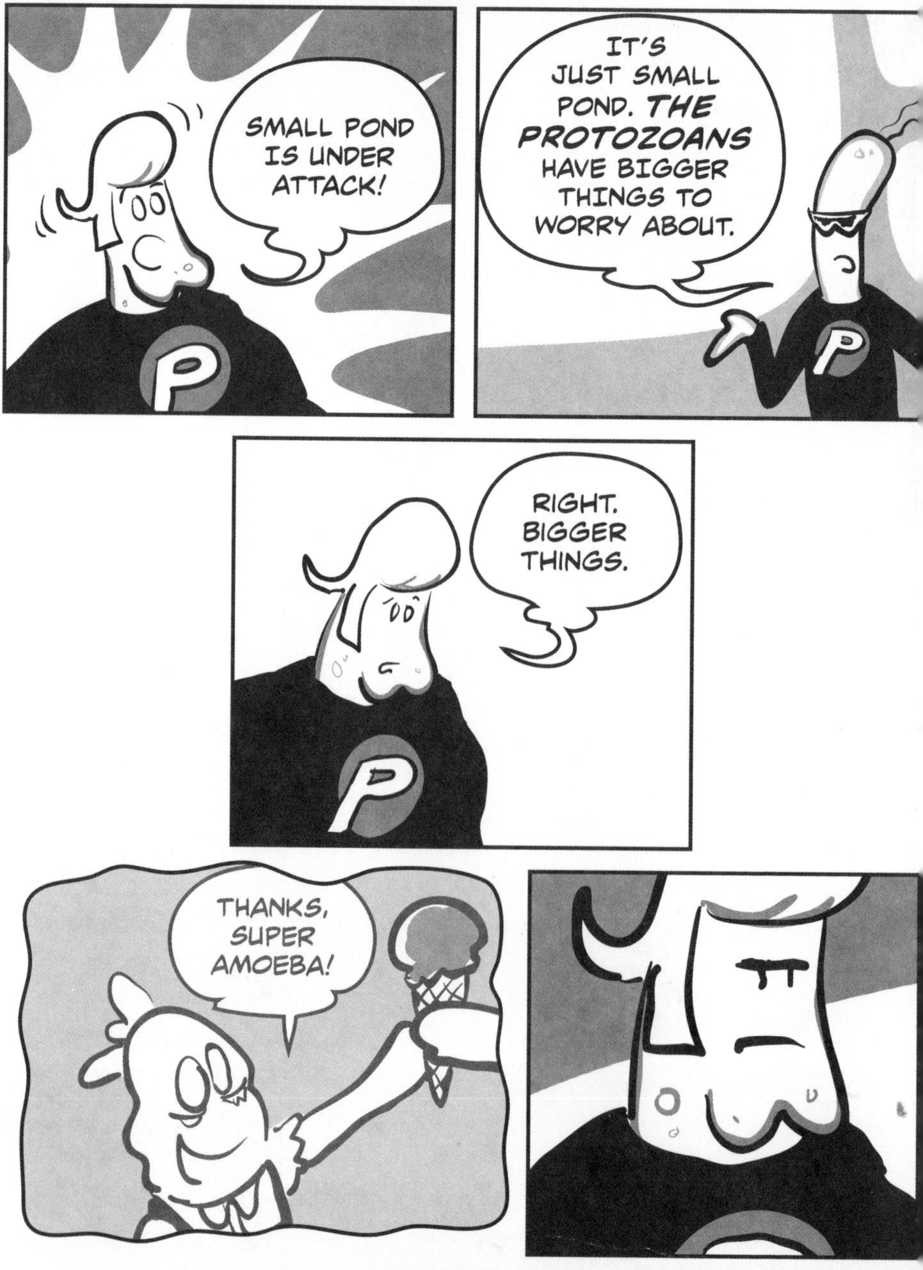
SMALL POND IS UNDER ATTACK!
IT'S JUST SMALL POND. ***THE PROTOZOANS*** HAVE BIGGER THINGS TO WORRY ABOUT.
RIGHT. BIGGER THINGS.
THANKS, SUPER AMOEBA!

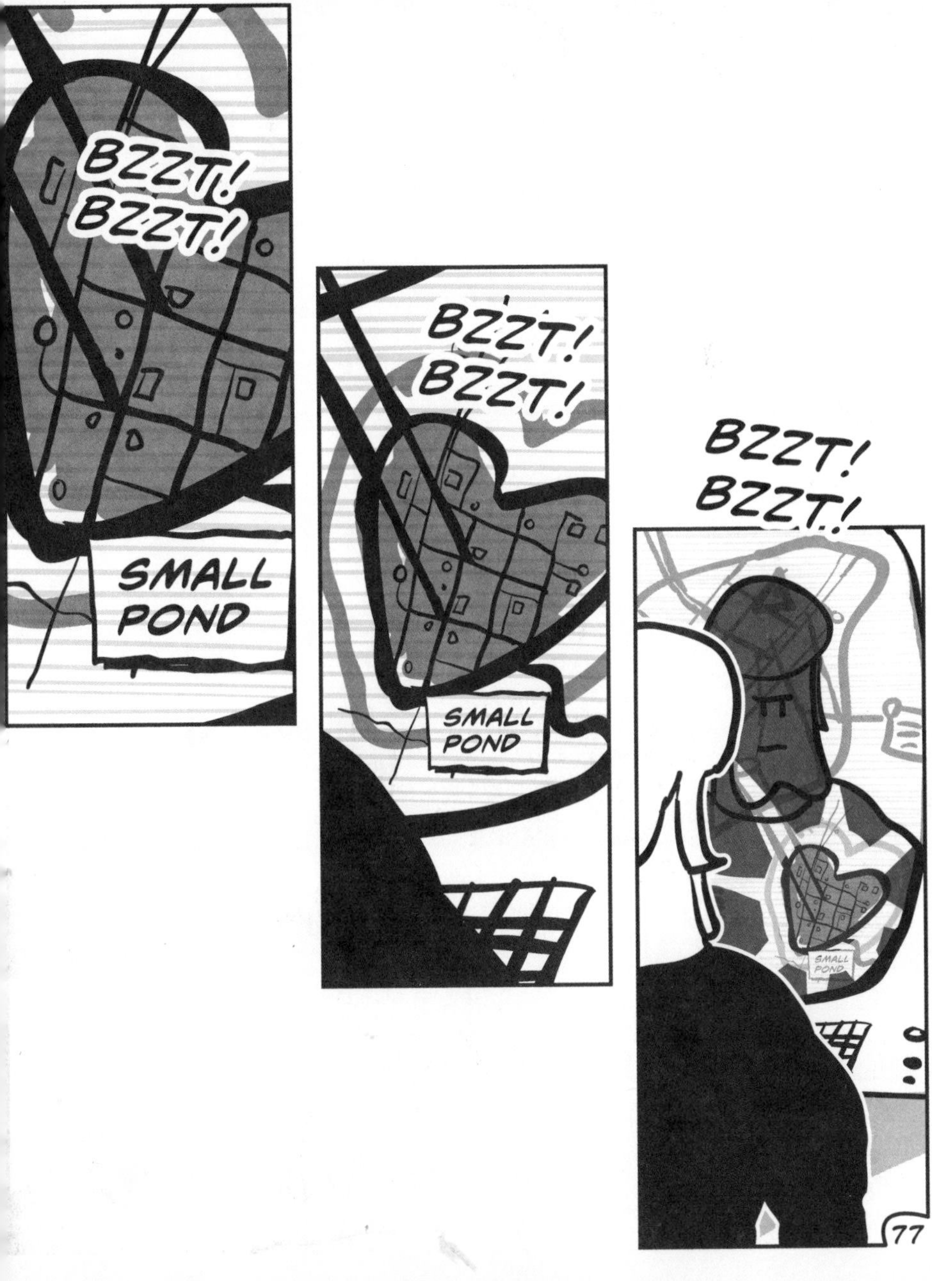
BZZT! BZZT!
SMALL POND
BZZT! BZZT!
SMALL POND
BZZT! BZZT!
SMALL POND

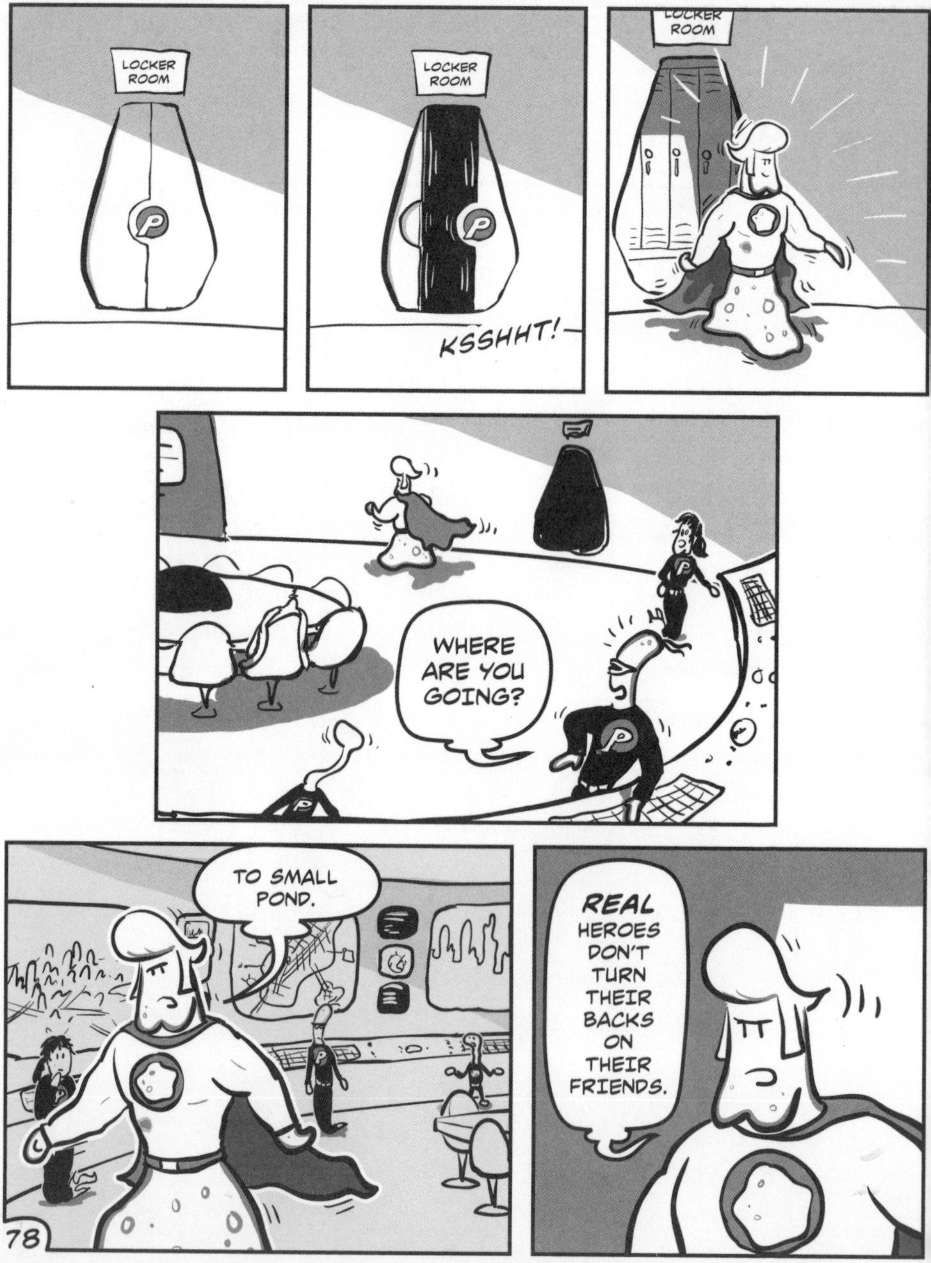
LOCKER ROOM
LOCKER ROOM
KSSHHT!
LOCKER ROOM
WHERE ARE YOU GOING?
TO SMALL POND.
REAL HEROES DON'T TURN THEIR BACKS ON THEIR FRIENDS.

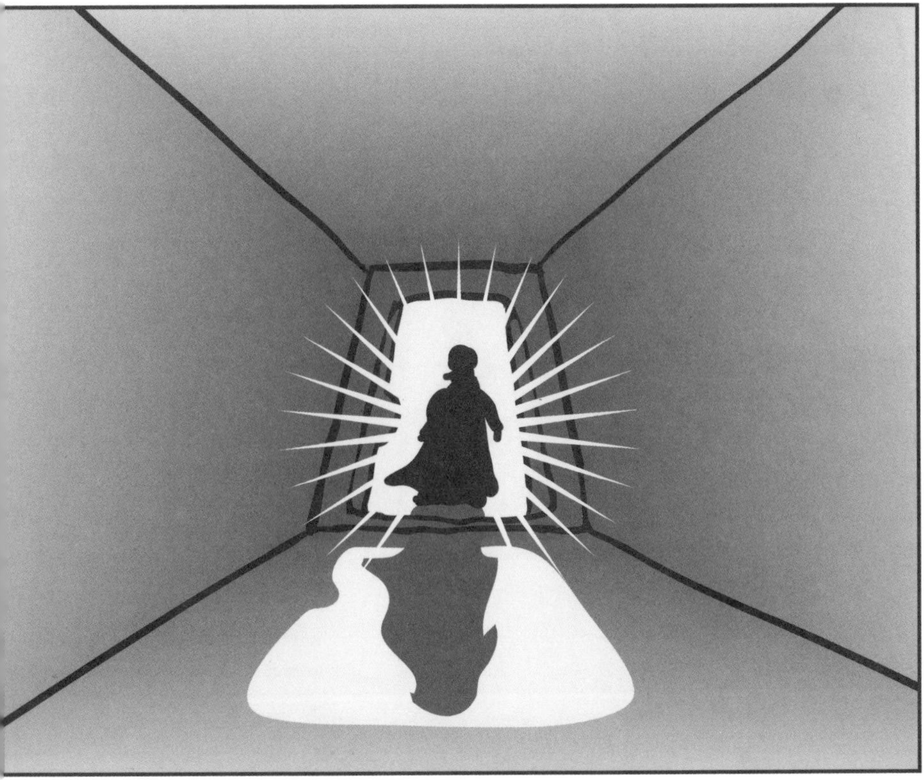

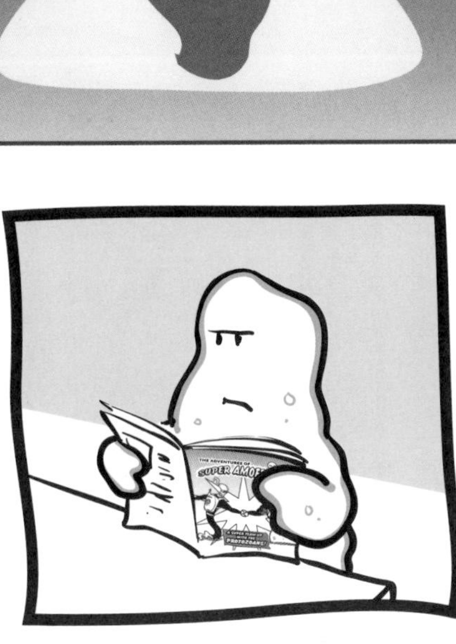

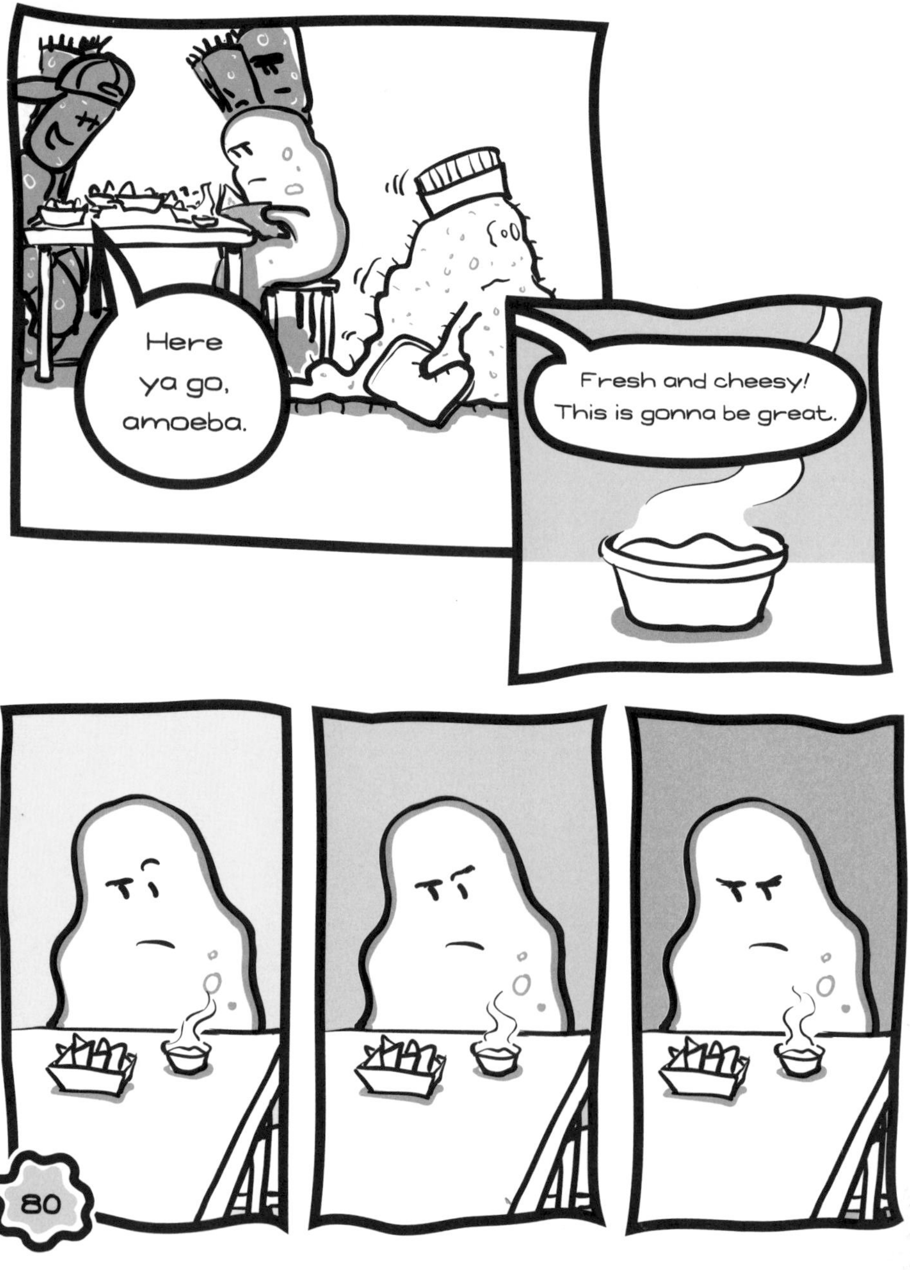
Here ya go, amoeba.
Fresh and cheesy! This is gonna be great.

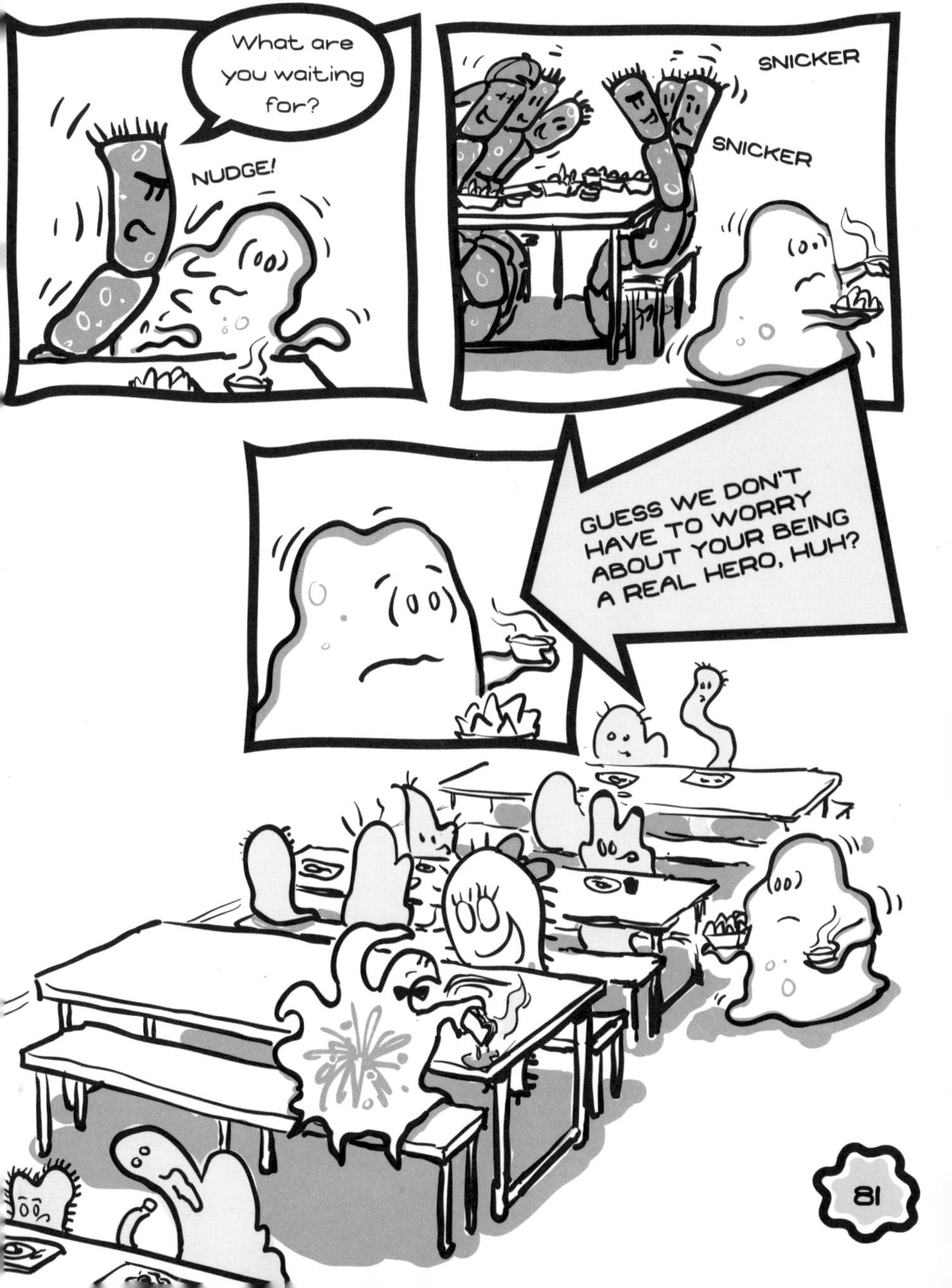
What are you waiting for?
NUDGE!
SNICKER
SNICKER
GUESS WE DON'T HAVE TO WORRY ABOUT YOUR BEING A REAL HERO, HUH?

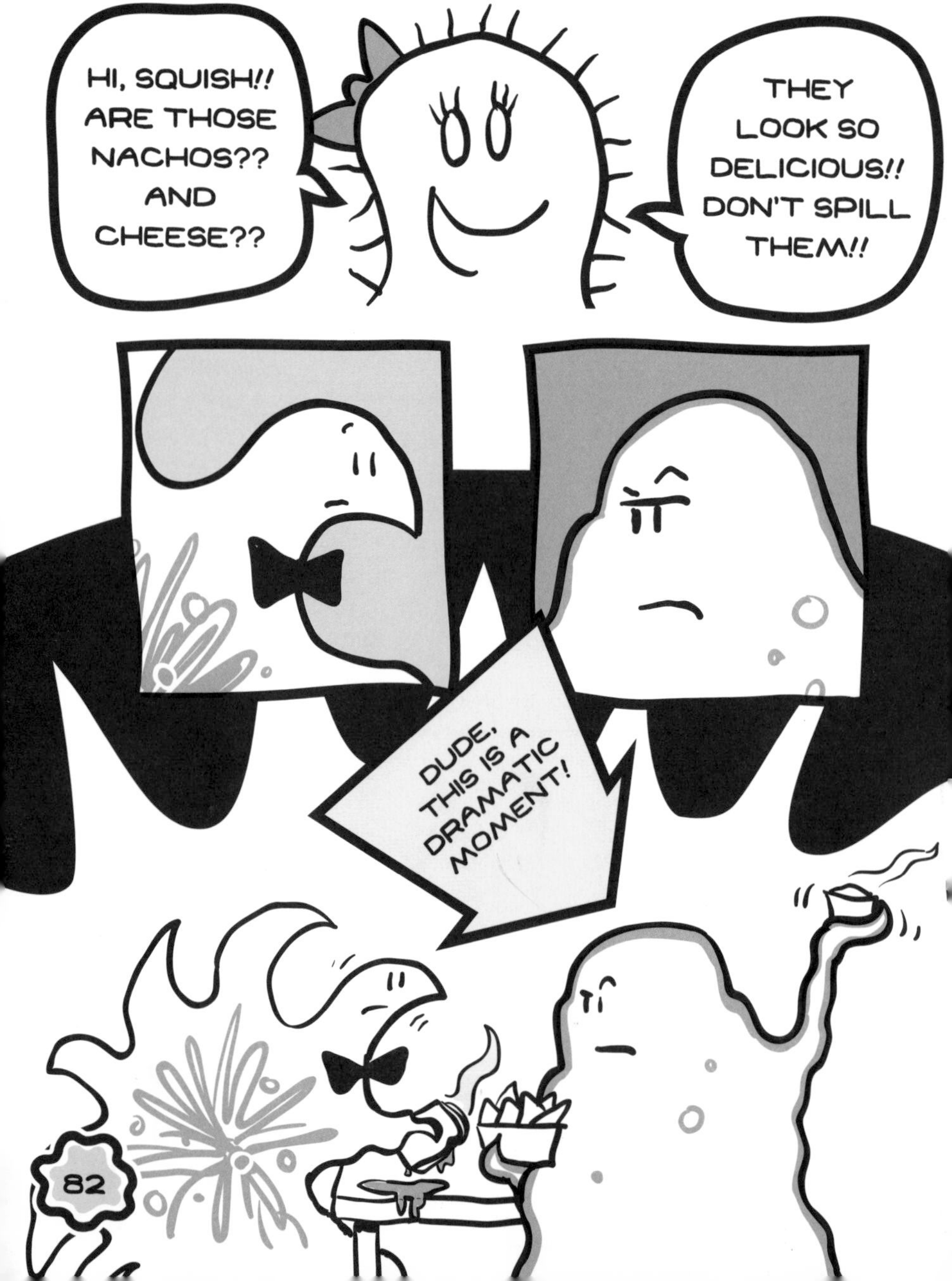
HI, SQUISH!! ARE THOSE NACHOS?? AND CHEESE??
THEY LOOK SO DELICIOUS!! DON'T SPILL THEM!!
DUDE, THIS IS A DRAMATIC MOMENT!

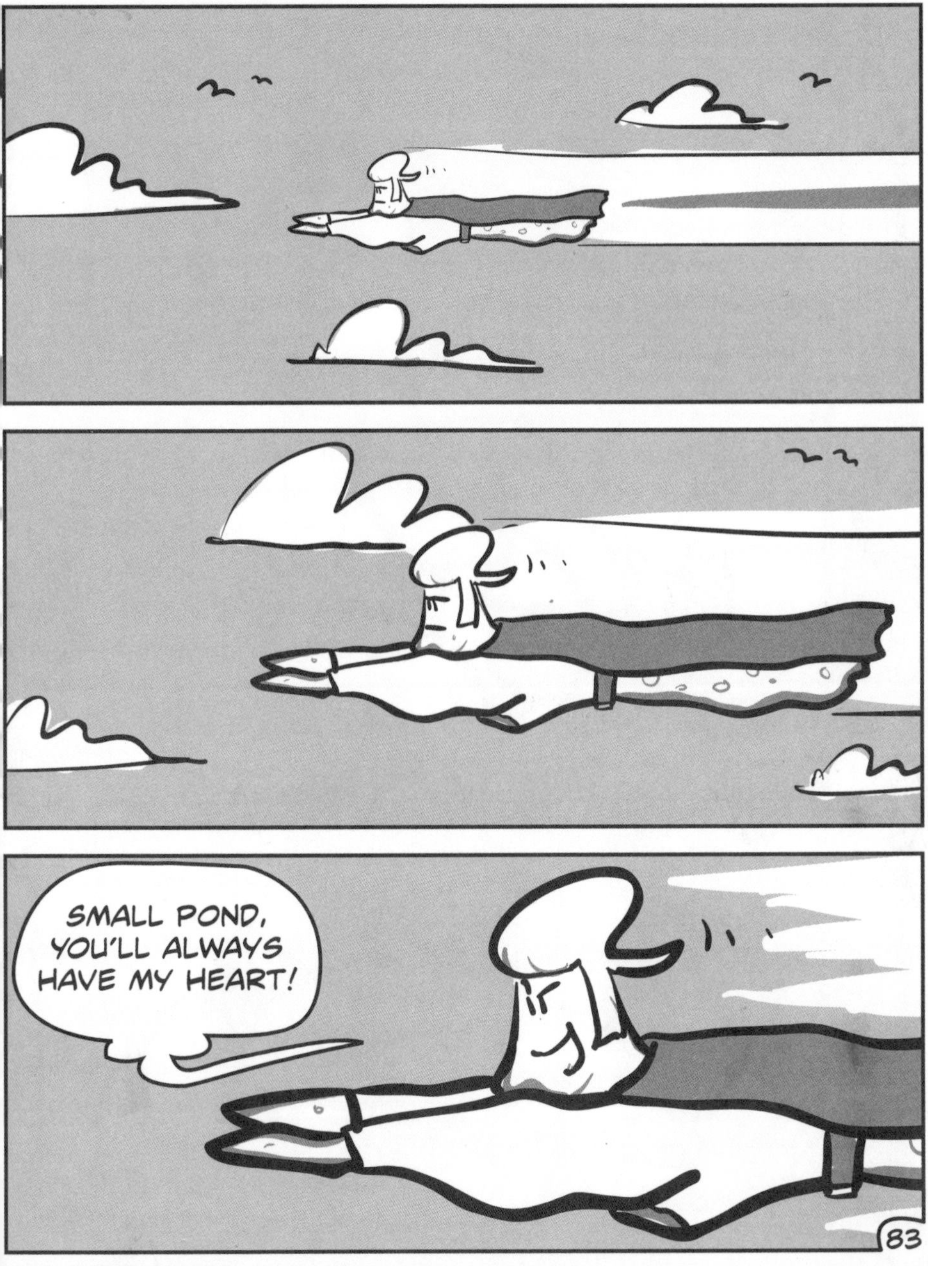
SMALL POND,
YOU'LL ALWAYS
HAVE MY HEART!

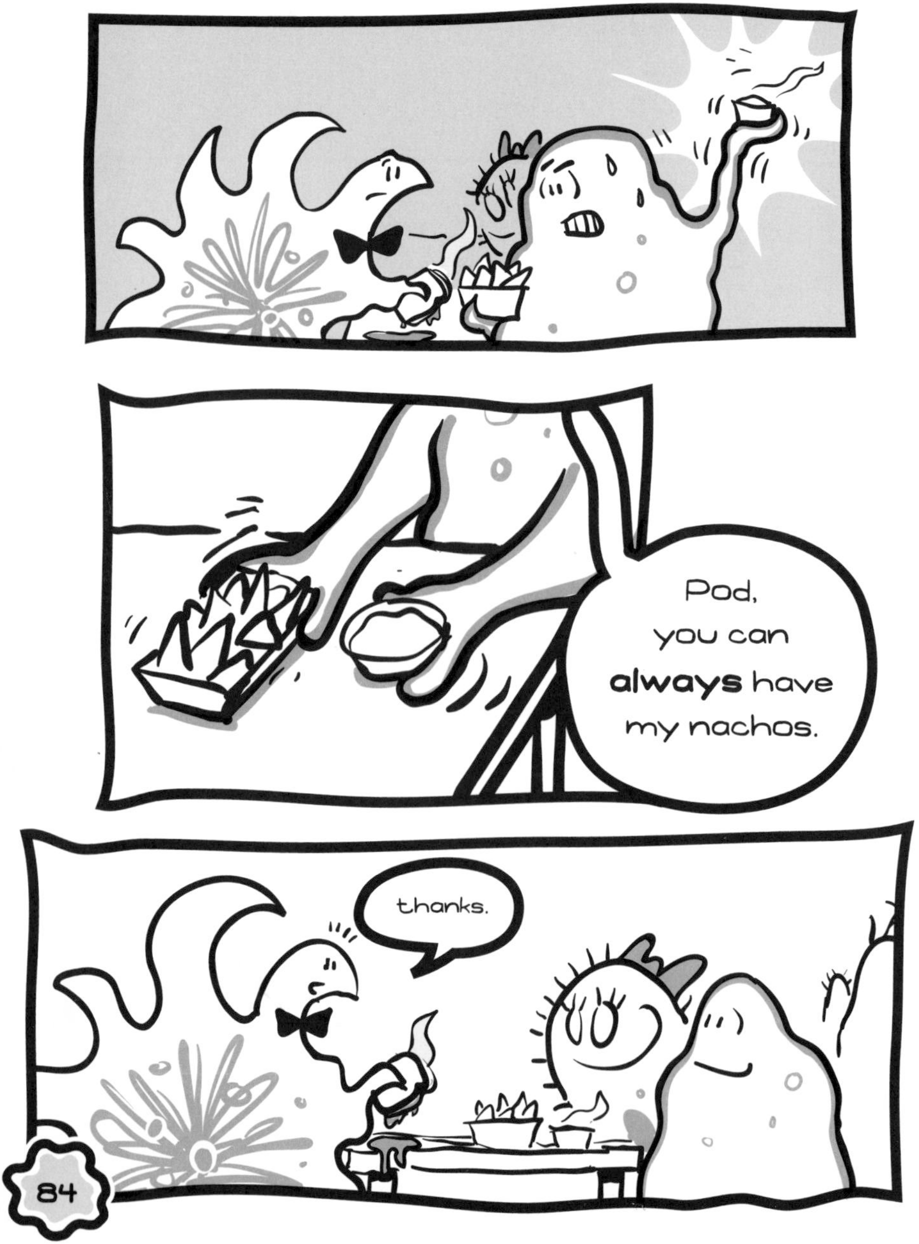
Pod, you can **always** have my nachos.
thanks.

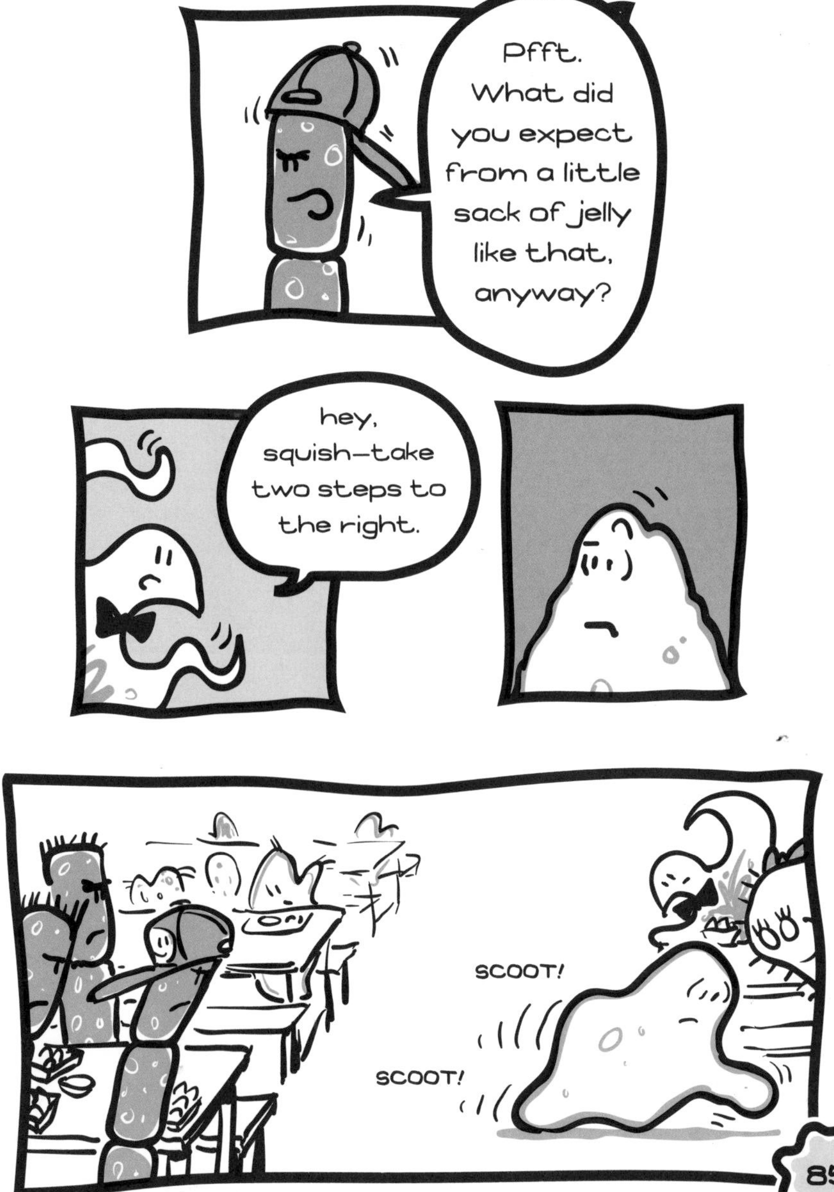
Pfft. What did you expect from a little sack of jelly like that, anyway?
hey, squish—take two steps to the right.
SCOOT!
SCOOT!

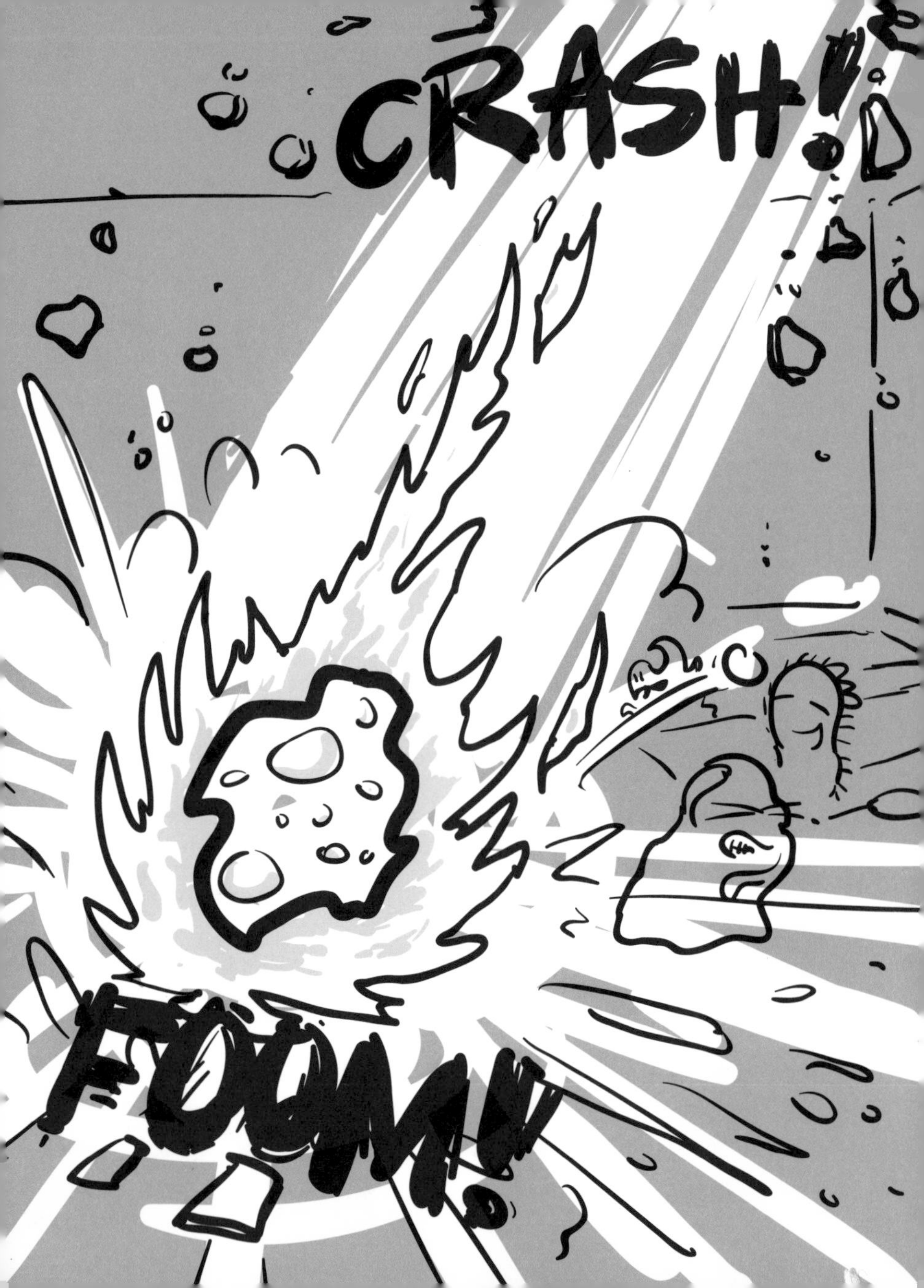
CRASH!
FOOM!!

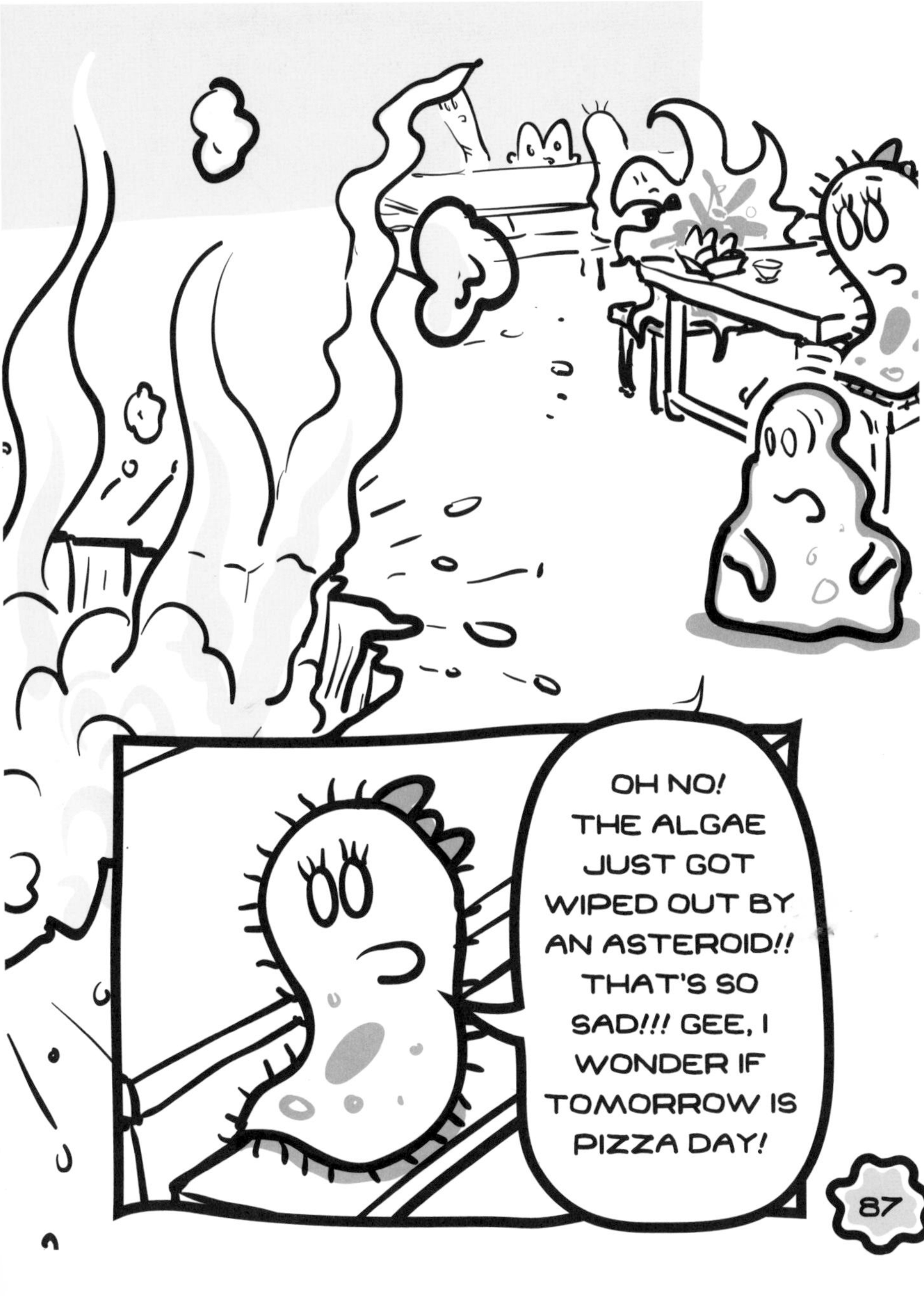
OH NO! THE ALGAE JUST GOT WIPED OUT BY AN ASTEROID!! THAT'S SO SAD!!! GEE, I WONDER IF TOMORROW IS PIZZA DAY!

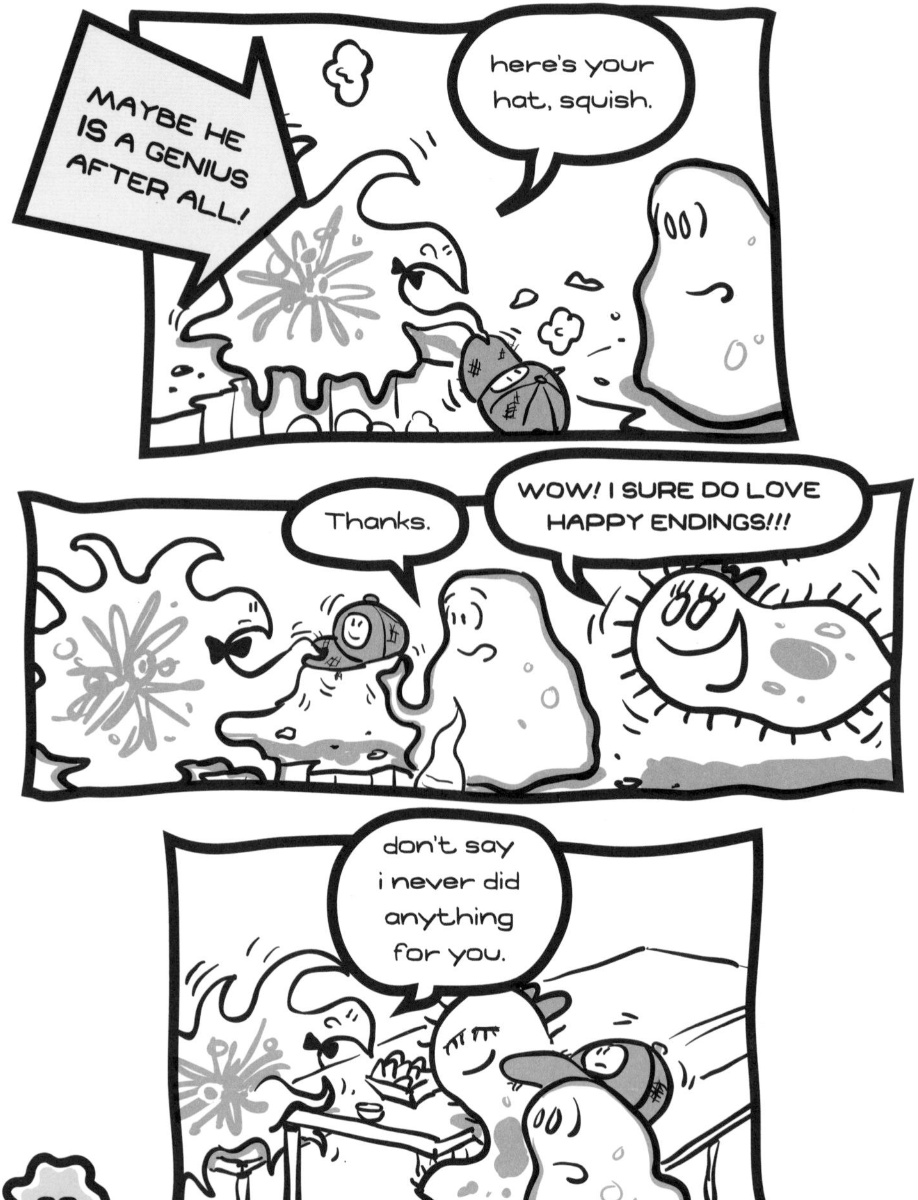
MAYBE HE IS A GENIUS AFTER ALL!
here's your hat, squish.
Thanks.
WOW! I SURE DO LOVE HAPPY ENDINGS!!!
don't say i never did anything for you.

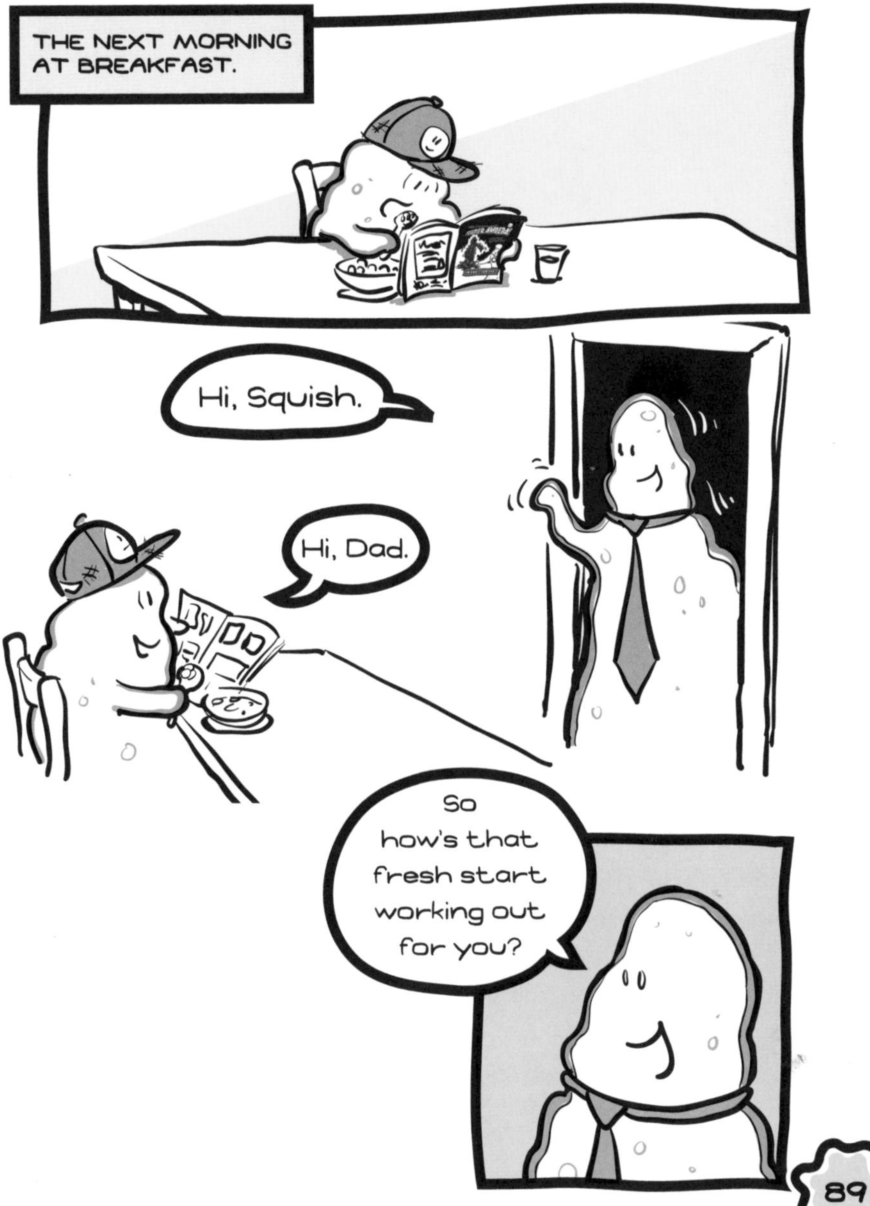
THE NEXT MORNING AT BREAKFAST.
Hi, Squish.
Hi, Dad.
So how's that fresh start working out for you?

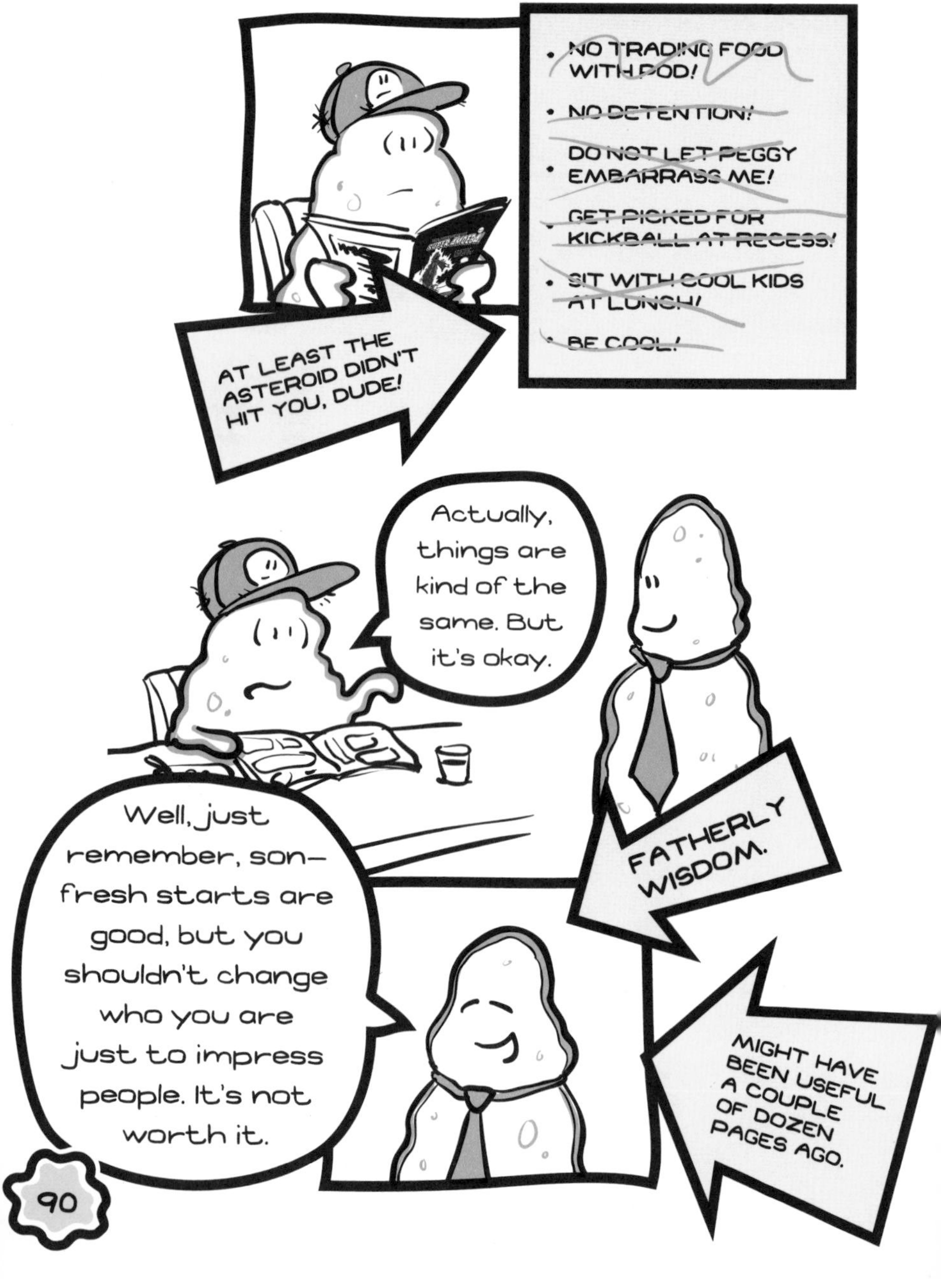
NO TRADING FOOD WITH POD!
NO DETENTION!
DO NOT LET PEGGY EMBARRASS ME!
GET PICKED FOR KICKBALL AT RECESS!
SIT WITH COOL KIDS AT LUNCH!
BE COOL!
AT LEAST THE ASTEROID DIDN'T HIT YOU, DUDE!
Actually, things are kind of the same. But it's okay.
FATHERLY WISDOM.
Well, just remember, son— fresh starts are good, but you shouldn't change who you are just to impress people. It's not worth it.
MIGHT HAVE BEEN USEFUL A COUPLE OF DOZEN PAGES AGO.

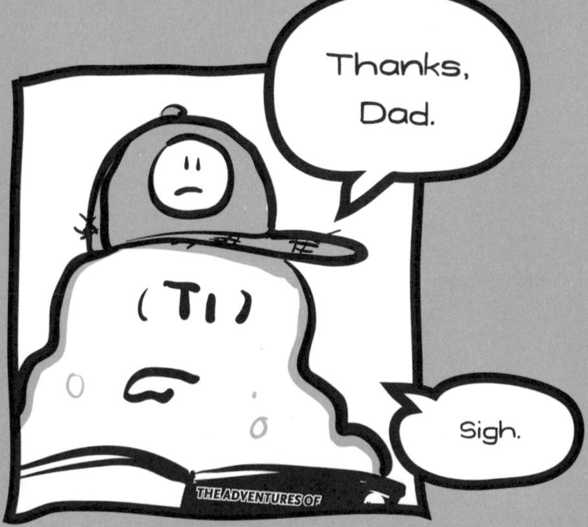
Thanks, Dad.
Sigh.
THE ADVENTURES OF

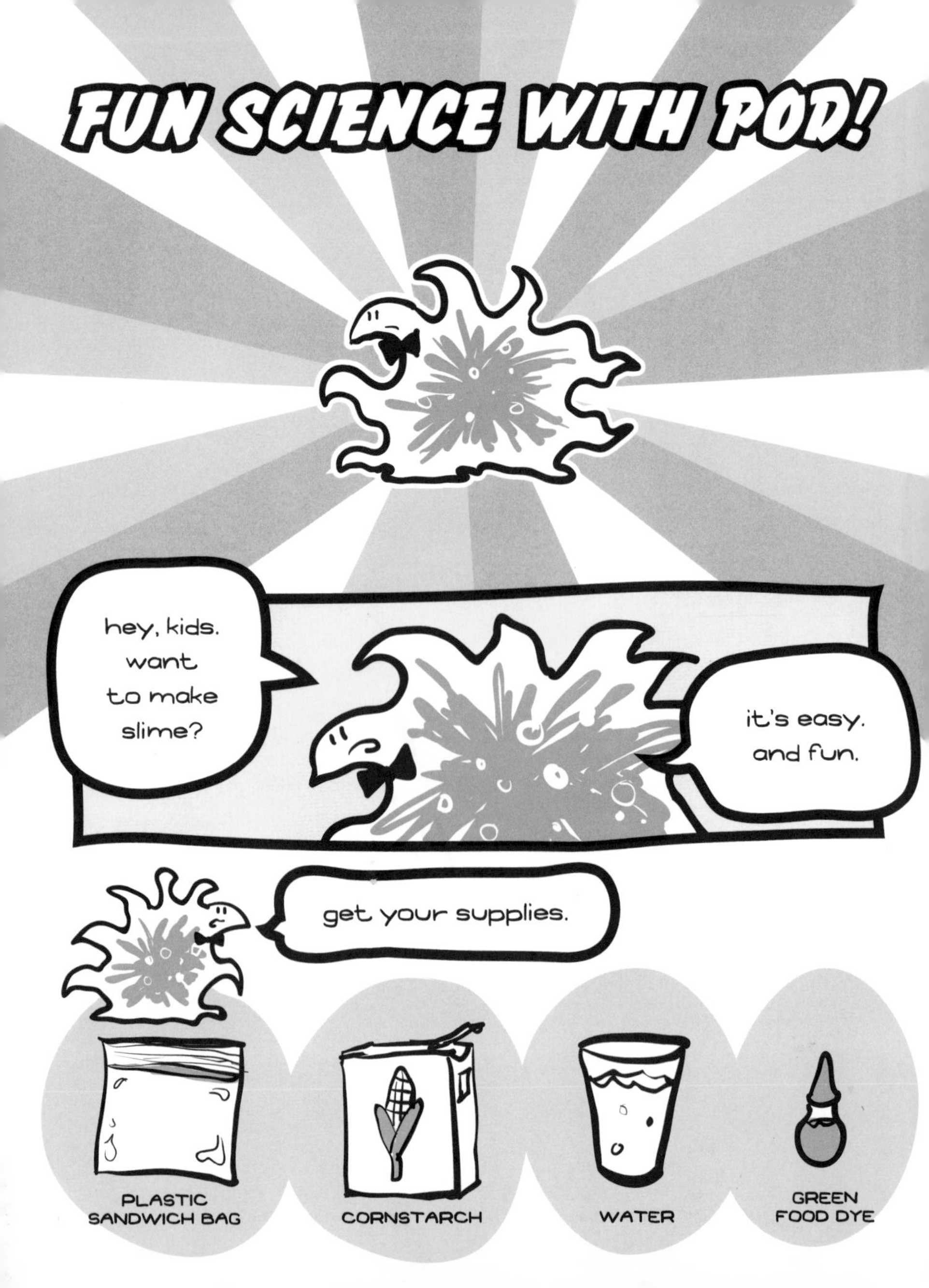
FUN SCIENCE WITH POD!
hey, kids. want to make slime?
it's easy. and fun.
get your supplies.
PLASTIC SANDWICH BAG
CORNSTARCH
WATER
GREEN FOOD DYE

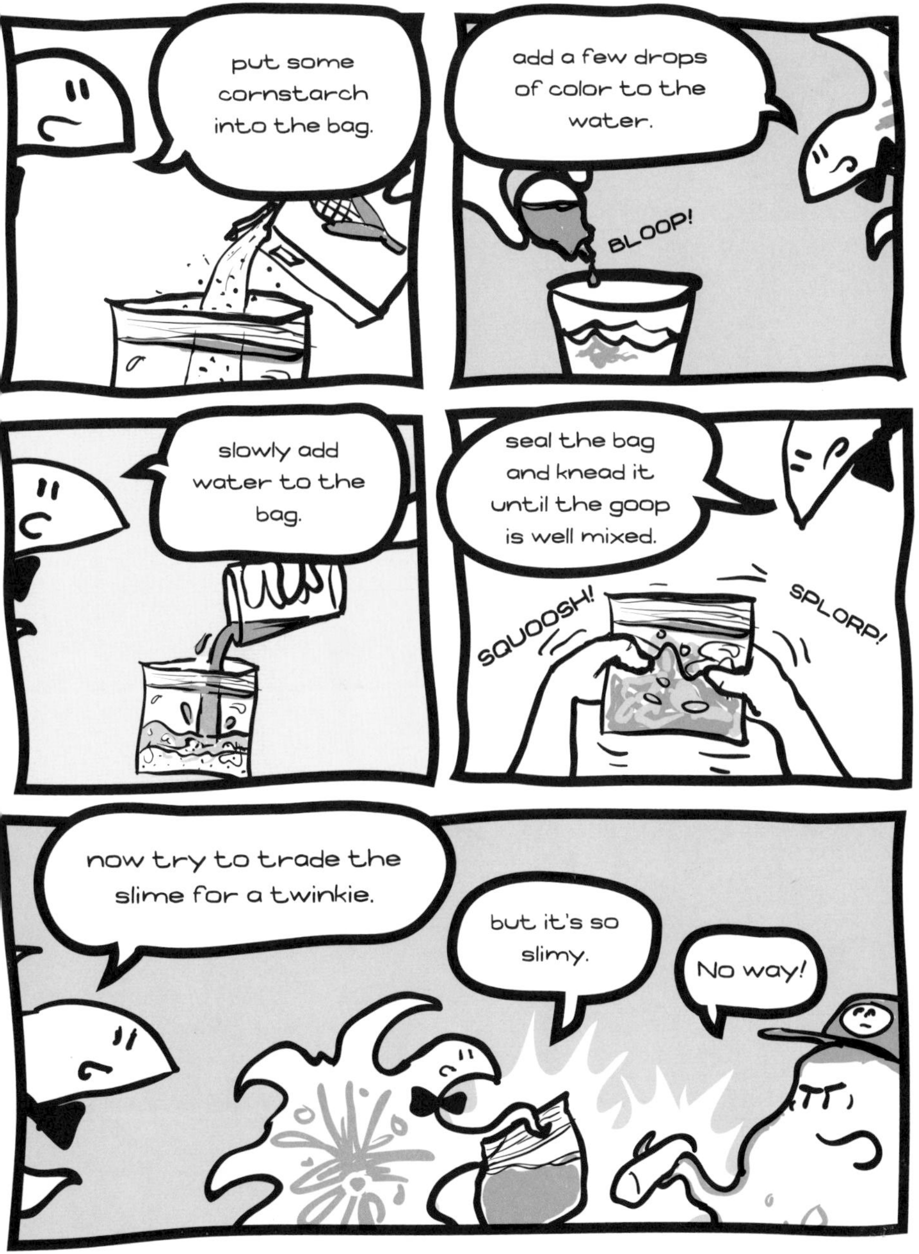
put some cornstarch into the bag.
add a few drops of color to the water.
BLOOP!
slowly add water to the bag.
seal the bag and knead it until the goop is well mixed.
SQUOOSH!
SPLORP!
now try to trade the slime for a twinkie.
but it's so slimy.
No way!

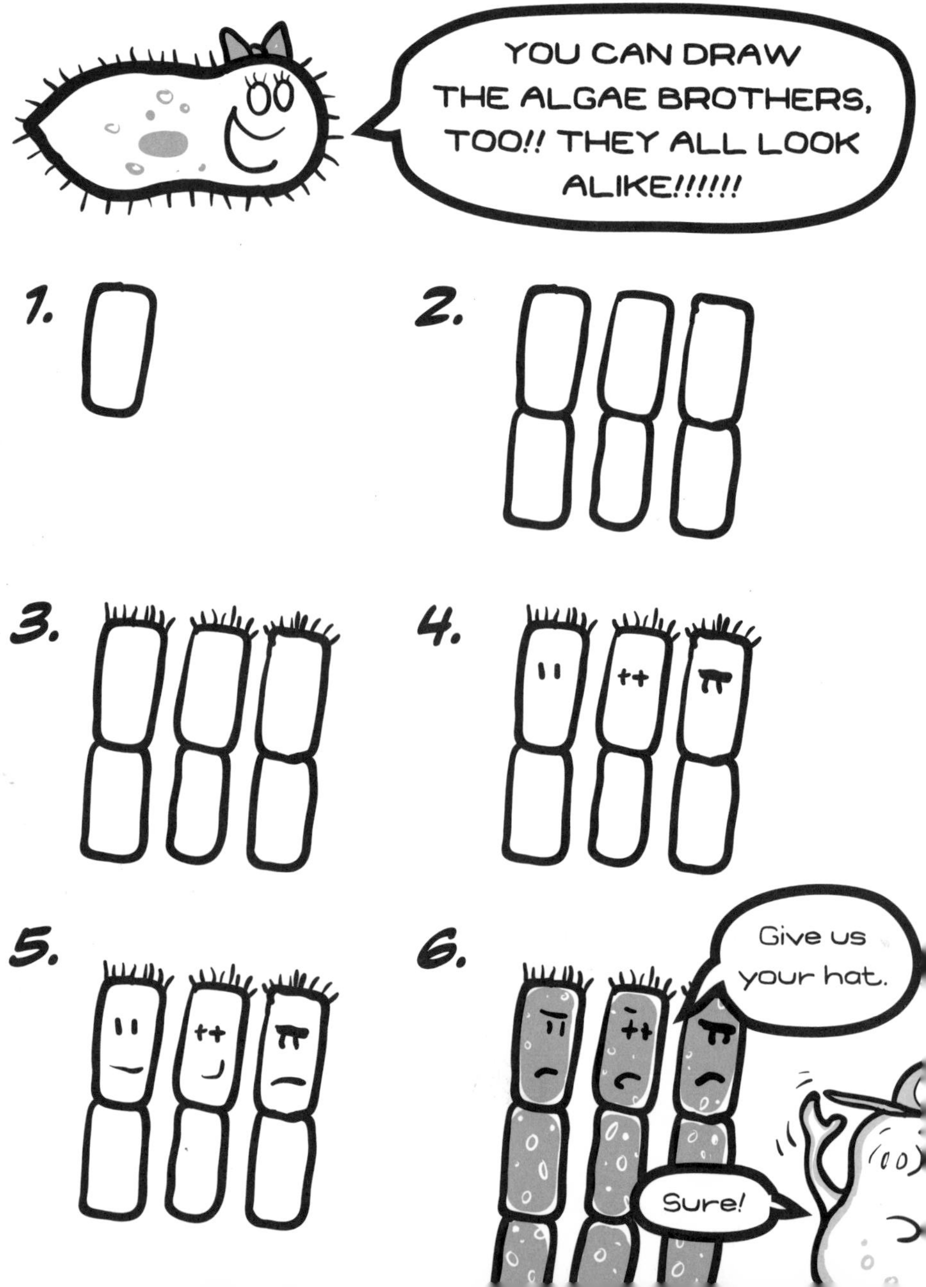
YOU CAN DRAW THE ALGAE BROTHERS, TOO!! THEY ALL LOOK ALIKE!!!!!!
1.
2.
3.
4.
5.
6.
Give us your hat.
Sure!

IF YOU LIKE SQUISH, YOU'LL LOVE BABYMOUSE!

#1 BABYMOUSE: Queen of the World!

#2 BABYMOUSE: Our Hero

#3 BABYMOUSE: Beach Babe

#4 BABYMOUSE: Rock Star

#5 BABYMOUSE: Heartbreaker

#6 CAMP BABYMOUSE

#7 BABYMOUSE: Skater Girl

#8 BABYMOUSE: Puppy Love

#9 BABYMOUSE: Monster Mash

#10 BABYMOUSE: The Musical

#11 BABYMOUSE: Dragonslayer

#12 BABYMOUSE: Burns Rubber

#13 BABYMOUSE: Cupcake Tycoon

#14 BABYMOUSE: Mad Scientist

#15 A Very BABYMOUSE Christmas

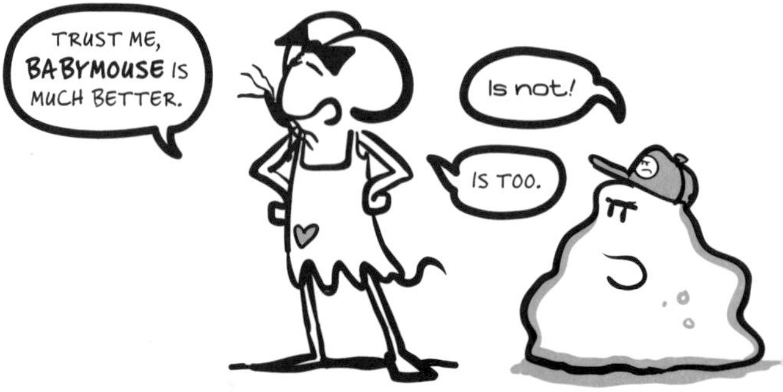
TRUST ME, BABYMOUSE IS MUCH BETTER.
Is not!
IS TOO.